THE DREAM FACTORY

PETE KRAMER

ISBN: 979-8-9884513-4-1 (Paperback)
ISBN: 979-8-9884513-5-8 (Ebook)

Interior Book Design/ Formatting: Tamara Cribley, *The Deliberate Page*
Cover Design: Eric Labacz, *Eric Labacz Design*

Any references to historical events, real people, or real places are used fictitiously. All characters, incidents, and dialogue are drawn from the author's imagination and are not to be construed as real.

AK Publishing
23 Leigh Drive
Smyrna, DE 19977

PRAISE FOR PETE KRAMER'S CHESAPEAKE BAY MONSTERS

"You get much more than you realize you're getting."

— Fantasy for the Ages

"The unique storyline was engaging
and had me guessing until the end."

— Reader's Choice

"These characters were really good. I really
enjoyed our three main characters."

— David's Book Reviews

"A heck of a fun read."

— Talking Story

"Go in blind and tell me this isn't a Banger!"

— Beard of Darkness Book Reviews

"A fantastic mer-beast creature feature that
also has twists, turns, and some dark humor
to round it all out. Highly recommend!"

— Horror Reads

For my Mom and Dad who took my brother
and I on family vacations seemingly every
year, including two trips to Disney World.

I didn't appreciate them at the time, but I do now.

TABLE OF CONTENTS

SOMEBODY DONE ROBBED YOU

The fat and sweating bald man was trying so hard to blend in that he stuck out like a cactus in a cornfield. His tight polo shirt and pressed jeans were far too clean, and he hadn't touched his plastic cup of beer in the over forty minutes he'd been sitting in the little booth Carl had agreed to meet him at.

The man, Mark Warner, like almost everyone else here, cashed his paychecks courtesy of the Bixby Company. But the typical regular at Rusty's was nothing like Mark. The people who drank here were the maids, the line chefs, and the people who cleaned up the puke when some weak-stomached dipshit took an ill-advised twirl around The Flying Pigs carousel.

Mark, on the other hand, was your typical Corporate America do-nothing who made eight times as much as anyone else in this shithole bar. Carl had been keeping an eye on him from the bar while Wade swigged Bud Lite on the stool next to him and watched the Astros game on the little muted flat-screen with the drooping cord that hung behind the bar.

For this kind of work, it was better when Wade was at least a little drunk. His bulldog face would get red and pouty, and his eyes would get this dead look that was perfect for scaring the nuts off yuppie pussies like Mark Warner.

Mark had finally taken his first baby sip of beer when Carl decided he'd made him wait long enough. "Come on," he said, tapping Wade on the arm. "Let's go talk to him."

Wade looked confused, then dipped his thick chin into his neck, indicating the screen. "But it's the ninth inning."

"Unless you want to pay for them drinks, you'll pick your ass up off that stool."

Wade's beady eyes were darting as he read over the rolling black-and-white captions flashing across the screen. "But he already been waitin' an hour," he said. "They just got back to the top of the order."

"And an hour is long enough. You can squeeze in next to him. You'll be able to see the game from there."

Wade shrugged before picking up his latest half-finished pint.

As soon as Wade had shoved himself into the booth next to Mark, Carl knew it was the best seat for the big man.

Mark's eyes had bulged and begun to twitch. "What is this?"

He looked scared, which was good. Carl slid in across from him. "You Mark Warner?"

"… Yeah," Mark said. "You were supposed to be here at 9:30."

"And I was," Carl said. "I been watching you. This is my associate, Mr. Johnson." Wade continued watching the game, impassive and imposing.

"But you're supposed to be alone."

"I ain't going to debate you, Mark. I do not debate." At the mention of his name, the fat little man sank deeper into the booth. "Now," Carl said. "You got the cards?"

Mark subtly lifted the top of a black plastic bag over the lip of the table.

"Let me see one."

Mark slid across the gift card, emblazoned with the cartoon-ish face of Wally Rabbit. Carl detested everything to do with the soul-sucking Bixby Company, but the card made him smile anyway. He turned it over with his fingers, pretending to study it. "There's a thousand dollars on this card? How do I know it'll work? We use too many of these … it don't set no alarms off or nothing?"

"No," Mark whispered. "People put even more than that on these cards all the time."

"Yeah," Carl said, tapping the plastic card on the edge of the table. "Rich fucking people."

"Where's the *package?*"

"So everything we done was legal?" Carl asked, ignoring Mark's question.

"Yes. Well … you *are* going to keep everything on the low down."

"Down low, Mark. It's down low."

"Me and Bert talked about this," Mark said, wincing. "He said you would keep this quiet."

"Well, Bert didn't talk to me about it."

In fact, Bert had told Carl over and over again that Mark urgently wanted to keep their little operation quiet, which meant there was an opportunity for additional negotiation. "I'm gonna need another thousand of these cards," Carl said.

"Another thousand?"

Carl bit off a loose thumbnail and spat the dirty curl onto the table. "We're debating again, Mark."

"This is … outrageous," Mark said, sputtering. "I need the package tonight. I don't have these preloaded cards just lying around."

"I don't get why you doin' this shit," Carl said. "Why you send me out there?"

Mark's palms slapped the table. "No questions. Bert said there'd be no questions."

"Yeah, well, Bert didn't go trouncing around on no swampy island in the middle of the fucking night. I did that. And I'm gonna need another thousand of these here cards with a grand on each of 'em."

Wade slammed his glass, and Mark jumped in his seat. The Rangers had hit a walk-off home run. Disappointed Astros fans were already trudging up through the stands to the exits.

"Look," Mark said. "I can probably get you another three hundred cards in two weeks. But I need the chip now."

Carl felt good enough about that. Best not to look this particular gift-horse in the mouth. "Fine," he said. "But don't try to fuck me. You try to fuck me, I tell everybody about every damn thing." He wasn't sure what exactly he had copied onto the chip, but it was obviously some top-secret corporate espionage type shit.

"We won't," Mark said. "Now: *where's the package?*"

"The shit's in the bathroom," Carl said, reaching over the table and taking hold of the bag. "Above the ceiling tiles in the handicap stall." He slid out of the booth, clutching the bag. "Come on, Mr. Johnson."

They returned to the bar, and Carl waited for the fat man to disappear into the bathroom before he tapped the card on the counter. Sophia, the bartender, leaned in. "And just what is that? That ain't no credit card. You know we don't take that shit here."

"I think you might." Carl guessed he could get close to six hundred bucks for most of the cards. He managed to sell that one to Sophia for five hundred and fifteen before Mark emerged from the bathroom and scurried out of the bar.

Sophia threw in two shots of Jameson on the house. Carl and Wade tinked glasses, and knocked the shots of burning liquor back in unison. "I think I done had enough," Wade said. He'd been watching the Astros postgame show in silent fury. Carl didn't understand his friend's intense interest in the sport. Wade had never played baseball, or any sport for that matter, and had never been to a professional game.

Carl had only promised Wade some free drinks, but decided he wouldn't do his friend like that. The exchange had worked out great. Carl was getting an extra three hundred cards that he wouldn't have to split with Bert, which would work out to well over six figures.

"Here," Carl said. "Take a card."

Wade looked at it closely. "But I never even been to Bixby Park."

"No shit you haven't," Carl said. "And why? Cause it's expensive as shit, that's why." He waved the card. "*Now it's free.* There's a grand on that card. You been to the sports bar at Bixby Harbor. They take this there."

Wade smiled at the prospect of a thousand-dollar bar credit and tucked the card into his pocket.

Outside and walking to the car, Carl thought it was fortunate that the yuppie had been able to find Rusty's. The barn-style building had only a single small window and no exterior lighting other than a deteriorating wooden light pole near the gravel entrance. The only signage was an old tarp hanging from a crude frame that read: 'OPEN' in red letters.

"You ain't got to drive me," Wade said, stumbling towards the dark street. "I can walk." The trailer park Wade lived in was less than a mile up the road, but there were almost no street lights.

"Come on," Carl said. "You could get your ass hit out here. You did good tonight."

Wade began chuckling. "Well shit," he said. "Looks like you walking too."

Carl was confused until he noticed the rear tire of his pickup. The axle was an inch above the ground, the wheel surrounded by a deflated tube.

"You got a spare?" Wade asked mid-hiccup.

The spare was already installed on the pickup's front driver's side. It was an annoying pickle, but Carl had hardly a moment to think of a plan before he heard the voice: sickly sweet and mechanical.

"What seems to be the trouble there, friends?" The voice had come from the open window of a beautiful black Navigator. Carl thought for a moment that it must have been Mark. No local would be driving a car like that, but it wasn't the sweaty bald man from the Bixby Company.

The man behind the wheel of the Navigator had a pale waxy face and shock white hair.

"It's a flat," Carl said.

"Do either of you think you will be requiring assistance?" The man grinned wide, pale pinkish lips stretching past the base of his earlobes. "My name is Tapper. I am here to help!"

Carl did need some way of getting home, but didn't want to go anywhere with the repulsive looking man.

The Navigator's doors unlocked with a click. "I would be happy to take you anywhere you would like to go," Tapper said. "There is a refrigerator in the back with some beer if you are interested."

Wade patted Carl in the chest and headed for the vehicle.

"What are your names?" Tapper's eyes trailed after Wade as he settled into the backseat.

Carl found himself momentarily lost for words before formulating a response. He didn't want to get in, but didn't want to leave Wade. "My name's Mr. Sanderson," Carl said. "That there is Mr. Johnson."

"Good to meet you both, and welcome aboard," Tapper said.

Inside the cabin, Carl's friend had already cracked open a can of beer. Tapper planted an elbow on the front seat and looked to the rear. "Address?"

"Old Country Road," Wade said, slurring. "One … four …"

"Nine," Carl finished for him. "One four nine."

"Absolutely, sirs," Tapper said, starting the car forward. "Just sit back and enjoy the ride."

"You think I can sleep at your place tonight?" Wade asked under his breath. "I think I might be a little tipsy."

Carl nodded but said nothing.

Tapper's reflection flicked into view in the driver's mirror as they passed a rare street lamp. "So, what do you boys do?"

"I just got a job," Wade said. "Work for the Bixby Company."

What?! Carl thought. "You didn't tell me that."

"I just got it." Wade finished the beer and crushed the can in his hand before tucking it into the door's side pocket. "Dish washing at the Ink Club."

"I also work for Max Bixby," Tapper said.

It was odd that he said *Max Bixby* and not the *Bixby Company* or *Bixby Park*, but Carl didn't say so. He wanted to say as little as possible and get out of the car with Wade and his cards.

"What do you do, Mr. Sanderson?"

"I'm an … *investor*," Carl said.

Wade laughed and cracked open a second beer.

"Hey," Carl said to Tapper. "You know where you're going? You didn't plug the address into no GPS."

"Of course I know where we're going, Carl."

Carl's blood went cold.

"I know my way all around these parts," Tapper said, looking up to the mirror. "What you have in the bag there?"

"Ain't no business of yours."

"No reason to get angry, friend," Tapper said. "I was only trying to get to know you is all."

Carl looked out the window as they passed a darkened Bob's Meat Market. "It's right up the road here."

"Of course, Carl."

"How you know my name?"

"You told me, of course."

"Hey, Mister," Wade said. "What was you doing out here? I didn't see you inside Rusty's."

"I'm looking for a man. He took something that didn't belong to him."

"We just met a Bixby Park security guy," Wade said. "You work security too?"

"Something like that," Tapper said. He passed his card back without looking.

Carl pinched it from the air. The card read: 'Tapper' in big and bold letters with an eight-hundred number scrawled beneath it. "Let me know if you need any more late-night pickups. I am out on this road all the time."

Carl was thrown forward as the SUV skidded to a stop. Outside, the only light came from the flash of fireflies, and the bathroom light Carl had left on in his trailer.

"Here we are," Tapper said. "You boys have a nice evening."

"You too," Wade said before staggering out into the thick air.

Carl bolted from the car and watched it turn and rumble away, leaving behind a trail of dust dissipating in red tail lights.

Carl's leg was shaking. *Who the fuck was that guy?* Behind him, he vaguely heard his squeaking screen door slap against the doorframe.

"What the shit happened in here?" Wade shouted, looking back over his shoulder. "Carl … I think somebody done robbed you."

INTERLUDE

OBITUARY

Maximilian 'Max' Bixby, 1905–1969
Visionary Animator, Inventor, and Entertainment Magnate

Maximilian 'Max' Bixby, the reclusive millionaire and creative genius who built an entertainment empire from humble beginnings, passed away at the age of 64 on December 12, 1969, at John Sealy Hospital in Galveston, Texas.

Bixby, who captivated the world with his whimsical animated creations and visionary approach to storytelling, died of acute circulatory collapse following a series of medical complications after surgery for a lung tumor.

Born in 1905 in Memphis, Tennessee, Max Bixby's rise to fame began in the 1920s with the creation of the beloved animated character Wally Rabbit. Wally's adventures captured the imaginations of millions and set the foundation for an empire that would span television, film, and theme parks. He was responsible for launching some of the most iconic animated films of the 1930s and 1940s, including *Chateau of the Moon* (1937) and *The Beast* (1948), both of which introduced groundbreaking animation techniques that revolutionized the industry.

While Max was known for his prolific work in animation, it was his ability to blend art with technology that defined his legacy. In the 1950s, he expanded his vision to in-person entertainment, creating Bixby Park, an immersive fantasy park that brought his animated worlds to life. Bixby Park's opening in 1955 marked the beginning of a new era for theme parks, making Bixby a pioneer of not only animation, but also of robotics and animatronics.

Despite his public success, after the deaths of his wife Evelyn and his oldest son Fritz, Max became known for his extreme reclusiveness, especially as his focus shifted to the development of The Dream Factory, an upcoming attraction on a small island within view of Bixby Park.

As his health deteriorated, Max rarely left the confines of his factory, delegating most of his company's day-to-day operations to family members and trusted advisors.

Surviving Max are his brother Lawrence Bixby—the newly announced CEO of the Bixby Company, and Max's three children: Joseph (35), Violet (25), and Lucille (20).

A statement released by the company reads: "We will continue to operate Max's company in the way that he has established. All the plans for the future that Max had begun, including the Dream Factory, will continue to move ahead."

A private funeral service will be held on a date and time to be announced.

"When you dream, dream big—and make it real."

— Max Bixby

PART ONE:
BIXBY PARK

CHAPTER ONE:

A MAGICAL WEEKEND

It was two months after Pops died that Jaxon's mom had suggested the 'funcation'. She'd brought it up in the kitchen after dinner, only a few days after that miserable Christmas, while pouring herself a glass of cloudy coconut water. "How do you guys feel about taking a little funcation somewhere over spring break?"

Dad, who despised going anywhere, had ignored the invented word and said, "We just got back from Florida."

Florida had nice enough weather, but Jaxon hardly considered Pops' funeral to be a vacation. Mom had agreed. "That wasn't a vacation," she said. "And it certainly wasn't a *funcation*."

"Hmm," Dad had said before returning to the glow of his phone. "Maybe it's something we can look into."

Spring break came and went, but that 'maybe' was a crack in the armor that Mom had kept hammering relentlessly, even deep into mid-August. The summer was nearly over when Jaxon's parents called him and his older sister down to the living room for the big news. They were going to the land of dreams and wonders: Bixby Park.

"Funcation here we come!" Mom had shouted.

Jaxon still wasn't sure what the difference between a funcation and a regular vacation was, and Dad had yet to refer to the event as anything other than 'that damn trip.' Still, Jaxon was thrilled. The best part of it all was that Bixby Park was close enough that they wouldn't need to fly. Jaxon hated planes. They crashed all the time … and if your plane crashed while you were on it … well, sport, that's it for you: fin-ee-toe … *you're dead.*

Despite Jaxon's relief, the car ride was proving far from relaxing.

"What the fuck do you mean!" Dad yelled into his phone, only one meaty hand on the wheel. For a word Dad often said he didn't like, he used the f-word quite a bit, in the car particularly.

So why can't I say it? Jaxon thought. It was hard for him to pin down what the word even meant. He was sure it had something to do with making babies, but he wasn't sure how. YouTubers would let it rip in all kinds of situations, none of which seemed to involve baby-making. They would say it when they were happy. When they were mad. When they were shocked. Dad had muttered it when he'd heard Pops had died. It seemed to mean both everything and nothing.

"What are you talking about?" Dad's voice had risen to a high shrill. "Of course you don't give them the fucking check!"

Mom brushed a wisp of blond hair behind an ear and offered an apologetic smile to Jaxon and his sister in the backseat. Dad normally had to be at least mid-level mad before he'd drop the forbidden word so flippantly, but the bumper-to-bumper traffic outside of Houston had pushed him well past that threshold.

The jam had started to loosen up at about the time the looming highway lights outside had ignited, and a thin arc of moon had begun following their car.

"Why would I pay them off before they're done? I told you not to hold up their money. I said, give it to them as soon as they're done. Not *before* they're done. We'll be lucky if we ever see their fucking asses again."

Mom leaned her wiry frame across the center console. "Hunnie, is there something I can do? You're driving."

"Just … give me a sec, will ya?" Dad fumbled the phone onto the dashboard and stabbed at it with a thick finger before it could slide away.

"Boss, you still there?" It was Joey, Dad's right-hand man.

"Yeah," Dad said. "I'm still here …"

Mom gave Dad a knowing look and shook her head. "I told you we should have set up the Bluetooth."

"I'm sorry, Boss. The check was there with his name on it. I didn't know not to give it to him."

"Look," Dad said. "I know I told you to give that check to them on Monday … *after* they'd finished."

"Sorry, Boss. I just didn't want to bother you with it."

Dad's fingers dug into the steering wheel, grinding into black leather. "It's fine," he said, his tone softening artificially. "Did everyone get to the mall okay?"

"Yeah, Robby was late as usual but they're all there now. Everyone's a li'l pissy working the night shift is all, but I got it under control. Should work out good. They're going to want to get finished tonight so they ain't gotta work the weekend."

"Good," Dad said. "I'll see you Tuesday."

"Night, Boss. Have fun—" The phone slid off the dash and landed in Mom's lap.

Becky perked up next to Jaxon. "He sounded real sorry, Daddy. People make mistakes." Becky loved to talk. Always quick with something to say. The most infuriating part was Jaxon could never seem to think of anything to say when there was an opening.

"I suppose they do," Dad said into the rearview mirror, the lines around his eyes folding together. "I swear, though. It's every single time I go out of town."

"Babe, relax," Mom said. "The bad thing hasn't even happened yet. It'll probably be fine."

"You're right," he said, forcing a smile. "We're going to have a fun weekend, no matter what. Guaranteed."

"*Funcation!*" Mom shouted.

"I do think it's going to be cool," Becky said. "I remember when we came here last time. *It was so fun.*" This was Becky's way of rubbing it in. Jaxon couldn't remember much from their last trip to Bixby Park four years earlier, and his sister had been scant about the details.

There were pictures, but they might as well have been of another person. Jaxon could recall little more than flashes: a distant factory on black water that puffed out rainbow smoke, a flying pig ride, and some kind of party where people threw fire into the sky and made it dance.

"It was fun," Dad said, scratching the salt-and-pepper hair above his ear. He seemed lost in a happy memory, before the buzzing came again from Mom's lap. "Fuck."

"It's an unknown number," she said, narrowing her eyes. "And stop saying that."

"Sorry," he said softly before reaching for the radio.

Jaxon needed to say something now or he'd miss his chance. In a flash, he remembered something Pops had once told him. If you can't think of anything to say: ask a question. "Dad, can I ask a question?"

Dad's eyes shifted back up to the mirror. "You don't have to ask for permission to have a question answered. Just ask it."

"How come you can say that word and we can't?"

"Because I'm the dad and you're the kids."

A typical answer, but Jaxon wasn't going to let it fly this time. "That's not fair," he said. "What does it even mean?"

Dad looked to Mom for help, but she smiled and looked away. "Okay," he said, slowly. "You're right. From now on when I say the f-word—"

Jaxon spelled out the letters "F-U-C-K," and Dad grunted out an amused chuckle.

"You're becoming a better speller than I thought, sport. And you're right: from now on, if you catch me saying that word, you have my permission to say it. One time and one time only."

Jaxon cackled maniacally. *This was going to be great.*

"I want that too!" Becky said.

"Okay. Fine. Both of you."

"This should be interesting." Mom was rolling her eyes.

"You're in this too," Dad said, pulling their car off an exit.

"You don't actually think I'll be the one to break, do you?"

"I think Daddy will win," Becky said.

I'm going to get to say 'fuck,' Jaxon thought. "This is going to be so hilarious."

Dad frowned. "It's not even going to happen, but let me be clear: you can't bank these words. If you hear it, you've got five minutes. That's it."

More fricking rules.

Becky straightened up. "What if it's in a place where we're not allowed to say it?"

"Well," Dad said, "you're *allowed* to say it almost anywhere, you just shouldn't. This is America."

"What if it's in school or something?" Becky said.

"You mean like if I come to your school, stick my head in the classroom and drop the f-bomb?"

"Yes," Jaxon and Becky said in unison.

"On that rare occasion, my children, you may scream the word as loud as you like."

"Be careful with your promises," Mom said. "You'll want these rules spelled out real clear. What about other variations of the word?"

"We don't need to draw up a contract, okay?" Dad said. "We all know the word in question."

"What about the other bad words?" Becky said.

Jaxon tried and failed to suppress a giggle. "What about 'damn'?"

"Don't push it, buster," Dad said, ice cold. "Anything I say, both of you can say once, and once only, within five minutes. Understood?"

Through the windshield, a glittering bright blue archway came into view. Sitting at its peak, an animatronic Wally Rabbit waved to the cars that passed beneath him. On his right, a smiling Regina Rat's whiplike tail flicked to and fro beneath the arch.

Jaxon read the speech bubble attached to Wally's head: *"Tune in to 101.1 for Bixby's Greatest Hits and Park News!!!"*

"Did you see that?" Mom said. "It's the Bixby Station."

"Or we could have a sing-along," Dad said. "When I was a kid, we'd always sing in the car during trips. Kids, your grandma was a fantastic singer."

They'd heard this all before.

"Dave, the kids don't know any of the old songs that you're going to want to sing." Mom leaned forward and tuned the dial. The bright music drifted cheerfully through the cabin, and Jaxon's heart swelled with joy.

It was going to be a magical weekend.

CHAPTER TWO:

A MAGICAL EVENING

"**M**an, will you turn that shit down?" Don sank deeper into the passenger seat, working to avoid the phantom stare of the woman stopped alongside them at the red light.

"Chill, man," Ziaire said, shifting his shoulders to the rhythm of the corny Bixby music. "It ain't that bad." He gave a friendly wave to the woman before accelerating through the light.

Ziaire could afford to be a dumbass. When you were over six feet tall, with money to throw around and an ESPN player page to boot, the girls would throw themselves at you, regardless of how much of a doofus you actually were.

"Motherfucker, someone gonna hear that shit."

Ziaire shrugged and thumbed down the volume from the steering wheel. The cheerful singing faded to a blissfully dull murmur. "Fine," he said. "But you gonna have to get into the spirit of this shit."

Don shouldn't have been surprised by his friend's goofy behavior. It was clear now that Ziaire had lost his mind since being called up. First, he'd given up smoking weed, then he had bought this ridiculously compact Boxster that he had practically needed to fold himself into … and now there was his new girl, Pam.

And her friend.

"I don't think many other guys on the team are listening to Bixby soundtracks."

Ziaire smirked. "Like you'd know."

It was a low blow, but Don was used to them. "Maybe I'll ask 'em."

"They listen to whatever they want, and they still get laid. Who are you to fucking judge me, man? You listen to musicals and shit."

This again. "*West Side Story* ain't no kids' movie, man. Got gangs and shit."

"Dancing gangs."

"Whatever. You like it too. I seen you tapping your foot."

"I'm just trying to get you in the groove, baby. Get you in the right head space. Have I ever played you wrong?"

Ziaire had certainly played Don wrong on more than one occasion, but it would have been a lie to say that Don had not been benefiting from his association with him.

Don had been successfully swimming in his friend's high-profile wake for the last five years, and things had only gotten better since Ziaire's call up to the Rockets. He had only played in five minutes of garbage-time against the Grizzlies, but that was enough for him to be draftable in NBA fantasy leagues and have a profile page on the team's website.

Ziaire shook his head. "These rich white girls don't listen to this gangster shit."

"That don't mean they listening to kids' music," Don said. "You think pretending to like this shit is going to help you?"

Ziaire snickered. "I mean it hasn't hurt. Maybe it'll work for you too if you let it."

"Maybe," Don said doubtfully. It had been over a month since he and Ziaire had last been out together. On that occasion, Don had ended up with Whitney. She had a big ass and juicy lips, but had bitten his left nipple so hard it had throbbed for a week.

"Honestly," Don said, "Princess Pam sounds psychotic."

Ziaire pulled a vape pen from inside his blazer and took a long drag, before expelling fruity-smelling vapor. "You just jealous."

"Why would anyone want to do that all day?" Don mimicked an exaggerated *Stepford Wives* smile and wave. "Creepy as hell, man."

"It's kinda sexy."

"It's sexy now," Don said. "But dude, I'm telling ya … crazy sticks the fuck around."

"Fool, she ain't crazy. It's her job."

"Okay. Her job. Fine."

"She has to work someplace."

The truth was Princess Pam was one of the rare girls either of them had hooked up with who had actually had a job. That was unless you counted having an Only Fans account as being an entrepreneur.

Don's typical cover story, when he was out with Ziaire, was that of an A-list scout.

No, don't bother looking it up. You ain't gonna find him on no website. My man is undercover, okay? Deep, deep undercover.

A week after Don's nipple had healed, he'd sent Whitney a 'what u doin' text.

There had been three dots, then a long nothing. Three more dots. Then a screen shot: his picture and bio on the George Ruby High School website. He looked stupid as shit in that picture.

Donald Williams, Health and Physical Education. Hello, my name is Mr. Williams. I graduated from Sam Houston State University with a degree in Exercise and Sports Science. I'm a proud former member of the Bearkats and your new basketball coach!

Fuck. He'd told his momma not to put his photo on the website … and then she went and wrote all that?

Ziaire turned off the highway exit onto Wally Boulevard.

"What you tell her I do?"

Ziaire blew out a bit of air. "I mean … the truth, I guess."

"The truth? Fuck, man."

"Yeah, the truth," Ziaire said. "And Rosie still wants to meet you. So chill, baby."

"How they know each other?"

Ziaire winced slightly. "Auditions."

"*Shhhe-it*. She's a Bixby Princess too?"

Ziaire hunkered closer to the wheel, and his rangy frame curled over it. "Not exactly," he said. "Rosie didn't make the cut."

Christ. That could only mean one thing. "She a Bixby Adult?"

"A what?"

"Motherfucker, a Bixby Adult. One of them crazy grown-up Bixby bitches."

"I honestly have no idea what you're talking about."

"Fool," Don said. "Where we going?"

Ziaire looked confused before indicating the gatehouse they were approaching. "What? You mean Bixby Harbor? What the shit it matter?" Ziaire came to a brief rolling stop as the gateman, smiling ear to ear, waved them through.

Don extended his index finger to the blue sticker in the corner of the windshield. "Bruh, you got a VIP pass."

"Pam gets them through the park. It's whatever, man. It's cool. They free."

This was going to be a nightmare. "Shit," Don said. "Rosie is going to be a six-hundred-pound former man. I know it."

"No, she ain't. Chill."

The GPS announced they'd arrived, and Ziaire slid into a preferred space twenty feet from the promenade. "And besides," he said, "didn't you have that *situationship* with—"

"Yo, you need to watch it with that shit. Cassie wasn't six hundred pounds, and she wasn't no damn man neither."

"Neither is Rosie," Ziaire said, opening the door. "You honestly don't deserve what I've hooked up for you." He uncurled himself from behind the wheel and skipped out onto the spotless sidewalk. "You ain't gonna embarrass me tonight, are ya? I like this girl. A lot."

"Come on," Don said, opening his door. "That's the last thing I'd do."

Ziaire smiled and slapped his door shut before sliding towards the bustling promenade. Don had to jog to keep up with his loping gait. "I appreciate you, man," Don said. "You know I do."

"I know you about to." Ziaire locked his Boxster with a *beep* and slipped the key into the chest pocket of his blazer. Behind him, in Bixby Cove, a fountain sent up a tower of water, and cartoonishly bright steamer boats paddled into their berths at Pirate Island's Snacks and Gift Shop.

Don swam through the throng to keep up with his friend. "Slow down, man. We early." He slid around a man wearing a Wally Rabbit earhat and a gray Bixby t-shirt that had been stretched over his dangling potbelly.

Ziaire retrieved his phone and held it up to show him. "We're not early. We're right on time."

"On time is early. You don't want to get there first."

"Why not?"

"Trust me, man. You want to make 'em wait."

"Now see … *that* is psychotic." Ziaire looked up from his phone. "They here already." His face split into a grin. "You ready for that picture you been after?" He angled the phone for Don and chuckled out a cough. "Not bad, right? Rosie's the one without the glasses."

Both of the women were stunning, but Rosie had massive breasts, practically bursting out of the Captain Proton t-shirt she was wearing. She smiled at the camera with shy, full lips. *Fuck*, he thought. *How tough are these princess auditions?* "You said she ain't got no kids?"

Ziaire hacked out another laugh before tucking the phone back into his blazer. "I told you she was fine." He hopped up to the maître d' stand at Captain Proton's Cafe and Command Store, passing an animatronic spaceman that announced, "Welcome, Space Cadet."

"We're meeting some people," Ziaire told the spacewoman at the desk. "They already here."

She nodded. "Do you know where they're seated?"

"By the space tank."

"I see," she said. "Mr. Crank will direct you after your security check."

Don was about to complain until he realized it was a joke. A thick brother, crammed into a stark white spacesuit, came forward holding a ray gun that didn't look much different from a grocery store scanner. He pointed it at Ziaire's head.

"Hold still a moment, cadet." A blue light ignited, and the scanner whistled, high-pitched and shrill. "Okay. You're all clear."

Don choked down a laugh as Mr. Crank scanned him. The trooper glared before cocking his head. "This way."

He led them past the Command Store through a hazy purple fog that filled the restaurant. The far wall was a void of blackness, save for the lime-green and ruby-red fish flittering through nothingness.

Pam stood first, hanging over the edge of the booth and waving in wide, enthusiastic arcs. She pulled up Rosie, who made a nervous wave, the beginnings of a Mona Lisa smile forming at the corners of her mouth.

"Go ahead," Mr. Crank said, scooting to the side. "Your waitress, Verotica of the Venus Belt, will be right over."

Rosie tucked a fallen strand of dirty blonde hair back into her messy bun as Don drifted after Ziaire through the beeping and buzzing space port.

"This my boy Don I was telling you about." Ziaire leaned over the booth's pulsing onyx table and kissed Pam on the mouth. "This is Pam and Rosie."

Rosie became rosy in her pale cheeks and exposed chest above her low-cut Captain Proton t-shirt. Don scooted around the booth next to her, and she flashed pearlish white teeth.

"Fan?" he asked, risking a brief look down at her rhythmically rising chest.

"I've been watching it since I was a kid."

"I heard you was more of the *princess* type."

"Oh, I wish." Rosie nodded to Pam. "Turns out she's the princess."

Pam had already curled herself against Ziaire.

"Which princess are you?" Don asked her. He knew at least a couple of them.

Pam removed her square-rimmed glasses and pulled her hair free of its ponytail, letting the strands fall around her face in twirling curls. She pouted her lips and narrowed her eyes.

Don studied the pose before shaking his head. "Sorry."

"Princess Saarkar." Pam frowned and replaced her glasses.

"That's the one with the singing camels, right?" Don said. "I haven't seen it."

Pam looked oddly concerned at the revelation. "You haven't seen *Jewel of the Dunes*? I think you might be in for a long night."

"You have to see it!" Rosie said, brightening. "We'll have to find somewhere to watch it when we leave. Oh my God, it's so good. The music is amazing!"

"We can rent it and watch it at my place," Ziaire said.

Don was relieved Ziaire had jumped on this so quickly. He didn't want to risk bringing a white girl back to his mother's house, even if she was asleep. His momma had a radar for white girls.

"You live all the way in the city," Rosie said, waving the notion away. Over her head, miniature star fighters came screeching by, twisting and sliding on a colorless track. "I practically live in the park," she said. "It's five minutes away."

"They have houses in the park?" Don asked.

Rosie pursed her full lips and nodded. "Who would ever want to leave the most magical place on Earth?"

A waitress in a sparkling white miniskirt and black knee-high boots came alongside the booth. "Welcome to Captain Proton's, space cadets." She pulled four laminated menus that had been tucked under a smooth bare arm and passed them out.

"You must be Verotika of Venus," Ziaire said.

"Of the Venus Belt," she corrected, pulling a space-pad with a twirling antenna from her wide black belt. "Something to drink?"

"You guys have to try the Moon Water," Rosie squealed. "It's out of this world!"

A hint of a frown formed at the corner of Pam's thinning mouth. "Rosie," she said. "They probably don't want—"

"Why not?"

Red heat brightened across Rosie's breasts. Whatever she wanted sounded like at least a moderately good idea to Don. "We'll take four of them," he said. "On me."

Verotika of the Venus Belt put the order into her whirring space-pad. "Alright, sir … coming right up. Anything else for now?"

Pam shook her head, her lips pursed in annoyance.

"Alright then, cadets. I'll give you a moment to look over the menus and I'll be back with those drinks." She marched back through an explosion of pink mist that sent the children three tables away into screaming fits of laughter.

Rosie edged around the table, and Don felt her bare knee graze against his thigh. "You can't come to Captain Proton's and not get the Moon Water. It's just not done."

Don leaned into her, inhaling a sweet scent of fresh laundry and soap bubbles. "I didn't know they had water on the moon."

Rosie's hand swatted his leg seemingly in jest, but now it was resting there, her fingers drumming on his kneecap.

A tall figure in silver armor and matching helmet emerged through a blast of neon-blue mist, holding a tray of glasses. Across the helmet's red visor, a blinking light flashed.

"Can you take a picture of us?" Pam said, holding up her phone.

The light passed across the visor a few more times before a digitized, feminine voice said, "Of course, cadets."

Pam handed the robot-woman her camera, and the group took hold of their smoking glasses and held them up, smiling as if in mid-toast.

"There you are," the robot-woman said. "As a special prize, your table has been selected for the Dream Factory drawing."

Rosie squealed. "OH. MY. GODDDD!"

"The what?" Don said.

Ziaire twiddled his fingers like an old-timey magician. "*A tour of the mysterious—and fantastical—Dreaaam Factory.*"

Don had seen the Dream Factory. Once. Right after his dad had left. Mom-mom had brought him to the park. "That's the building on the island," Don said. "The one with the rainbow smoke. I guess I thought it was just a big prop or a dressed-up maintenance building or something."

"Are you crazy?" Rosie snaked a hand around his bicep. "How is it possible you don't know this?"

The robot-woman began ripping perforated tickets free and handing them out. "One ticket per guest. Good luck."

The others were scratching at them with their silverware before Don even had his in hand:

*One Million Dollars and a Trip
To the Land of Dreams and Wonders
Scratch here:*

The others were groaning, all losers. In a flash of inspiration, Don tucked the scratch-off card into his hip pocket.

"What are you doing?" Rosie said.

"I'll open it later." The card probably was a loser, but if Don was scratching it later—alone with Rosie—that would be a win.

She wrapped a hand around his thigh. "Can we order?" she said. "I need something hot and sweet."

The robot-woman turned on her heels, starting away. "Verotika will be back in a moment."

Rosie pointed to the menu. "Let's get the Europa Puffs."

Europa Puffs:

Original Cubes
Synthesized All-Beef Space Cubes, $19.99

Reuben Space Cubes
Original Cubes with Russian Dressing,
Coleslaw, and Swiss Fondue, $22.99

The Works
Original Cubes with Russian Dressing, Coleslaw, Pickles,
Bacon, Hot Sauce, and Swiss Fondue, $24.99

What the hell is a Space Cube?
"What are they, even?" Ziaire said. "I like Reub—"
Pam nudged him hard in the ribs. "I'll have the Galactic Nuggets with the potato strings," she said.
"Yeah," Ziare said, rubbing his midsection. "I'll take that too, I guess."
Don didn't care what a Europa Puff was. But whatever they turned out to be … he'd decided it was going to be a magical evening.

CHAPTER THREE:

ZZZZZZZZZZZ...

The man in the sparkling gray dinner jacket fixed a smile on Jaxon, his deft fingers dancing over piano keys. The sound was pure happiness: Christmas mixed with a wedding.

"I'm sorry, sir," a hotel lady said to Dad, raising her voice over the ascending music. She was wearing the same gray jacket and matching bow-tie as the piano man and displayed the same unrelenting smile. "I'm afraid check-in ended at seven."

Jaxon scooted closer to the lobby's reflective front desk. Every surface in the hotel seemed to be polished to an impossible sheen.

"It's seven thirty," Dad said. He looked, exasperated, toward Mom.

She frowned at him. "I told you to call them."

"I'm afraid there was a waitlist, sir."

"I was here by seven!" Dad said. "I was here. The bus you people put me on got stuck in the parking lot." He threw a thumb back towards the illuminated pink Regina Rat bus sitting outside under the glass-covered archway. "Calling shouldn't have made a difference. I was here."

The hotel lady cocked her head high and to the left. Grandma Betty-Ann had a similar move that she used whenever Jaxon had told her that he was very sure about something.

It was the 'I don't know about that, dude' look.

"It should be clear on our website," the hotel lady said. "We recommend arriving at least two hours early.

Dad's jaw worked side to side. "What the ... *flip*."

"Sir, please ... I've already arranged accommodations for you in the Dark Forest. And you are on our waitlist here."

"The ... Dark Forest?"

Becky perked up. "Are you scared of the Dark Forest, Daddy?"

Dad grunted.

"Sir, putting you on the waitlist is the best I can do right now."

"Yeah, the waitlist," Dad said. "So, I can steal a room from the next poor son of a ... *guy* ... *whatever* ... that comes in here fifteen minutes late?"

"Sir... the bus is waiting for you. The Dark Forest is one of our most popular resorts. You're going to love it."

A thick cord of muscle was protruding and twitching under the skin of Dad's neck. He was going to say a bad word soon. "But we need the Skyline access," he said. "We have reservations at Canyon Jane's at eight tomorrow morning."

The hotel lady cocked her head again in an 'I don't know about that, dude' sort of way.

"Mother ... flipper ..."

Come on, Dad.

Say it.

The hotel lady gestured for them to head back towards the glass doors. "I am afraid, sir, that with the festivities this weekend, a room here is unlikely to become available for you, but rest assured you are on the list."

"What the hell's going on this weekend?"

"Hell!" Jaxon said instantly. Dad glared down at him, and Jaxon's breath caught in his throat.

Dad rubbed his tongue along his teeth beneath the upper lip. "At least use it in a sentence, son."

Jaxon began formulating a string of words when Dad said, "No ... not now. You had your shot. Next time." Becky was shaking like a busted soda can. "Do it," Dad said. "Once. Now."

"Hell," she whispered, gleefully.

"Great. All done." Dad gave the hotel lady an apologetic smile that she returned. "It's a little … little family game."

"I'm sure it is, sir. All the information regarding the event is in your treehouse."

"Our … *treehouse?*"

• • •

The boyish bellhop held down his red-and-black pillbox hat as he slid the golf cart to a stop along the sidewalk. The twisting pavement had been cut through a dense mass of dark, chirping trees. "Here we are, folks," the bellhop said. "Better late than never."

Jaxon leapt off the cart and jumped up onto one of the flat-topped light bollards that curled along the path. The place didn't seem scary at all.

Dad slung his leather bag over his shoulder and indicated the path. "It's right through there?"

"Yes, sir," the bellhop said. "I'll take you up."

"That's not necessary." Dad put up a hand. "Just tell me where it is."

The bellhop frowned for a moment before rediscovering his magical smile. "As you wish, Mr. Kinney. It's the third villa on the left: seven-oh-eight. Follow up the ramp into the trees. The rest of your luggage should arrive in the next thirty minutes or so."

Dad's loafers scratched across the sidewalk, and he lifted Jaxon off the warm bollard as Becky darted past his swinging legs. "Me first!" she yelled.

Jaxon wiggled free of Dad's hands and bolted ahead. The sidewalk widened into a broad clearing where wooden ramps climbed toward the structures perched in the branches. Becky sprinted ahead of him, clunking up onto the elevated decking toward the glowing treehouse villas.

"That's not fair, Becky!" Jaxon ran as hard as he could, but it was an impossible challenge against Becky's spindly roadrunner legs.

She thudded past three of the cottages built along the deck and smacked both hands against the fourth's forest-green door below the gold-trimmed '708'.

"That wasn't a fair race," Jaxon said, trudging forward. "You gave yourself a head start."

"Yes, it was."

"No, it wasn't, Becky. You're always cheating. You're such a cheat."

"Becky don't tease him," Mom called. Dad speed-walked ahead of her, adjusting the leather strap on his shoulder.

Becky perked up, her scowl replaced with the mask of a perfect daughter. "Can I put in the code, Daddy?"

"That's not fair!"

Dad shook his head and flipped down the weather protector above the polished latch. "I'm not in the mood, gang." He punched five keys with his thumb, and the lock blinked green and beeped.

Becky threw herself forward, slammed down the latch, and rumbled inside the dark cottage.

"That's no fair!" Jaxon stormed after her as Dad hit the lights.

The room had tall ceilings with exposed wooden beams held up by thick, knotty columns. All of it, and the furniture too, looked as if it had been carved by a wood elf.

Becky was already seated at one of the shiny wooden stools at the open kitchen's raised counter. "This place is amazing."

"Yeah," Dad said, rolling his neck, as if trying to loosen something stiff. "Amazing. I'm just glad the code worked." He dropped his bag next to a gnarled floor light shaped like a tree branch.

"Would you lighten up?" Mom said, stepping inside. "Hey … this is nice, guys. There should be a room with a bunk bed …"

Becky was already off her stool and in a full run toward the back half of the cottage. She had reached the top rung of the ladder by the time Jaxon had made it inside the room. She smiled, flipping a leg over the twisting log that was the top bunk's guardrail.

Whenever Jaxon and his sister stayed at their cousin Ava's house, Becky would get to share the bunk bed with Ava, while Jaxon would be banished to sleep on the floor next to his aunt and uncle's bed.

Becky got everything.

"That's not fair!" Jaxon said. "You get to sleep in bunk beds all the time."

Mom came in and patted Jaxon on the shoulder. "They're bunk beds. You can both sleep in them. That's the point."

Jaxon groaned. "I don't want to sleep with Becky if I don't get the top bunk. She's a slob."

"There's three rooms in this house," Dad called from the kitchen. "I really don't want to listen to this crap tonight."

"Crap," Jaxon said.

Mom chuckled. "Keep practicing, hunnie."

"That's not even a bad word, dum-dum," Becky said.

"I'm not a dum-dum!"

"Becky, please," Mom said. "Stop antagonizing him."

"Yeah, Becky! Stop antagonizing me!"

"I wasn't, Mom. I just got here first. He's the one with the attitude problem." Becky threw out her arms and laid out dramatically over the log rail. "And besides, there's plenty of room down there."

"No way. I want the top bunk."

"Are you guys hungry?" Dad called from the kitchen. "They can bring out a pizza."

"I am," Mom said. She smiled, looking down to Jaxon. "Pizza sound good to you, little man?"

Jaxon nodded.

"I want fries," Becky said.

"We'll see." Mom turned back to the kitchen. "Work this out with your brother."

"Fine," Becky said, smiling sadistically. "Okay, Jaxon. You can sleep on the top bunk. You're right. It wouldn't be fair of me to take it."

Jaxon sensed a trap but couldn't think of what it could be. With the rails, he probably wouldn't fall out of bed, and if there were monsters in the Dark Forest, they would certainly eat the kid on the bottom bunk first.

"Mom," Jaxon called. "Becky says I can have the top bunk."

"Wonderful," Dad said. "You want mushrooms?"

"Gross." Jaxon ran back to the kitchen. "Don't put that on it!"

"Relax, I'm only kidding," Dad said into his glowing phone. "Okay so we've got a half pepperoni, half cheese. Is there anything else?"

Mom looked over the big, plastic menu. "Becky wants fries."

Dad thumbed over his phone. "I didn't see fries."

"They come with the Mystical Forest Platter."

"Mystical Forest Platter? Oh, come on." Dad looked up from the phone. "We don't need Wizard Skewers and Goblin Fingers."

"I don't want any of that either," Jaxon said.

"That's not really what it is, sweetheart." Mom scooted over and pointed to the big plastic menu she was holding. "It's only twenty dollars. It's not that bad. And if we have enough left, we can save it for breakfast."

"Breakfast?" Dad said. "We're going to Canyon Jane's. I was looking at the map." He pointed to the thick leather binder at the edge of the kitchen counter. "We'll be able to make it. We just have to be waiting at the ferry terminal by seven to make it out of here on the first boat."

Mom shrugged and snuggled under Dad's shoulder. "Whatever you say, hunnie. Do you want to get a bottle of Sorcerer's Poisoned Oak? It's a cabernet."

"It's poison?" Jaxon said.

"How much is it?" Dad asked, ignoring him.

Mom snuck away and tucked the menu back into the top pocket of the leather binder. "You don't want to know."

"Oh, I see … yes," Dad said, scrolling over the phone and finding his answer. "You were right, I didn't want to know." He blew out a sigh.

"Well … we *are* on funcation. Let's do it." The fabricated Frankenstein-word sounded wildly unnatural coming from him.

"That's the spirit," Mom said, grinning. "*Funcation!*"

Dad indicated the leather binder. "Did you see that event sheet in there about this factory thing?"

"The Dream Factory?"

Dad nodded. "They're finally opening it up to a few guests this weekend apparently."

"Really? I thought that building was just for looks."

"Seems like there's something in there," Dad said. "But I'd be more interested in the cash—a million dollars."

The number seemed unfathomable. Jaxon had three hundred dollars in a checking account that Mom had started for him, so he had a place to put the birthday-card money from his grandparents.

Jaxon snatched up the binder and found the brochure, tucked in the back pocket. It was bright and oddly heavy, as if a gold brick had been hammered paper thin.

Dream Factory Set to Be Open to Guests for First Time

I, Lucille Bixby, have decided to open my father's factory for the very first time to a pair of lucky guests, so they can see all the secrets and magic of the factory on September 15th. At the end of their tour, as a special present, each winner will be gifted a one-million-dollar cash prize. Tickets will be given out randomly at most of the park's restaurants. If you scratch and find a wand, you'll unlock the magic beyond!

- Lucille Bixby

September 15th? "That's this weekend …" Jaxon said.

Dad scoffed. "Do you have any idea how many Bixby nutcases are in this park right now, trying to win those tickets?"

Jaxon had no idea, but before he could answer Mom pulled a short rectangular box from under the TV. "Look," she said. "They've got Bixby Monopoly."

Jaxon was tired, and he hated Monopoly. But Mom looked desperate to play, and Jaxon loved to make her happy.

All four of them played the game on the deck outside and ate pizza under string lights that cast bobbing circles of gold across the deck boards. Beyond the buzzing trees in the lagoon, lighted steamer boats paddled by, slapping against the water.

"That'll be twelve hundred." Becky smirked, her hand held out.

Jaxon didn't need to count his money to know he didn't have enough. "Fine," he said. "Whatever. I lose."

It hadn't been fair. Dad had made the trade that allowed Becky to take over the corner of the board around the jail, which in this edition was called the Silly Slammer and had a picture of Marty Duck behind bars in black-and-white prison-stripes. Dad was letting Becky win. Like always.

Dad stood from his wicker chair, bones cracking. "Well, Becky," he said, "if you've got all that, I guess you win."

Whatever.

Jaxon was relieved the stupid game was over. He was exhausted. It had still been dark when Mom had woken him that morning for the drive to Texas.

Mom flipped off the deck's string lights, leaving only the thin slice of moon glowing above them through the crowded trees. "I like the moon better when it's full," Jaxon said. "I hope it's full tomorrow."

"There won't be a full moon for weeks," Becky said.

"How would you know?"

"I read it in a book."

Dad pulled open the cottage's sliding glass door and leveled his eyes on Jaxon. "Reading makes you smart."

Yeah. Blah blah blah. Reading makes you smart. Reading was boring, and Becky didn't read half as much as she pretended.

Back inside the cottage, the four of them sat on the couch and started to watch TV. After only a few minutes, Becky was asleep, and Jaxon didn't think he'd be far behind.

Dad carried Becky off to bed, and Jaxon laid his head on Mom's lap. He wanted to fall asleep out here with her and the TV.

Dad sank back on the leather couch, and from behind closed eyelids Jaxon detected a subtle change from fuzzy color to monochrome. His eyes fluttered open.

Dad had put on something old—black-and-white. A man dressed like a southern gentleman walked on screen carrying a cane capped with the marbled head of Wally Rabbit.

Jaxon yawned.

Above the man's shoulders, an animated rabbit and rat popped into existence. "Hello there," the man said. "My name is Max Bixby. These are my friends … Wally and Regina." Each cartoon waved enthusiastically. They looked something like the Wally Rabbit and Regina Rat that Jaxon knew, but this earlier duo wore unnaturally wide and impish grins.

Bixby pulled off his white hat and bowed. "Allow me to welcome you to Bixby Park and its World of Dreams and Wonders. You're currently staying in one of our Dark Forest Treehouses."

"The Dark Forest?" Wally squealed.

"Relax, Wally," Bixby said. "There are little surprises around every corner, but nothing dangerous."

"W-well," Wally stammered, "if you say so, Mr. Bixby."

Regina Rat slithered onto Wally's back. "I'll protect you, Wally."

Jaxon's eyes drooped shut, and then flashed open when Dad flipped to the next channel. Another old-timey black-and-white Wally Rabbit cartoon. In this one, the rabbit wore a funny engineer's hat and smiled sadistically from the helm of a howling choo-choo train.

A thick bead of sweat ran down the head of a black duck tied across the tracks.

"This looks fun," Dad said. "I used to watch these with Pops."

"Dave, this is too old even for me."

"Fine." Dad flipped to the next channel.

A brunette woman appeared on screen in color so vibrant it was blinding. Behind her, a distant factory shifted in and out of view, and colorful smoke reflected across black water. "*That's right, James,*" the woman said into her microphone. "*Neither winner has yet to come forward, but Bixby insiders tell us there is no chance the tour will be put off.*"

The camera pulled back for a full view of the factory. Its four smokestacks blew out beautifully colorful purple and blue clouds that lit up the night sky.

Dad grunted. "The park is going to be packed tomorrow."

"*We caught up with CEO Roy Allen a few moments ago, and he guaranteed us that the two winners would be found before the start of the tour. When asked how, he replied simply: 'magic'.*"

Jaxon looked up to Dad, fogging into and out of view. "Dad."

"Hmm?"

"How can they do it?"

"Just a sec, sport. Need to download the park app." He looked up from his phone's glowing screen. "How can they do what?"

"How can they open a factory that no one's ever seen?"

Dad released a guttural chuckle. "People have seen it, kiddo."

"But they said …"

"It's a commercial, sport. They're just ginning up interest in a ride is all."

What is this factory?

Jaxon's eyes grew impossibly heavy as the woman disappeared from the screen, replaced by an overweight man in geometric glasses. "*Thanks Barb,*" the man said. "*The Master of Dreams, Max Bixby himself, could not have put together a more exciting contest. In other news, a new collection of clothes, toys, and accessories themed to the new film Pirate Cove 2 has arrived at Bixby Park ahead of next month's digital release …*"

– Zzzzzzzzzzzzzzzzz …

CHAPTER FOUR:

MAGIC ALL OVER YOU

Charlie stepped out of the locker room and into the night, amazed that her task had gone almost exactly as Lucy had said it would. She was out of the hot, heavy costume and back in her jeans and t-shirt. The parking lot was less than twenty yards away. She'd made it without a hitch.

"New here?" a woman called.

Shit.

The woman smiled with perfect straight teeth that seemed to ignite the darkness. "I'm Destiny," she said, starting forward. She had perfectly done-up blonde princess hair, but Charlie wasn't sure which princess she was. Charlie hadn't watched a Bixby film since the turn of the millennium, and this particular princess was holding a cigarette and wearing only a pair of ruffled bloomers and a tank top.

Princess Destiny pointed to the little tattoo beneath Charlie's left ear—a pale-green spiral of thin vortexes. "That's pretty. How'd you get hired with it?"

Charlie pulled a strand of black hair over her ear, and covered the tattoo up.

Destiny tossed down her cigarette and smushed it into the sidewalk with a toe of her slipper. "I knew a girl got fired for having only a little thing on her ankle," she said. "Casting director saw pictures of her on the beach while she was on vacation."

The operation had all been going so well. Until now, no one had seen her face, and there were no cameras permitted, not even cell phones, in the area of Bixby Park that corporate referred to as 'backstage'.

Charlie had taken the cast trolley from the backstage parking lot all the way to and from Bixby Harbor without any park employees speaking to her or questioning her at all.

The trolley driver on the ride back to the park had looked at her a bit strangely, but that was likely because Charlie had left her helmet on. They were between shifts, and no other cast members had been riding the shuttle.

Charlie quickened her pace, head down, towards the parking lot. Lucy had told her only five phrases were permitted when interacting with park employees or security:

1. Good evening

2. Thank-you

3. You're welcome

4. No, thanks

5. I have to go, my shift is over

"They don't have any authority to detain you, and no one will even try," Lucy had told her.

"Good evening," Charlie said to the woman, without stopping or turning her head. Charlie scarcely heard Destiny mutter something under her breath, but she was already too far away to even guess what it was.

Past the gate, in the employee parking lot, the black Navigator was where it was supposed to be. Waiting for her.

Charlie expected a silent trip, as Lucy's driver always kept the privacy partition up, but when she opened the door Lucy was there, hunched forward in her seat.

The old woman pursed pruned lips, waiting for Charlie to enter. When she did, the car was off before she had even a moment to buckle.

"I'm a bit distressed, Charlotte."

"Oh," Charlie said, startled. "I don't think that woman back there suspects anything."

"Woman? What woman?"

Charlie had said too much. It was always best with Lucy to say as little as possible. "I thought you meant the woman outside the locker room," Charlie said. "Her name's Destiny."

"Who in the hell is Destiny?"

"A princess. One of the ones with blonde hair. I'm not sure which one she was."

"What did you tell her?"

"Good evening."

"Anything else?"

"No."

"Then I don't care about her." Lucy waved a veiny hand. "I'm talking about the man you gave the ticket to. He hasn't come forward yet."

"He didn't scratch the ticket," Charlie said. Lucy had never told her to make sure that happened.

Lucy made a guttural, throaty sound, like a grind of stone shifting before a collapse. "You're sure he has it, at least?"

Charlie nodded. "Tucked it into his pocket. I'm guessing he'll scratch it soon, assuming he doesn't lose it." Charlie didn't find it at all surprising that a contest like this would be rigged. What she didn't understand though was why it would have been rigged for this particular man.

The selection had come in through the one-way earpiece she had been wearing under her helmet: 'Table 42, shorter black guy.'

As it had turned out, the shorter man at table 42 was quite good looking, with a neatly shaped beard that defined his jaw. He wasn't short by most standards, and was athletically built in the kind of way that suggested strength even while he was sitting still.

At the time, Charlie had thought it fortuitous the man had tucked away the ticket. It had made it much easier for her to disappear from the scene.

"Keep your phone on tonight," Lucy said. "I may need you."

Charlie had learned a long time ago what Lucy's favorite sentence was, and when in doubt, she said the magic words: "Yes, Lucy."

Charlie suspected the remainder of the trip would be in silence. The long silences had been unnerving at first, even though she had been prepared for them. When her brother's friend Lou had hired her a decade ago, he had explicitly told her not to ask Ms. Bixby any questions. Back then, Charlie had been paying exquisite attention.

Three months before being hired, she and her boyfriend Danny had been evicted from their apartment. Danny had soon disappeared but only after he had cleared out what little was left in their joint checking account.

By the time Charlie had broken down and called her brother in Lafayette from her room at the Howard Johnson, her Texas Capital checking account had been down to its last $19.92, her credit cards had been federally fucked, her Honda Civic had been repossessed, and checkout had been the day before.

It had been humiliating to call her brother, but rock bottom was rock bottom. Lou was a friend of his from business school ... and Lou, as it turned out, was looking for a girl just like her.

Charlie had never had any job with a big corporation. Her only jobs before working for Lucy had been cutting hair, and a short stint at Mario's Pizza that had ended when Mario put a hand down her pants.

Compared to that, Charlie didn't have much of a problem with most of Lucy's requests or restrictions. No communication other than with her company-issued phone, no social media or chat sites of any kind, and a pinprick of blood that Lucy would collect every Monday and place between a pair of microscope slides.

At first, the blood had been the most unusual thing, but Charlie had stopped worrying about it years ago. She had missed her Instagram account for a long time too, but had soon found more soothing things to look at on her phone.

She slipped out the iPhone, and it opened immediately to the Zillow app. She thumbed away and over to her Texas Capital account and refreshed: **$704,892.58**.

Whatever the reason Lucy wanted the black man, it was none of Charlie's business.

• • •

Don had only been able to choke down a handful of Europa Puffs, and their effects had been making him queasy on the ride to Rosie's house. There hadn't been anything *puffy* about the mushy, multicol-ored cubes. They had smelled like burnt plastic and tasted like cold hotdogs that had been dunked in a bowl of sugar.

Rosie rolled her Mini Cooper to a stop at her neighborhood's gatehouse. 'PRINCESS GROVE' was emblazoned across the chalky pink bricks in raised golden letters.

A plump woman wearing a matching bubblegum-colored vest slid open the gate window. "Well, lookie here," she said. "You're back pretty early, Ms. Rosie." The woman's mouth split into a patronizing smirk. "And I see you have a new friend?"

Rosie giggled. "This is Donny. Donny Williams. I'm taking him home to watch a movie! Can you believe he's never seen *Jewel of the Dunes*?"

Donny. He hated that fucking name.

Hey-yo … here comes Dopey Dribble Donny.

Still, Don didn't know where all of the other basketball kids back at Hill Crest had ended up, but it damn sure wasn't the NBA. And none of those guys were taking Rosie home tonight. So, for now, she could call him Wally Rabbit if she wanted.

"A wonderful film," the gatewoman said. "I'm sure he's going to love it. Does he have his ID?"

Don thumbed his wallet out of his back pocket and passed over the license.

The gatewoman leaned back into the booth and passed a blue scanner over it. "Well now," she said, above the glow of the scanner. "This looks fine. Enjoy your movie, Mr. Williams." The gatewoman handed Rosie back the license. "Do you think your friend will be needing to arrange for pickup later?"

Rosie turned and eyed Don playfully. "I don't know."

"I see," the gatewoman said. "Well, if he does, I'll be happy to arrange a car for him. I'm here all night."

Rosie waved twiddling fingers goodbye and proceeded down the wide stone-paved drive.

Don had a lot of questions but wasn't sure how to ask them. He didn't want to offend her. Not tonight.

He had sent a few texts to Ziaire during the ride from the harbor, but there hadn't been any replies. During dinner, Rosie had mentioned she was an artist, but after almost two hours, the only other things he knew for sure about her was that she was hot as hell … and that she *really* liked Bixby shit.

Don: *Where does the money come from?*

Ziaire: *Pam says her dad owns a couple hotel resorts in Vermont. She doesn't like to talk about him. Be cool. She likes you.*

Rosie definitely liked Don right now, and he wasn't going to risk screwing it up.

Rosie rolled the car over the bronze curb and up a short drive-way. The house was huge, with white bricks and expansive windows adorned with thick black grilles.

"Here we are," she said. "Home sweet home."

The lights of the two-story ante room came up as they stepped inside, and a voice from the vaulted ceilings announced, *"Welcome home, Princess Rosie."*

"Magic Mirror," Rosie said, "play the soundtrack for *Jewel of the Dunes.*"

"Playing Jewel of the Dunes, Original Motion Picture Soundtrack *by Igor Rubenstein and various artists."*

The cheery music came up, and Rosie pivoted, walking backwards and swaying her hips as she started towards the sunken living room. "Maybe we could just listen to the soundtrack. The music's the best part of the movie."

"Do you think I'll like it?"

She bit her lip. "I know you will."

He followed her reflection across the gold-framed mirror that ran the length of the foyer bar. At its nearest corner, a small spiderweb of cracks was etched into the glazing. He set the bag of leftover Europa Puffs on the bar's marbled counter.

Through the glass sliders behind her, the pool area was bathed in sensual blueish light.

"I wish I knew to bring my trunks."

She eyed him playfully. "You want to go swimming?" She pulled loose the top button of her jean shorts as wailing horns swelled over the speakers. "Magic Mirror, activate exterior speakers. Volume five."

Don pulled off his polo shirt as she was stepping out of her shorts. At the outer edge of his field of vision, he saw the colorful blur of the painting.

Christ.

"What the fuck."

On the wall above the kitchen, on a canvas the size of a ping-pong table, a ravenous Wally Rabbit was performing oral sex on a very pleased-looking Regina Rat. Her pink jumper had been pulled over her head to reveal grotesque furry breasts.

"You don't like it?" Rosie asked, sounding wounded.

"No … I … I didn't say all that," he stuttered. "I mean … it's a little … I mean, did you *paint* that?"

"Yes …" Rosie slid forward and pinched the polo from Don's flaccid hands. "Do you like it?" she said, dropping the shirt to the carpet. "How does it make you feel?"

Uncomfortable, Don thought. *Very uncomfortable.*

He forced a laugh. "Good … but … I … uhm …" He pointed a thumb backwards. "This is a little embarrassing. Is there a bathroom? Moon Water ran right through me."

Rosie smiled and pulled off her tight-fitting Captain Proton t-shirt. "To the left of the bar," she said working the clasp of her bra. "On your way back, bring me a drink." She spun away revealing a silhouette of Wally Rabbit peeking above her panties at the base of her back. "Plastic cups are in the cabinet."

"Absolutely." Don tripped on the short step out of the sunken living room before recovering. "Be back in a minute." He rounded the corner past the bar and tapped Ziaire's name on his iPhone. Don's friend didn't answer until the third attempt.

"*What the fuck is it, man?*" Ziaire said. "*As you can imagine, I'm a bit busy at the moment.*"

"Bruh," Don whispered. "This bitch is crazy."

"*What?*"

"I said… *this bitch is crazy.*"

"*I told you. It's hot, right?*"

"What? No … I don't mean like sexy crazy. I mean like actually fucking crazy. Has Pam ever been to her place?"

"*I don't know. Probably not. I done told you they only met a couple weeks ago at auditions.*"

Reflected in the mirror above the sink, Wally Rabbit smiled as he plowed Regina Rat from behind. "She's crazy as hell, man. Fucked-up pictures and shit."

"*What?*"

"Pictures! You know, on the walls. Paintings."

"You're at the home of a hot, rich girl that's ready to fuck you and you're hung up on the wall decor?"

The point was not lost on him … *but still* … "Man … you ain't here."

"Come on, bruh. Whatever it is, deal with it. Don't fuck anything up for me."

"I already told you we was cool, man."

"Alright then. Goodnight. Text me in the morning."

Don tucked away his phone before tossing handfuls of cool water across his face and the back of his neck. *Okay. It's not so bad. We can work with this. Everyone's got a thing … she's horny and has a thing for cartoons. Lot of white people were like that.*

Don headed back into the atrium. A warm breeze was now blowing across the foyer through the living room's open doors. Outside, Rosie, smooth and naked, came to the edge of her diving board, bouncing idly on her toes.

Could definitely be worse.

She dove in and swam to the edge. "Are you afraid to get wet?" she called, tucking damp hair behind her ear.

He whipped himself behind the bar. "No, ma'am. What are you drinking?"

Everything was going to be fine. Better than fine.

"Redbull and Mountain Dew on ice," she called. "Make yourself something too."

Redbull and Mountain Dew on ice? Don opened the minifridge at his knees and set the cans on the counter before scanning the bar for liquor bottles. All Rosie had on hand was a re-corked bottle of yellowish wine.

Don wasn't thirsty anyway. "Coming right up." He mixed her drink in a red plastic cup and slipped around the bar, unbuttoning his pants before remembering the ticket. He pulled it out and tossed it on the bar.

Rosie hauled herself upward out of the pool, resting her midsection on the concrete like a beached mermaid. "You haven't scratched that yet?"

"Not yet."

It had been the right decision to wait on scratching the ticket. In moments, Rosie was out of the pool, leaving a trail of water dripping across the concrete and carpet.

Don pinched away the ticket only a moment before Rosie could pick it up. She slid her wet arms around him. "I'm so cold," she said. "Warm me up."

He felt the unmistakable stirring of his loins, and she felt it too.

"Oh hello, there," she said, before looking up at him. "How about we make a trade?"

"You want my ticket? What will you give me for it?"

She pushed away and smiled. "What won't I give you?"

"A million dollars is a lot of money."

"I don't care about that. I want to see the factory."

"I'll tell you what," Don said. "If I win, you can take my place on the tour … but I'm keeping the money."

"They might not let you."

"It's the best I can do." Don looked around the bar. "Do you have a coin?"

She kissed him, dragging nails across his chest. "Let's do it. Right now." She put her hand in his, whilst gyrating against his thigh. "Use my nails."

Don rubbed Rosie's pink thumbnail against the ticket. In a flash, he remembered this ticket wasn't going to be a winner. The chances were infinitesimal. "Alright," he said, scratching. "You don't think it's going to spoil the magic if …" His words became a gnarled ball in his throat when he saw the wand.

"Oh baby," Rosie said, scratching faster. "I'm going to magic all over you."

CHAPTER FIVE:

INTO DARKNESS

Jaxon heard Grandma Betty-Ann's sweet sing-song voice floating through the Florida condo. In the living room, Pops' leather recliner, pockmarked and scratched by their cat, was empty save for a wide, butt-shaped indentation.

Jaxon drifted towards the kitchen pass-through window, the singing growing louder. Something had changed. The voice was no longer a soprano. It had become high, almost squeak-like, as if the singer had sucked in a mouthful of helium.

Framed by the pass-through window, Wally Rabbit pressed a gloved hand against his black tuxedo as he hit the final notes of 'Be Our Friend'.

So come on, friend, don't hesitate,
The fun's waiting for us—let's celebrate!
Be our friend, let's laugh and sing,
Together forever, that's the thinggggggg!

Raucous cheers and applause came as Wally took a deep bow. In the living room, Max Bixby finished clapping and rose from Pops' chair. His skin and hair were still black-and-white, but the Santa suit he was wearing was so bright red and vibrant that it choked off the rest of the room, sending it into a smear of smoky crimson.

Bixby held out a ticket. "I think this is yours," he said. "The magic is inside, waiting for you."

Jaxon reached for it, but it was gone. Bixby was gone too.

Becky had the ticket, holding it high above her head. "Are you going to cry now, crybaby?"

"Give it to me."

She pulled the ticket away, smiling wickedly. "You know you'll never win."

It wasn't true. He had as much chance as anyone else—more than anyone else even. He wanted it more.

"When you lose, you know you're going to cry, right? Cry, cry, cry. It's all you do. Scared little crybaby."

"I'm not a crybaby!"

Becky unfurled her tongue before flinging herself forward. She hit Jaxon hard, knocking the wind from his chest.

Jaxon jolted upright. Dark shapes and unfamiliar clawlike shadows huddled around him. Beyond his window, dark cypress trees shifted in the breeze.

He was fine. He wasn't in Florida. He was in a treehouse in the Dark Forest. Sleeping in the top bunk. Exactly where he was supposed to be.

A hard thrust came at his lower back. The mattress bounced up before cracking back down against wooden slats. "What the heck, Becky!"

"What ... what ..." she muttered.

He hung over the side of the bed letting blood run to his head. Becky nuzzled her face deeper into her pillow.

"I know it was you," he whispered. "You're so mean."

She retorted with an exaggerated, snotty snore.

She wants you to yell. Don't do it.

Jaxon wasn't going to fall into one of her traps this time. He climbed down the ladder of logs with his pillow tucked under his arm. "That's not how you sound when you sleep," he whispered. Becky returned another exaggerated snore.

"You sound like a pig."

Another snore, louder and even more theatrical.

There was nothing Jaxon could do. Dad would blame him if he got angry. Daddy's little princess could do no wrong.

Jaxon crept into the darkness of the hall.

Zric … Zric ….

It's just a cricket.

Zric … Zric …

A giant cricket and right on top of him! He hit the lights. The chirping stopped, and Becky screeched, "Turn them off, Jax! I'm sleeping."

He winced and dropped a limp finger over the switch.

Zric … Zric …

Mom and Dad's room remained dark and quiet.

Jaxon crept down the hall, stopping for only a moment to consider the third, empty bedroom. Inside, branches beyond the window tapped on the pane with waving, skeletal fingers.

He scampered into his parents' room and crept around to Mom's side. She was snoring soothing, genuine snores. He could tell the difference. Mom was the real princess. Jaxon curled himself around his pillow on the floor and listened to her rhythmic breathing …

Becky had his ticket again. She was leaning over the railing of one of the park's paddling ferries. "No, Daddy," she said, her voice thick with mocking sweetness. "I haven't seen Jaxon's ticket. What does it matter? It's not a winner anyway."

"Put it down, Becky!"

"What?" Becky said, holding a cupped hand to her ear.

"I said put it down!"

"What!" Mom's sharp voice jolted Jaxon from sleep.

"Cream!" Dad called from the kitchen. "Do they have any?"

"In the cabinet above the fridge," Mom yelled from the bedroom's connected bathroom.

On the nightstand, the clock blazed 5:38 am in digitized red letters. *So early.*

Wooden cabinet doors outside the room slammed in rapid succession as Jaxon elongated his body into a blissful stretch. Even on a school day, he would have had until at least 6:30 to sleep. Dad was normally gone for work well before then. Not today though. Today they were on funcation.

Jaxon found Dad in the kitchen, slapping shut another cabinet door. "Found it!" he yelled, tearing open a crinkling baby-blue pouch of sample coffee. "Morning, sport."

Jaxon winced. "Why are we up so early?"

"Well, you can sleep for another couple minutes if you want."

Fat chance. "Do they have YouTube?"

"You're in the Dark Forest. What do you need YouTube for?" Dad inserted the pod into the coffeemaker. "Did you sleep in our room again?"

"I can't sleep with Becky. She's awful."

Dad gave a heavy sigh. "I really wish you guys could just get along."

That was easy for him to say. Becky enjoyed a few activities—horseback riding, reading, puzzles—but what she enjoyed most of all was torturing Jaxon. Dad seemed to be able to see everything, but when it came to Becky, he wore princess-colored glasses.

"Go ahead and get yourself ready," Dad said. "Shirt, pants, underwear."

"I know, Dad. I know." Underwear was such a stupid waste. What was it even for?

In the bunk-bed room, Becky was wheezing beneath her web of brown tangles. Her snores were real this time and much more disgusting than the fake ones. Jaxon crept across the room towards his shark-shaped travel bag.

A sharp pain shot into his foot. "Yow!" He kicked the bristly hairbrush he'd stepped on across the room.

"Would you shut up?" Becky moaned. She threw a tasseled pillow at him, before rolling over. "I'm sleeping."

Fricking monster.

Jaxon snatched up his bag and headed for the hall bath to get ready. When he emerged, Mom was already in the living room, pulling her blonde ponytail through the back of a pink Bixby cap. "We're going to have so much fun today!"

"I know, I know. Can I have my iPad?"

"Don't give it to him," Dad called from the kitchen. "He doesn't need that today."

Jaxon made enlarged sad eyes, which Mom returned. "Sorry, sweetie," she said. "He's right."

Dad scooted into the room, sipping gingerly at a steaming cup. "Underwear?"

Jaxon dropped his shorts to his ankles. "Okay, okay," Dad said, holding up a hand. "I would've believed you."

Mom bent down to Jaxon and hugged him. "You're getting so good at getting ready in the morning. Have you seen your sister?"

"Last time I saw her she was still sleeping."

Mom stormed off. "Becky, I told you to start getting ready." The bedroom door banged open. "*Girl, that hair is a mess.* Let's get moving. If your dad misses this ferry he's going to lose it."

Jaxon listened with delight to Becky's screeches as Mom tore tangles out of her hair.

There was a moment when Jaxon was sure Dad would finally break and drop the coveted f-bomb, but he had instead said they were going to miss the *flutin' flippin'* ferry. It was only going to be a matter of time before Dad said the magic words, and Jaxon wasn't going to miss his chance.

After Mom had finished with Becky, Dad rushed them all out of the treehouse. A few minutes from the villa, they found a knotty dock carved into the trees. It stretched long across buzzing, blackish water that stank of mud and rot.

Not so magical out here so far.

They were the first to arrive at the dock, but within a few minutes, a clamoring line began forming behind them.

A distant sound of splashing came from beyond the buzzing trees. A royal-blue steamer ship chugged into view, its red paddle wheels puttering across still water. Emblazoned on its hull in bright crimson letters:

S.S. Gumdrop
Destination: Bixby Park

They were loaded first, seated on the upper level at the back of the ferry. "I think we're going to make it, gang," Dad said. After a few minutes, the ferry paddled away, leaving behind about thirty guests on the dock. "That's why you leave early, kids."

The ferry chugged beyond the chirping lake into open water. The factory sat on the horizon. In the early light it didn't appear particularly magical, only a dead building with four inactive smokestacks that poked into the gray sky like gun barrels.

The park, however, was a different story.

Colorful cable cars sent shadows sweeping over sparkling water before disappearing behind the park's towering outer walls. Imprinted on bubble-gum-pink blocks, 'Bixby Park' had been spelled out in crisp, sweeping letters alongside a royal-blue gate that was tall and wide enough to admit King Kong.

The ferry's intercom scratched to life. "*Everyone please be patient when disembarking, and remember to have a magical day!*"

Jaxon counted six more ferries converging on the docks at the base of the wall. They all began unloading their passengers in near unison. Unfortunately for Dad, he hadn't taken into account that the first guests to board the ferry would, by design, also be the last to get off.

"Stupid …*flipping* system. Worse than the … *darned* DMV."

So close.

By the time Dad led them off the ferry, there was already a crush of bodies ahead of them, massing towards the front gate. Jaxon lost sight of the entrance behind an enormous butt stretched over high-riding elastic shorts.

A kid somewhere yelled, "It's moving!" over the whine of grinding metal.

Loud, playful music seemed to come from everywhere all at once, floating over the squealing crowd like a fog of happiness.

Jaxon's heart pounded with excitement.

The chattering crowd shifted glacially forward. "Okay, gang, stay close." Dad tugged on Becky's wrist, pulling her to his heels. "Close together now." Dad arched up on tiptoes, peeking around a man in a wide-brimmed hat. "Why is this gate so narrow?" he said to himself. "This is ridiculous."

Mom gripped Jaxon's shoulders and sandwiched him behind Becky. After what seemed like a million baby steps, they squeezed through the gate, spilling out onto the immaculate cobblestone street of Bixby's Town Square.

Guests tore past the distinctive buildings without a glance: an old schoolhouse with a ringing bell, a colonial-style restaurant, a movie theater with flashing lights, and a barber shop with a red-and-white swirling pole that spun into and out of infinity.

"It's this way," Dad said, dragging Becky up the street. "Come on! We have to move!"

By the time they'd made it to Canyon Jane's Tavern, a line had already formed, extending well beyond its saloon-style doors.

The cowgirl at the front desk smiled at Dad when he finally approached. "How we doin' there, partner?" She was pretty, like all the park ladies, with perfect teeth and skin that seemed to glow. "Do you have a reservation?"

"Kinney," Dad said. "There are four of us."

Her plushy pink cowgirl hat bobbed up and down as she scanned her ledger. "Yes … I see. I'm sorry, sir … your reservation has expired."

Here we go.

"What are you talking about?" The veins in Dad's neck pulsed. "You just opened!"

"Sir … your reservation was for ten minutes ago."

"I had to stand at the back of this line."

The woman curled her head around Dad to see that no one else had stepped in line behind them, before smiling diplomatically. "How did you arrive at the park today, sir?"

Dad grunted. "The ferry."

"I see, sir. Well, we do advise everyone making breakfast reservations here at the tavern to take the skyline."

"I couldn't *take* the skyline. I'm at the goddamned Dark Forest."

"Goddamn right, Dad," Jaxon said.

Dad sneered down at Jaxon for a terrifying moment, before releasing a long sigh and turning back to the hostess. "How long is the wait?"

The cowgirl's lips twisted together. "Some groups typically get finished faster than others, but I would say it's aboouuuut thirty minutes, partner."

"Would you stop ... *fluting* calling me that?"

So close.

"Look, Dave." Mom extended her iPhone over. "There's almost no one in line for the Pirate Cove Cruise."

"Of course there's no one in line," Dad said. "The park just opened. We can go after breakfast."

The cowgirl's eyebrows arched upward in the '*I don't know about that, dude*' sort of way.

"Are they giving out tickets here?" Jaxon asked.

The cowgirl looked down at him with a sympathetic smile. "I'm sorry, partner. We don't have any left."

They were going to run out! At least two people in the park *today* were going to win them. The TV said so. "Let's go, Dad."

Becky moaned. "I'm not goddamned hungry either. Let's go do something!"

Dad huffed out a weak noise and started out of the tavern. "Fine," he said, offering the cowgirl a no-look wave. "Let's go. Where's this ride?"

"This way." Mom looked up from her phone and led them past a group of swanning park ladies dressed like peacocks.

Dad's phone vibrated.

"What is it?" Mom asked.

Dad read and seemingly reread the message.

"What is it?"

The phone hummed again, and Dad's lips vibrated like a motor. He tapped at the screen before tucking the phone into the back pocket of his cargo shorts. "It's … it's nothing," he said. "It's work. It's fine."

"Work?" Mom looked down at Jaxon and smiled. "We're not working today. We're on *funcation*!"

They followed the flow of foot traffic, swept along by the noise and motion of the park. A vendor selling rainbow popcorn called out flavors as they passed, the sugary smell trailing after them. From somewhere ahead, cheerful music drifted over the crowds, bright and bouncy in a way that didn't match the urgency in Dad's stride. He kept urging them forward, guiding them through the archway for the Pirate Cove Cruise.

They rounded the first corner and stopped short behind a wall of bodies.

"I don't understand this," Mom said, reading her phone. "It said it was only a five minute … Wait." She returned the phone to the black pouch hanging below her waist. "Now it says thirty minutes."

Dad hissed and looked over the massive line of guests ahead of them, snaking between the shiny black chains linked to fat oak barrels.

"Is there gold in those barrels, Dad?"

Dad was scrolling through his phone.

"*Dad?!*" Jaxon repeated.

"Gold comes in chests not barrels, son," Dad said, without looking up.

Becky laughed with mocking delight. "They're just decorations, dum-dum."

"*Stop calling me dum-dum!*"

Dad looked up, his face darkened. "Enough yelling, Jax. That's the only warning you're getting."

Jaxon always got blamed for everything. Becky had started it. She curled her fingers into a hook. "Pirates are in there, Jax." She sliced her fingers across his belly. "They'll cut you limb from limb."

"Becky, stop scaring him," Mom said. Jaxon felt her warm fingers on the back of his neck. "It's just for fun, sweetie."

The fiddling sound of pirate music intensified as the line passed through towering double doors and into a cavern with swinging pendant lights that sent a jungle of shadows dancing across slick, cavernous walls.

Ding.

Mom glared at Dad. "I thought you silenced that."

"Babe … I've got a little situation here. Bear with me."

The sound of dripping water began to overpower the music as they made their way deeper into the cavern. *Why is it so dark in here?* "Mom … is this cave haunted?"

Becky cackled. "Bro, you've got a micro brain."

Ding.

The next chamber stank like the pool at the YMCA. Pirates greeted guests at the end of the line, loading them into sloshing black boats.

Ding.

Ding.

The phone rang.

"Dave. Don't answer it."

Dad answered it. "How in the heck do they even know anything about it yet?"

"Dave … *get off the phone.*"

Dad put up a hand and repeated "unh-huh" into the phone every few seconds until they reached a short, bony pirate. He wasn't scary-looking. Jaxon had imagined real pirates would be thick and hairy. This one looked more like a YouTuber at a Halloween party, gangly with a thin, patchy beard.

"Look," Dad said into the phone. "I need to get on this ride … yeah, a *flippin'* ride. I'll call you when I get off. Yes, when I get off."

"How many in your party, sir?" one of the pirates asked.

Mom angled around Dad and answered for him, "Four."

"Aisle three!" the pirate called to his mateys. They replied with a "yo-ho-ho".

Mom led the four of them into the tight stall as a boat splashed to a stop and the stall's steel gate squeaked open. Laughing tourists disembarked on the opposite side of the cave river.

They seemed happy, Jaxon thought. No decapitations.

Up close, the craft didn't seem like a real boat. It had no engine or sails. It had to have been running on some kind of track. Jaxon could hear humming machinery under the swishing water.

Mom rocked aboard, and Jaxon scooted across the damp bench next to her. She gripped his arm. "Will you protect me?"

"Yeah," Jaxon said. "I'll protect you."

Dad boarded last, and the YouTube pirate said, "No flash photography, sir. I'm going to have to ask you to stow your phone."

"Fine, fine." Dad patted around for a spot, ultimately slipping the device into the shallow breast pocket of his shirt. He stepped onto the boat and as he bent forward to sit, the fabric bowed.

Oh boy.

The phone slid right out, skittered off the lip of the craft, before dropping into the water with a soft, *plunk*. Dad's eyes went wide.

"Oh God." He lurched toward the side, reaching for the water.

The pirate caught him by the wrist. "I can't let you put your hand down there, sir."

Dad froze, face tightening into a strained, furious magenta. "*Motherfucker.*"

Jaxon screamed the word joyfully as the boat rattled forward down the black river and into darkness.

CHAPTER SIX:

THE FINAL FRONTIER

Charlie imagined the girl, Rosie, had been raised by perfect parents in a perfect house with brothers and sisters. Aunts and uncles. Maybe even a golden retriever. The young woman was beautiful, polite, and utterly grating.

"Donny, look at this one!" Rosie released an idiotic giggle and pointed to a framed animation cel of the original Wally Rabbit, his eyes as big and black as an eight ball and his ears flopped over like clipped linguine.

Lucy tottered over to the picture and nodded. "That's one of my favorites too."

The 'show office' of Bixby Manor was dressed like a shrine to the company's gilded past—rare toys posed in glass cases, oil portraits glowing under warm sconces, brass fixtures polished to a buttery shine. The air even smelled faintly of old varnish, as if someone had tried to bottle nostalgia and spray it around for effect.

Charlie couldn't have cared less. The whole place struck her as a museum built for people who actually cared about the old theme park, and she wasn't one of them. Judging by the flat look on Don's face, he wasn't either.

Charlie guessed that Don, like herself, had not grown up in a house with a golden retriever.

"So," Don said. "The tour's been great, and I don't mean to be the kind of guy that gets right down to real talk, but … *what's the deal with the money?*"

Rosie's little-girl voice sank into a painful whine. "Donny!"

God, Charlie thought. How can he stand it?

Lucy eased herself into an oversized art deco chair. "I completely understand your excitement," she said, indicating the leather couch opposite her. "Please sit, Mr. Williams. I understand you've requested to have Ms. Rosie here take your place. Fortunately, you are both in luck … there will be room to accommodate the both of you on the tour."

Rosie giggled and clapped her hands as she flopped onto the couch. Don eased down gingerly at the edge of the cushion. "Fine," he said. "But what I want to know about is the money. No one will tell me anything. They kept saying I had to talk to you about it. Where is it?"

If the questions were bothering her, Lucy wasn't showing any sign of it.

'*Whatever you do, don't ask her any questions, especially about the Dream Factory,*' had been the mantra of Lou's one-day training ten years earlier. Charlie had soon learned the wisdom of this advice. Lucy didn't answer questions; she gave orders and instructions.

But not today. Today she was pleasant as a rainbow. "I can assure you," Lucy said, "a check will be waiting for you tomorrow evening after the tour."

"Honestly, Ms. Bixby," Don said. "I really couldn't care less about this ride you got going on. You can make Rosie the winner for this part. She can—"

"Oh, Donny!"

"What?" he said, wincing. "Bring Pam or something."

Lucy shook her head. "I'm afraid the money can only be awarded to the winner. And only after a successful tour."

"What you mean: a *successful* tour?"

"This should have been clear in the paperwork you signed earlier."

"Ain't nobody got time to read all that. They rushed us through it all."

"Well," Lucy said, "a successful tour would be one where you stay for the duration of the event."

Don leaned forward. "When ... *when exactly* ... do I get this money?"

"For this evening, we've arranged accommodations for the both of you in a luxury suite at the Safari Lounge. In the morning, you'll take a private car to a small airfield a few miles from here. From there, we'll fly over to the island. At the tour's conclusion, a check will be waiting for you. If it's important, I can see that it's right outside the door as soon as we step out of the factory."

Don's eyes became as big and black as Wally's. "Fine," he said. "But I want to know what's in there."

You and everybody else, Charlie thought.

"It's a bit of a surprise," Lucy said. "But trust me ... it'll be worth the wait."

An officious knock came from the door, and Mark Warner's head peeked inside. It wasn't even 10 am yet and the man was already sweating. "Pardon me, Ms. Bixby—Mrs. Allen would like a word."

Lucy frowned at Don. "I'm afraid, Mr. Williams, I have quite a bit of doing in preparation for your tour. Charlotte, will you show our new friends out?"

"Yes, Lucy."

Charlie walked Don and Rosie down the manor's north portico to a waiting black Navigator. The two of them seemed like an odd match, though Charlie suspected it may have been her own envy talking. She had never had tits quite as large as Rosie's or legs quite as toned, but she had been young once and missed it.

She waited at the base of the stairs until the Navigator curled around the drive disappearing behind the manor. The building was a corporate office pretending to be a fairytale mansion. Its steep gables and creamy stonework gleamed under the Texas sun, every window polished to a storybook shine. A decorative turret speared upward for no practical reason except to look good in park brochures. Beyond the hedges, she could hear the distant shrieks from the coaster loops.

When she returned to the portico, Mark Warner was at the base of the steps, wiping a damp sheen from his forehead like he'd jogged the whole way to catch her.

"Ms. Cooper, I'd like a word."

Charlie walked past him and up the stairs. "No thanks." She could hear Mark huffing out wheezing breaths behind her.

"Wait!"

Charlie kept moving.

"What's it matter if you talk to me?" he called after her. "It's your last day anyway."

You're almost there. Charlie hustled faster up the stairs.

"Who was driving that car?"

How the hell should I know?

Charlie stopped at the top of the stairs and looked back: Mark was four steps beneath her, looking expectant and hopeful that she might slip up and give him more than one of Lucy's canned and pre-approved phrases.

Charlie didn't need Mark Warner to tell her that her contract was coming to an end. It was something she knew all too well, but it changed nothing. She didn't know who was driving that Navigator. It wasn't her business to know.

Charlie continued up the stairs.

"Wait!"

Mark lunged weakly after her, but Charlie scurried away and had lost him completely by the time she'd made it back to the show office. On the other side of the office's thick door, Violet Allen was shouting.

Charlie had only seen Lucy's sister three times in ten years, but the grating sound of the old woman's voice was burned in her memory. She eased the door open.

"Rules are rules, dear," Lucy said.

Violet Allen ripped off her ruby-red glasses. "Rules? Who gives a fuck about rules? Do you know the problems with Legal you're causing?"

Charlie was unsure for a moment if Violet had noticed her. Her face was a difficult one to read. The skin was unnaturally smooth, as if it had been stretched back and stapled behind her blonde wig.

"What's she doing here?" Violet said, not bothering to glance in Charlie's direction.

"I need Charlotte with me," Lucy said. "She's here to take notes."

Charlie felt a brief stab of panic. "I didn't bring anything to write with."

"That's okay, dear." Lucy waved a hand. "Take mental notes."

"Yes, Lucy."

Violet's phone buzzed, and she read the message. "That's interesting," she said, looking up. "It seems the second winner has been found."

"That's impossible," Lucy said.

"The ticket seems genuine," Violet said, holding up her phone. "Forty-five-year-old cashier from Dallas. Would you like me to have him brought up?"

"Of course not. It's a fake," Lucy said. "And if there's nothing else, I've reserved the office for the day. Charlotte and I have some private matters to discuss."

"Private matters to discuss? With the assistant?"

"If you don't mind," Lucy said. She waited for Violet to storm out before turning her attention to Charlie. "Continue with the operation as planned."

"Yes, Lucy."

For a brief moment, Charlie had been hopeful that, with a second winner found, there would be no need for her to carry out her latest assignment.

She would need to hurry if she was going to catch the next trolley. It had been folly to think, even for a moment, that Lucy might change her plans. Charlie had never known the old woman to change her mind about anything.

Charlie headed for the maintenance stairs. When she shoved the door to the stairwell open, Mark Warner was waiting for her, resting his thick backside against the flaking yellow handrails. "You're a tough woman to catch up with."

Charlie slid past him and hurried down the stairs.

"I know you're headed for the cast trolley," Mark said.

Charlie kept moving.

"And I know you gave Williams that ticket. What I don't know is why. Who's getting a ticket this time?"

Charlie said nothing. She didn't know, and she didn't care.

* * *

Dad had taken possession of Mom's iPhone on the pirate ride and hadn't given it back. When they stepped through the cave's exit and into the Seven Seas gift shop, he jogged towards the blinding glass storefront, putting the phone to his ear. "I need a second. I'll be right back. Grab yourself something."

Mom clapped her hands together and smiled, looking over the gift shop. "You heard him, kids." She reached for a long-sleeve t-shirt and held it below Jaxon's chin. '*Dead Men Tell No Tales*' was stamped across the chest in wispy pirate letters. "What do you think, sweetie?"

"It's fine, I guess." Jaxon had more clothes than he knew what to do with. At home, he preferred to lay about in his underwear more than anything else. It was the only time underwear was any use.

Becky picked out a small silver bracelet of jeweled skull and crossbones, and Mom bought a t-shirt for herself that said, '*Looks like a Mermaid, Parties like a Pirate*'.

Outside, they found Dad sitting on a metal bench, his head in his hands. Mom tapped his shin with the toe of a sneaker. "Babe, what is going on?"

Dad forced a smile. "Demolition disaster last night," he said. "The entire food court is coated with concrete dust, and they haven't been able to open yet. I've got a cleanup crew heading over now to take a look."

"The mall's closed because of dust?"

"It's the *food court*. It's a health thing. Got into the vents too apparently."

"You're still going to make money on that job?"

Dad waited a long beat and nodded. "Sure. It's going to be fine. Just having a rough morning." He held up her iPhone. "I need to hold onto this."

Mom offered a reserved smile. "Where to next?"

"There's only a forty minute wait to get on the Skybreaker," Dad said. "It'll be way longer than that if we sit around talking about it."

The Skybreaker sounded dangerous and it also didn't sound like a place where Jaxon could get a ticket.

"Jax is too small for that," Mom said.

Jaxon forgot his objections. "I am not!"

Mom nodded sympathetically. "You are, sweetie," she said. "Need to be fifty-four inches."

"He'd be too scared anyway," Becky said. "And I want to get my picture with Princess Sarkarr."

Jaxon couldn't think of anything more boring or embarrassing than waiting in line to see a park lady in a ballgown pretending to be a cartoon princess.

Dad thumbed over Mom's phone and shook his head. "Geez … looks like even that is a thirty-minute wait. Who the heck would want to wait that long for an autograph?"

Jaxon's heart swelled with love.

"Lots of people would want to, Dave," Mom said. "People like your daughter."

Princess Becky grinned victoriously, and Dad's shoulders slumped. "Do you really think Jaxon wants to wait in line to have a Bixby princess give him a signature?"

"No way," Jaxon said. "I want to get some breakfast."

Mom sighed. "You just want a chance at one of those tickets."

"We're around the corner from the Space Park," Dad said. "The Galactic Cruiser restaurant has been down since the park opened, but it just came back online." He held up Mom's phone to show her the estimated queue time: 'five minutes'. "We're close," he said. "We can probably get right in."

Becky screeched, "I don't want to go there! We're always doing what Jaxon wants to do. It's *funcation*! That's not fun!"

The idea that Jaxon got whatever he wanted, and Becky did not, was fricking laughable. If there had been a scoreboard as to which of them got their way more often, Becky would have been winning in a blowout.

"Okay, okay," Dad hoisted himself off the bench. "This way." He slipped around a group of four women Grandma Betty-Ann's age. Each was eating a long piece of fried sugary dough wrapped in greasy paper.

"Dave," Mom said, hustling after him, "where are you going?"

Dad stopped under a cartoonish four-way directional sign that pointed to each of the park's four '*lands*'. A miniature cutout of Captain Proton stood on the top with a thumb cocked towards an open gated archway labelled: *The Final Frontier*.

"Let's split up." Dad pointed back in the direction of Never Land. "The Princess Theater is straight back that way. It should only take me and Jax about half an hour to get something to eat if we head over now. After we're done, we can meet on one of those benches under that spaceship."

At the entrance to The Final Frontier, a wide-bellied flying saucer had landed on four metallic legs, creating an expansive picnic area buzzing with tourists.

Mom shook her head. "My phone …"

"Hun, our parents managed to raise us without constantly being on the phone."

"It was a different time. It was easier then."

"Babe … we're talking about us. Your mom thinks the Democrats are building a weather machine." Dad pulled off his metallic wristwatch. "Me and you will be fine."

"Easy for you to say; you'll be the one with the phone."

Dad held out the watch, letting it hang from a hooked finger.

"Please, Mom," Jaxon said.

Mom sighed and snatched the watch, tucking it into the black pouch hanging from her hip. "One hour," she said.

Jaxon watched Mom and Becky disappear into the throng, and his stomach rumbled. It wasn't hunger. He couldn't remember Mom ever not having her phone. Everyone always had them. What if something happened?

"Come on, sport. We don't want to miss the next shuttle." Dad grabbed Jaxon's shoulder and steered him towards The Final Frontier.

CHAPTER SEVEN:

MAGIC IS REAL

Dad guided Jaxon through the windowless corridor. The only light came from the pulsing hanging fixtures, alternating between a neon blue and a dark purple.

At the end of the hall, two men in cueball helmets, holding laser rifles, saluted Dad in unison. "Good morning, Corporal."

"Morning," Dad said. "There are two of us. Any room left on the shuttle?"

One of the spacemen nodded, his trailing yellow mustache hanging below an angular chin. He shot a serious look to his partner, a black man almost twice as large. The black man considered the question a moment before nodding in agreement. "They need to hurry."

The mustachioed spaceman ran a scanner over Dad and then Jaxon. After each scan, the device made an affirmative beep. "You'll need to run," the spaceman said. "Pintonian shock troopers have entered the park."

"I see," Dad said, unfazed.

"What about Mom?"

"She'll be okay."

"She doesn't even have a phone."

Dad squeezed Jaxon's shoulder, as the dead end of the corridor opened upward, sending in blinding light. "She'll be fine, sport."

The mustachioed spaceman ducked under the ascending door. "Through here, Corporal. Lieutenant Green, will cover our flank."

Lieutenant Green pointed his laser rifle back down the corridor. "Go, quickly," he said. "I'll hold them off."

Dad led Jaxon outside into a beige courtyard—an expanse of space rock studded with craters and glowing strips of neon embedded directly into the rocky terrain like alien circuitry.

A flying saucer with twinkling yellow and blue lights had lowered its ramp. The spaceman stopped at the base of the plank and waved them forward. "Up there, Corporal. Hurry." He made an odd two fingered salute: a balled fist with the pinky and ring finger standing perfectly upright. "Freedom to the Galaxy!"

Dad winced as he attempted a return salute. "Freedom to the Galaxy," he muttered before pulling Jaxon up the ramp.

"Dad … is Mom okay?"

"They're fine."

Everything did *seem* fine, and Dad would never really leave Mom or his sweet princess behind. It was all part of the show. It had to be.

They stepped inside the spaceship, and the door whooshed shut from above. Through the tinted side and rear windows, they saw the spaceman run back into the building.

"Dad …"

"It's fine. Trust me."

A misty pink light hissed above them, illuminating the cabin. The saucer was much smaller than it had appeared from the outside. There were no seats, only handrails along the perimeter, like on the monorail at the airport in Florida.

The blank window at the front of the ship fuzzed to life, and a scaly alien with bulging bug eyes came into focus. "Welcome aboard," it said. "As you've no doubt learned, shock troopers have taken over the park. The only safe place left to eat is on board the *Reliance*. Please strap in for takeoff. We'll try to secure the park during your meal."

The lizard-man made a perfect salute with two extended fingers as long as hotdogs. "Freedom to the Galaxy!"

The ship rumbled, and Jaxon instinctively grabbed hold of the nearest handrail. "Dad ..."

Outside, bluish smoke filled the courtyard, blurring the surrounding buildings in a darkening fog.

"Relax," Dad said. "They'll probably be giving out tickets on the cruiser."

The ship jolted hard, and through the window, the park shrank beneath them. In seconds the clouds fell away in a blur, replaced with a sea of stars.

What the heck ...

Dad pointed through the window. "Look there." A sharp-angled ship sitting on two glowing nodules floated towards them. "That must be the *Reliance*."

"We're preparing to dock," the alien said. "Enjoy your meal."

Jaxon's heart hammered. The ship hovering outside shot forward in a flash. In an instant, the paneled hull was snug against the window.

"All guests, please step to the center of the cabin."

Jaxon peeled his hand from the handrail, and the window split open to reveal a smiling park lady in a sparkling white mini-skirt. "Welcome aboard the *Reliance*," she said. "I'm Vaal of Europa. I'll be your server. If you'll follow me, please." She spun on clacking heels and led them through a glowing archway.

"Dad ... are we on Captain Proton's ship?"

Dad chuckled. "I don't know. Maybe."

Jaxon hated being so stupid. He should have known not to ask such a dumb question. It wasn't real. It couldn't be.

Still ...

Vaal of Europa led them into a room the size of a gymnasium. The ceiling arched high overhead like the inside of a giant metal whale, pulsing with soft blue lights that chased each other along the ribs. A glowing bar curved along one wall, its neon tubes bubbling with color, and clusters of smooth white tables sat scattered across the floor like landing pads. A window ran the length of the wall, the glowing Earth and moon sat beyond.

Vaal smiled at Jaxon and pulled out an egg-shaped chair near the window. The *Reliance* was passing over Australia.

Jaxon had almost forgotten about the ticket. But not quite. "Do you have any—"

Vaal stopped him with a perfect smile that told him everything. "In fact, we do have a sentinel that's just come aboard to give them out," she said, before making a subtle wink. "I'll see that they make their way over to you. Would either of you like something to drink? The Star Drive is my favorite."

Dad grunted as he folded his bulky frame into an egg chair. "I'm guessing that it's non-alcoholic?"

"It is, sir. Yes." She handed Dad a big plastic menu. "Drinks are on the back."

Dad scanned the menu and nodded. "Bring a Star Drive for him and a Bloody Pintonian for me."

Vaal input the order on her spacepad before turning away towards the bar.

"What's a Bloody Pintonian?" Jaxon asked.

"A Bloody Mary with Pintonian bacon," Dad said. "It's no wonder they're trying to take over the park if we're eating them."

"So ... *are we in space*?"

Dad laughed. "Of course not," he said. "This is a ride, son."

A sharp, embarrassing heat flashed across Jaxon's cheeks. They were always laughing at him. *Hardy-fricking-har.*

"Hey," Dad said quickly, smile fading as a shadow of something wounded crossed his face. "It wasn't a dumb question. I'm sorry. I don't want you to feel like there's anything you can't ask me. It's just that ... going to space is really hard."

"Astronauts do it all the time. How hard can it be?"

"As hard as it would be for a school of fish to take over the beach."

Jaxon thought for a moment. "The fish have never even tried."

"Yeah." Dad nodded. "I suppose you are right about that."

Vaal brought the drinks on a wide silver tray. Purple berry-scented smoke chugged over the top of Jaxon's glass. He took a tentative sip. The Star Drive was thick, cold, and disgustingly sweet.

Dad pulled a thick slab of bacon encrusted with glistening crystals from his glass, and bit off the dry end. "Is this the same bacon that comes in the Interstellar Breakfast Wrap?"

"It is, sir," Vaal of Europa said.

"Alright then," Dad said. "I'll have the breakfast wrap. Do you have Cheerios?"

"More or less."

"He'll have that with milk."

"It's from a cow, right?" Jaxon asked.

"If that's your preference," Vaal said, tapping her whirring space-pad with inch-long nails. "I'll go grab that all for you."

It was rare for Jaxon to be alone with Dad. On weekdays, he normally didn't see him until dinnertime. Jaxon wasn't sure what to say, so he sucked down another grotesque swallow of sugary sludge.

After a minute of silence, Dad asked him about school. Jaxon said it was fine, though that was far from the truth. He was in love with a girl who didn't know he existed, was terrified of Dodgeball Day, and he was pretty sure he'd already lost his art textbook after only being back in school two weeks.

Dad picked up his phone, when Jaxon remembered Pops' advice: *ask a question.*

"Is everything okay at work?"

Dad's eyes trailed down to the phone. "You don't want to know about my work."

"Why not?"

"Because," Dad said, eyes drifting slowly back up, *"we're on funcation."*

"Are we going to lose all of our money and die?"

Dad broke into a startling fit of laughter that sent Jaxon deeper inside his egg-shaped chair.

"Of course not," Dad said. "It's just one job. Everything's fine."

A slim figure in silver armor approached the table. "Good morning, space cadets. Any interest in a chance to win a tour of the Dream Factory? One raffle ticket per guest."

"YES!"

Dad chuckled. "He's pretty excited."

The robot woman tore a pair of tickets from a whirring futuristic-looking box and handed them out. "Best of luck to both of you," she said, before turning away.

"Before you scratch that," Dad said. "You should know … it's almost impossible that that's the winning ticket. Fifty thousand people visit this park every day."

That many? "Really?" The number seemed impossible.

"Something like that," Dad said. "All I'm saying is—"

Mom's iPhone dinged. Dad frowned, reading over the screen.

"What is it?" Jaxon said. Maybe they *were* going to lose all their money and die after all.

Dad held up the phone to show him, it was opened to the Bixby app: a ticker along the bottom read: *Second Ticket Found!!!!!!!!*

Frick.

No!

Jaxon felt his lips begin to quiver. He was going to cry. Dad never cried about anything, and Jaxon was going to cry in front of him. The frustrating knowledge of the coming tears made them come harder.

"I told you," Dad said.

The hot streams ran down Jaxon's cheeks. "It's not fair."

"That's life, kiddo. Just be glad you're you. Trust me, it's better than you think."

Jaxon didn't care about finishing the disgusting drink or eating breakfast. When his Cheerios came, he managed to choke down only a few bitter spoonfuls. He wasn't hungry, and he wanted to go home.

There was nothing magical here. He wasn't in space. He was in an expensive building drinking sugary slop.

Dad's breakfast sandwich didn't look particularly otherworldly either. Eggs, bacon, and cheese stuffed into a burnt folded-over pita. Dad was always a quick eater but was all the faster when he had someplace to be. "We need to hurry," he said between chews. "We don't want your Mom waiting for us long."

The phone buzzed again.

Dad took a long look at the screen and picked it up. "This is Dave." Dad listened intently and threw down a crumpled wad of cash onto the table. "I understand. Yes. I understand. I know how much this has cost …" He headed for a sign labelled 'Escape Pods' and blindly waved for Jaxon to follow him.

Jaxon took one final look at the infuriating pair of unscratched tickets on the table. He wanted to rip them up and throw them like confetti.

Outside the dining hall, three car-sized escape pods were waiting. A spaceman beckoned them inside the nearest pod. "A platoon of sentinels has repelled the Pintonian invaders on the surface, sir. Should be safe down there now."

Whatever, Jaxon thought. *This is all so stupid.*

They boarded, and the spaceman frowned at Dad. "No communications on board the pod, sir."

Dad grunted. "Call you back in five minutes—yes, in five … *darned* minutes."

The spaceman secured both their harnesses and stepped back giving them a perfect, stupid salute.

The pod's glass canopy whooshed down, and all air left Jaxon's lungs. They were in free fall, hurtling towards the Earth. He was going to fly out of his seat!

The pod jolted upward a few feet above the park and eased down to a landing. The doors opened, sending in a blast of warm air tinged with vanilla cookies.

Dad tore off his harness and answered the phone. "I'm here, Brad. Okay. Fine. Do what you have to do. I'm waiting for my guy to give me a call back. We're going to get this taken care of today."

Dad's neck and face were beet red by the time they reached the patio under the spaceship. It thundered with the sounds of tourists and the ship's hammering mechanical underbelly. At the rear, thrusters belched out pink plumes of smoke.

"*One sec!*" Dad yelled into the phone before holding it to his chest and turning to Jaxon. "We're here early!" Dad tapped the nearest empty picnic table. "Wait right here. Mom will be coming from that four-way sign. Don't move unless you know she's seen you."

Jaxon's fingers knotted together. "Where are you going to be?"

"Right over there."

A few feet off the edge of the patio was a roped-off bit of cobblestone labelled 'Stroller Parking'.

"I'll be watching you," Dad said. "I just need to finish this call."

Jaxon nodded and watched Dad intently as he snaked around the smattering of bulky park-issued baby strollers. He was likely trying to get away with a few freebie f-bombs. The forbidden word was one of the easiest to lip read.

Dad released his bottom lip, letting off a doozie, at the exact moment a small boy plopped down on the other side of the picnic table, obscuring the view.

Jaxon looped his head around him, annoyed. The patio was busy, but there were plenty of empty tables.

The mechanical beat above them fizzled out, and the rear engine let out a final pop of purplish smoke. Jaxon could hear Dad's voice now but couldn't make out the words. *He's yelling.* Jaxon wouldn't have wanted to be that guy …

"Hi," a high voice said.

Jaxon turned to look at the boy. He was about Jaxon's age, but a little shorter, with hair so blond it was almost white, and bright green eyes that caught the sunlight like glass.

The boy said, "What's your name?"

"Jaxon."

"I'm Alex," the boy said. "Where's your mom and dad?"

Jaxon pointed. "My dad's over there, with the strollers. My mom's supposed to meet us here. He's got her phone. Where are your parents?"

"My mom's around," Alex said. "She works on the *Reliance*."

"Your mom lets you outside without her? *That's dangerous.*"

"Not really," Alex said, laughing. "There are cameras everywhere in this park." The boy turned, getting a better look at Dad, who was gesturing emphatically with his hands as if to an invisible man.

"Why's your dad got your mom's phone?"

"He dropped his on the pirate ride," Jaxon said, laughing. "He was so mad." He wanted to repeat the magic word, but Dad had ears like Wally Rabbit.

"Epic," Alex said, before he laid a single ticket on the table.

"Is that for the factory?" Jaxon asked. "You know they already found all the winners?"

The boy looked uncomfortable. "I know," he said. "It's sort of why I wanted to talk to you. This ticket's yours. I nicked it."

Why would it matter? It wasn't special anymore. "You couldn't steal it," Jaxon said. "I left it. Finders keepers, bruh."

Alex pushed the ticket across the table with a finger. "My mom saw me scratching the other one at your table and told me to bring this one out to you."

"I don't want it."

"Tell that to her." Alex slid the crinkling slip of paper closer. "She said unscratched tickets could end up being collectibles some-day." He picked up the ticket and pressed it against Jaxon's chest. "Please?" he said. "I'm real sorry. My mom will kill me if you don't take it back."

Jaxon took the ticket. The words curled across the surface of the ticket in looping, old-fashioned letters, and a silver oval gleamed below them:

*One Million Dollars and a Trip
To the Land of Dreams and Wonders
Scratch here:* ▮▮▮▮▮

"Jaxon!" It was Mom. She pulled Becky around the four-way sign and was making straight for him. "What are you doing all by yourself?"

"I'm not all by myself," Jaxon said. "Dad's right over there." He pointed to where Dad was weaving between the carriages.

"Who was that you were talking to?"

Jaxon looked back across the table, but Alex had already hopped away and was disappearing into a throng of tourists.

"I see you managed to get your ticket," Mom said. "I'm surprised you haven't scratched it yet?"

"The app said the winner was found."

Becky reached forward. "If you don't want it—"

"Stop it, Becky," Mom said, smiling at Jaxon. "The app was wrong. It's all anyone is talking about. Someone created a fake, apparently."

Oh my God. This is a winner.

Jaxon scratched the ticket with a bitten-over thumbnail. On his third swipe, he saw the tip of the wand peeking through the flecks of black powder. His heart hammered faster as he scratched, but he said nothing until he had finished completely, scraping off every bit of the thin coating from the little box: a magic wand suspended mid-flick, surrounded with blue stars.

If you scratch and find a wand, you'll unlock the magic beyond!

When Jaxon held it up to Mom, he felt sure it was a winner, but he still couldn't manage to choke out any words. Mom was saying something to Becky, when her mouth dropped open mid-word.

Dad jogged over, but Mom's expression startled him. "What?" he said. "I could still see Jax where I was. I was just right there."

"Could you ... check his ticket?" she said. "I'm not sure what it means."

Dad pushed up his sunglasses and squinted. "Let me see that, sport." He took the little ticket as if it were a bomb, but in moments he was flipping it over to and fro with accelerating alacrity. "Hun … I think this might be a winner."

Magic is real.

CHAPTER EIGHT:

YES, LUCY

Mark Warner was sitting on the little bench outside the locker room 'backstage', when Charlie emerged. In the sun, his bald head had turned a boiled lobster red.

"You wouldn't believe it," he said, getting to his feet. "But it turns out that winner from earlier was a fake after all. Colby Ellis from Dallas was escorted out of the park about fifteen minutes ago. And did you hear the latest winner has been found?"

Charlie kept moving to the parking lot, head down. "My shift is over." It was true. *Her shift was over.*

Mark shouted after her, "*Why the kid?*"

Charlie didn't look back till she had opened the rear door of the Navigator sitting along the prison-like wire fencing.

She didn't want to think about why Lucy had selected the little boy, but there had been no escaping the command.

The stranger who spoke to her over the headset was a man, Charlie was sure of that, but he'd had a girlish sing-song voice: "*Nine-year-old boy, sitting along the window with his father in one of the white egg chairs.*"

It didn't matter why Lucy, or whomever, had picked the boy. Charlie was in the business of that not being her business.

Instead she boarded the idling Navigator and opened the Zillow app on her phone. She had been contemplating marking the house on Peck Boulevard as one of her coveted favorites.

The French colonial would have been perfect, with its recessed ceilings, refurbished floors, and those sink bowls that sat right on the counter. It had an outdoor kitchen too, which was good because the indoor kitchen did not have a proper hood, only a dingy microwave fan. But did she really want to have to cook all the greasy stuff outside?

She scrolled back, her thumb hovering over the heart-shaped favorite button. In the pictures, a pair of outdoor fans lined the colonial's breezeway and an elaborate lattice cast hexagonal shadows across the pavers.

The little boy and his family would be at Bixby Manor by now, signing their paperwork. If they'd previously signed up for Bixby TV, they might already be with Lucy in the show office.

It was none of Charlie's business. Today was her last day. Her shift was over.

She had been anxious for over a year about the status of her contract. At the start of the summer, she had begun to suspect that Lucy had simply forgotten that the contract was expiring.

But Lucy had not forgotten. On July 4th, Charlie had prepared Lucy a rack of lamb resting on Greek-style lemon-roasted potatoes. After she'd delivered it, Lucy had said: "Fetch the Merlot, Charlotte. I'd like to celebrate our last fourth of July together."

Our last fourth of July. The point was not reiterated, but the message had been loud and clear.

Charlie supposed she would have to leave the guest house in the morning. The thought caused the muscles in her stomach to contract and release. The truth was, she had only ever marginally considered what she would do when her contract ended.

She knew there were other people working for Lucy, but she never saw them, and there had been no apparent effort made to replace her. Would a new person take over making Lucy's dinner? Would they schedule her doctor's appointments?

It would not be hard work for Charlie to pack up all of her things in the morning. In her ten years with Lucy, Charlie had not acquired many possessions. In the early years, she had assumed the employment would end at any moment. That she would be fired, as so many of Lucy's previous assistants had.

Lucy didn't talk much, but when she did it was normally to complain about the ineptitude of her past assistants. She never praised Charlie's job performance, only addressing it if she wanted some adjustment made: "See if you can get the grass cut later in the week," or "I prefer my steak cooked a touch more."

But none of that mattered anymore. Tomorrow when Charlie woke up, she would have to leave the guest house and go … *somewhere.*

She would need to find a hotel. There were few other options. She had plenty of money, but scarcely accessed it. Lucy provided her everything she needed to live: food, shelter, internet. She would need to get her own phone too, and hadn't put any effort into seeing how much or how long that would take.

Soon the Navigator sped through the front gate of Lucy's compound, parking at the crest of the drive overlooking the big house.

Only a moment after Charlie stepped into the sun and shut her door, the thickly tinted Navigator jolted forward, looping around Lucy's circle drive before speeding away back through the front gate.

Charlie pulled her phone and trudged towards the little guest house that had been her home for a decade. She thumbed over to the Zillow app again.

This is what you want. It's time to go.

She staggered inside the house and to her room, and sat cross-legged on the bed, scrolling through the pictures. The final exterior shot of the house on Peck Boulevard was a view from the front porch: a red ranch house in front of farmland that stretched towards the horizon.

Why not?

She entered her contact information and sent it. In less than thirty seconds, the phone rang, and her hands froze.

So fast. Am I serious?

Of course she was serious … she just needed a moment to think. The phone continued to ring and vibrate in her hands. When it stopped, she lay down on her back, stretching across the bed.

The phone buzzed, and she angled her head to read the message: *Hi. I'm Paul. I saw you were interested in 390 Peck Boulevard in Deridder, LA. There's been a lot of interest in this property. Is this something you'd like to see tomorrow?*

Tomorrow? How was she going to get there by tomorrow?

She'd need to get a car. She needed to go to the bank too. She'd sworn off getting another credit card.

But there *was* the debit card. The bank had sent it to her without even asking. She slid to the guest house's little foyer and found the card exactly where she'd left it: in the small console table by the front door, sitting on top of a crinkled Chinese menu with red lettering. The card's now curling sticker read: 'Call 1-888-582-3912 any time, 24hrs to activate.'

Lou had told her it wasn't like a credit card.

"It's pretty simple," he'd said, flapping the card at her. "With this, you need the money in your account. That's not the case with credit cards. You can't go into debt with this."

It at least made sense to make sure the number worked. She picked up the card and padded back to the bedroom. The phone buzzed. Buzzed. And buzzed again.

She picked up. "Hello."

"*Hiyah there, is this Charlotte?*"

"Yes," she said, stiffly. "Well, I go by Charlie."

"*Oh, okay,*" the voice said. "*Hey Charlie. I'm Tom Zimore from Bayou Home Real Estate. I saw you were interested in 390 Peck Boulevard. Is that a property you think you might want to see?*"

"Well … yes I would like to see it? Is it still available?"

"*My screen shows it is, but I'll be honest with you, it's been on for ten days and these things go fast right now. Can you see it tomorrow?*"

"Well … I'm trying to think about how I would get there."

"Oh, well, shucks. You don't live nearby?"

"No … I live outside Dickersville. Tomorrow would be hard for me. But I could probably make it by the end of the weekend?"

"Dickersville? Anywhere near the park?"

"Yes … I sort of work there."

"Oh, how much fun is that? I took my kids there once when they were little. What a magical place. It sounds like you'll need to make arrangements. I can email you a hotel recommendation, if you need one. My sister is the manager at the Imperial. She can get you a really good weekend rate. You're going to want to look at more than one house if you're making a trip, am I right? My whole Sunday is pretty much wide open. I can show you anything you'd like to see in the parish. What attracted you to this house?" He was talking so fast, firing out the words like a machine gun.

"The land," Charlie said. "I really like all the space."

"Yeah, I can see that. Great spot for kids. Have any little ones?"

"No," she said. "It's just me."

Charlie had been pregnant eleven years earlier. After Danny had left, she'd told herself it had been for the best that she'd lost the baby, but now, at thirty-seven, that point of view was less appealing. Now she just didn't like to think about it. She wasn't sure that she wanted a baby, but she was sure that she hated not being able to choose.

"You're just by your lonesome?"

"… Yes …"

"Oh," Zimore said. "Well, it's just this place on Peck is awful big for one person. Do you need something this big? Going a little smaller might give you some more options."

"Sure," she said. "I guess that would be okay."

"I can see in the system you tend to stay in the six hundred to seven hundred range. Have I got that right?"

"Yeah … I mean I'd like to keep it closer to six hundred if I could."

"Okay, let me just update that so I remember … are you paying cash?"

"Yes. I've got seven hundred in my checking."

"*You have seven hundred ... thousand?*"

"Yes."

He was silent for a long moment. "*You say it's in your checking?*"

"Yeah," she said, alarmed. "Is that an issue?"

"*Well ... no, ma'am, I didn't exactly say that. It's just quite a big egg to have in a checking account.*"

"I can send you a picture if you need it."

"*Please do,*" he said. "*So ... you're not going to want to get a loan?*"

"I'd rather not. I have investments if I need more money."

"*Well, hokay then,*" he said, happily. "*If you're paying cash that makes this entire process a lot easier. Now do you know about closing costs?*"

The realtor talked and talked, and by the end Charlie's head was spinning. She needed a car. She needed to call Lou to see how hard it would be to pull out more money. She needed to see how far the nearest grocery store was from Peck Boulevard.

"*Alright,*" Zimore said. "*I'll see you on Sunday at two. Keep marking houses as favorites and I'll try to add them to the tour. I'm also going to go ahead and pull you off the list.*"

"What's the list?"

"*Trust me, if I don't do it, you'll have to bat the other agents off with a stick. I'll see you this weekend.*"

The realtor was right. Only whatever he did to stop the messages did very little. There was a new text message seemingly every few minutes.

This is Bob Coffey from Re/Max First—Delete.

Hi there. Sally Ryan from New Home—Delete.

I'm all finished up here and will be on my way home shortly. I think I'd like coconut shrimp and rice. Have dinner ready by 6. I'd like you to eat with me this evening.—Lucy Bixby.

Charlie's breath caught in her chest as the thought occurred to her. Maybe this was when she was going to be offered the extension. Charlie would normally eat her meals alone in the kitchen. It was a rare thing for Lucy to invite her to dinner.

Charlie used Lucy's Amex and had fresh jumbo shrimp delivered to the big house. The pantry had everything else she needed: corn starch and tempura mix for the batter, coconut cream, condensed milk, and sugar for the coconut sauce.

Charlie was scooping fried shrimp out of hot oil when Lucy came into the kitchen. "Oh good," Lucy said. "It looks like it's about ready. Grab a bottle of wine as well. Make sure to pour some for yourself. It's our last night."

So it isn't a contract extension.

Charlie set out the plates and poured the wine.

After Lucy had eaten a few mouthfuls of rice she said, "You have been an excellent employee, Charlotte. I worry I do not tell you enough." Lucy had, in fact, never offered Charlie anything approaching that level of praise. "Who was the last girl before you? Did I ever mention her?"

"Janice," Charlie said.

"Yes … that's right. Janice. Just dreadful. Couldn't cook rice without burning it. Set off the smoke detectors. And she had so many questions. Cluck-cluck-cluck."

"Yes, Lucy."

"Have you made plans for tomorrow?"

"I only just began to make them," Charlie said. "I guess I'm going back to Louisiana."

Lucy nodded and speared a shrimp dripping in creamy white sauce. "Before you go," she said, "I'd like you to come with me to the factory tomorrow as my guest."

Charlie wasn't sure how to respond without asking a question. "I see," she said.

"I'd like to reward you for your good work. It would do me a great honor if you'd come with us in the morning."

"Yes, Lucy." Charlie had said the words without thinking. She had only meant to say that she understood the request, but Lucy very clearly took it for an acceptance.

"That's wonderful," Lucy said. "I needed to reward you somehow. And I'm sure you're … *curious* about the factory. How could you not be?"

"Yes, Lucy."

It was true. Charlie was curious about all of it. More than curious. But she followed the rules. The contract she had signed with Lucy had been short and sweet. One page with two lines at the bottom for signatures. Lucy had already signed with an elaborate swooping cursive.

I, Charlotte Cooper, pledge my loyalty to the signee, Lucille Catherine Bixby, in consideration of $10,000 paid monthly for a term of ten years. I, Charlotte Cooper, pledge that I will ask no questions and not discuss my employment with anyone, even after the contract's expiration. This contract can be terminated by the signee, Lucille Catherine Bixby, at any time.

"I'm so excited to finally give you some answers."

"Yes, Lucy."

CHAPTER NINE:

HAPPILY EVER AFTER

It was the greatest day of Jaxon's life.

After Dad showed the ticket to the nearest park person, Mom and Becky were given gold badges that allowed them to skip all the lines in the park, while Jaxon and Dad were sent to meet an old woman named Ms. Lucy at a massive mansion near the center of the park, in a room filled with toys.

The little old woman had called herself the original Bixby princess, but she hadn't looked much like a princess at all. She'd been wearing slacks and a cream-colored blouse that smelled like hairspray and mothballs.

After Dad had signed Jaxon's paperwork, the two of them were sent to the front of the line for the Jungle Rapids cruise. Any trouble Dad had been having at work had seemingly been swept away.

At dinner in the Royal Hall, Mom and Dad ate Wagyu steaks from Japan and drank red wine from France. Princesses Sakhaar and Winnie made personal appearances at their table, but Becky had only smiled with strained politeness, barely touching her goopy macaroni-and-cheese.

It was glorious.

Becky was miserable, and except for perhaps their wedding photos, Jaxon had never seen Mom and Dad happier.

Funcation had finally and truly begun.

After dinner, they went to their new accommodations at the Grand Victorian Beach Resort. Jaxon had been disappointed to leave the Dark Forest, but he understood why they had been moved as soon as their town car rolled through the resort's golden gates.

The Grand Victorian, with its sharp angles and red spires, was infinitely fancier than the treehouse had been. The front-desk man said they would be staying in their most prestigious suite. "Max Bixby himself stayed in the room for six months while the factory was being constructed. Beautiful views. You're going to love it. Just love it."

The suite was pungent with melon and clover, and looked out onto the bay. The factory sat on the shifting black water, sending up beautiful plumes of glowing red-and-blue fog from its smokestacks, like fireworks that had forgotten to explode.

The rest of the suite felt like something out of an old movie—the kind like Pops had often watched—where everyone wore sparkly dresses and danced on shiny floors. Gold trim curled along the ceiling, and the lamps were shaped like upside-down champagne glasses.

The suite had no bunkbeds, but the ginormous mattresses were aggressively soft, the kind you could jump on and sink into all at once, like falling into a sponge cake.

Jaxon felt sleep pulling at him as soon as he laid face-first on the cold satin pillows. He had almost slipped away when he heard Becky's nasally breathing.

Jaxon propped himself on his elbows and found her standing in the doorway, flashing a radiant perfect-sister smile. "Can I have a pony?"

It was definitely the best day of his life. He laid back down, putting his hands behind his head. The golden fan spun lazily above him. "I don't think so."

"Can we trade?"

"I don't want anything from you."

Becky stomped alongside the bed. "If I won, I would share with you. It's not fair."

Jaxon slid off the mattress to face her. "It is fair," he said. "You wanted to meet boring, dumb princesses … *dum-dum.*"

In a flash, she barreled into him, tackling him off the side of the bed and pinning him to the floor.

"Get off me!"

She leaned in, suffocating him in noxiously sweet-smelling princess perfume. Dad had told him that at some point he would be able to handle his sister easily, but that day was not today. Jaxon despised how much stronger she was than him.

Becky pursed her lips. "Are you sure you don't want to trade?"

"No!"

She drooled out a thin, swinging pendulum of spittle.

"Gross! Get off!"

She slurped it back between her lips before releasing another.

"Stop it!"

The swinging stream touched his nose.

"GET OFF!"

"Quit screwing around out there!" Dad yelled from across the hall. "Time for bed."

Jaxon heaved Becky off and took a step towards her before stopping himself. She wanted him to do something dumb, like hit her or start to cause a ruckus. Despite everything that had happened today, Dad would blame him if he hit back or yelled.

Not this time.

Instead, Jaxon produced his best version of what Grandma Betty-Ann would call 'a shit-eating grin'. "I don't have to give you anything."

He sauntered into the hall, leaving her to fume. This money was his. All his. No one had given it to him. He had won it.

From the hall, Jaxon heard his mother inside her bedroom. "Did you hear from Brad?"

"Yeah," Dad said, over running water. "The sanitary guys have already been in and out. I think everything's going to be fine."

Fine? Of course everything was fine. It was better than fine. This was already the best weekend of Jaxon's life, and tomorrow was the tour. Things were only getting better.

His parents were in the bathroom when he entered their room, so Jaxon took the opportunity to crawl to the center of their bed.

The humming bathroom fan was cooing him to sleep when Mom spoke again, "Did they say how much?"

"It wasn't cheap," Dad said. "But I can't complain on a day like today. We'll have plenty after this weekend."

What the hell did that mean?

"Right," Mom said. "But how much did this cost us?"

Dad gargled and spit in the sink, before turning off the water. "About ten grand. We'll probably make it up by the end of the job though, honestly. And this trip has been too profitable to complain."

Too profitable?

"We haven't seen any money yet."

They're talking about stealing my money.

"Hunnie, come on. It's Bixby Park. They'll—"

"*That's not fair!*" Blood drummed between Jaxon's temples and his chewed nails dug into his palms.

Dad stuck his head out of the buzzing bathroom. "I told you to stop yelling. It's time for bed, sport."

"You're trying to steal my money!"

"Your money?" Dad lumbered into the bedroom, shirtless, his chest covered in bearlike hair. "You don't have any money," he said. "You're a kid. My kid."

"That's not fair!"

Dad's eyes narrowed. "Welcome to the real world. Do you think clothing and feeding you is free? Do you think this weekend getaway was free?"

"Dave, stop it." Mom leaned against the bathroom's doorframe. "Jaxon, sweetie, we just need to hold it for you. You're too young to have a bank account."

Dad didn't want to hold it for him. He wanted to keep it. He was a cheat, like Becky. Jaxon wasn't going to let him get away with it this time. "I'm not going on that tour if I don't get the money. All the money. It's mine."

"The hell you're not."

"The hell I will."

Dad's face darkened, and he leaned in, breathing out hot fumes of mouthwash. "You will do whatever I say."

Mom darted forward and sank onto the bed. "Jax, we're just keeping it for you. We're a family. We share—"

"He didn't even ask!" Jaxon screamed. "People that share stuff ask permission."

Dad bit the inside part of his cheek and chewed on it a moment. "Alright. Fine," he said. "Sounds like you can take care of yourself from now on."

Darn right. He could take care of himself. He'd prove it.

"So I guess in that case … there's no reason for you to sleep in here tonight?"

Jaxon stormed from the room, blood pounding in his ears.

• • •

Dinner at the Ivory Table was Don and Rosie's first time out of their suite since they had arrived at the Safari Lodge. After a ravenous afternoon, they had managed to work up quite an appetite.

Don stuffed himself with Moroccan lamb and crackly bread smeared with black salt butter, but still Rosie had insisted they order dessert.

And why not? It was all free.

Rosie ordered the chocolate sorbet sprinkled with passion fruit. She offered Don a tangy bite before licking a trail of dark cream from the bottom of her spoon. "It's getting late, isn't it?"

It wasn't even nine o'clock, and they had already done everything two people could do alone in a room together. Yet Don was hungry for more of it. He tossed a twenty on the bamboo table and pulled her out of the lounge and up to their room. He grabbed her hips as the door was clicking shut.

"Wait," she said, pulling away and sauntering to the bedroom. "I grabbed something from the gift shop earlier." He followed her eagerly. "I think it'll be fun to put on." She slipped into the master bathroom. "You'll like it."

Don thought she looked best with nothing on, but she closed the door before he could say anything.

He tore off his jeans and briefs in one swift motion and dove onto the turned-down bed. He scooped up the square chocolates wrapped in green foil and tossed them to the floor.

After a few moments listening to the croaking frogs and chirping crickets outside, he remembered the music. He fumbled for the remote and flipped on the TV, still set to the Bixby Music Channel. The speakers immediately blew out a sticky sweet fog of the cheery melodies they had been playing before dinner.

Don had tried playing other music, but nothing revved up Rosie like the Bixby stuff. Why songs like 'Be Our Friend' or 'Can't Wait To Be a Woman' would get anyone's sexual impulses firing was beyond him, but it turned Rosie wild.

She slipped out of the bathroom and spun so he could get the full view of the blue lace panties that rode up her backside deliciously.

"You got that from the Bixby gift shop?"

"Oh fine," she said, pouting out her lower lip. "I've had it for a while." She tugged at the fat ponytail she had tied with powder-blue ribbons and pulled over her shoulder. "You never asked me what princess I auditioned for."

In a hot flash, the name popped up. "Winnie," he said. The princess's signature look was a big ponytail and a light blue two-piece dress with an exposed midriff. As a kid, he had imagined what Princess Winnie would look like in the flesh. Now he knew.

She fell onto the bed and crawled towards him as 'Can't Wait To Be a Woman' began playing, sending a shudder through her. "Oh, baby. Say it again."

"Winnie." He pushed himself on top of her and pressed his lips to hers, tasting peach-flavored gloss. She arched her back, the warmth of her building to—"Oh … Donny."

That fucking name.

"What's the matter?"

He had to say something. The burning desire for her had gone immediately limp and ice cold. He rolled off her, and she sat in rapt attention.

"Listen," he said. "I just really wish you'd call me Don. I hate that fucking name."

"What? Donny?"

A muscle in his neck spasmed. "Yeah," he said. "Motherfucking Donny. I don't like it."

She laid her ass across his crotch. "Do you want to spank me?"

He pushed her off. "No. Will you just please stop calling me that?"

She made a playfully wounded face. "Okay," she said. "I won't. Now can I make it up to you?" Her warm hand slithered up his thigh, and she set to work doing just that.

• • •

Charlie normally fell asleep around 8:30, but midnight had come and gone. She'd spent hours drifting through home listings, barely absorbing any of it. Front porches, granite countertops, and backyard fences all bled together until she couldn't tell one house from the next.

Several times she had picked up and closed the book she was reading. Sloane had just discovered that Tucker had secretly been a billionaire the entire time.

No shit, Sherlock.

She couldn't read anymore. The words on the page had begun spiraling like water snakes. She laid her head back, dozing as the wicker swing hanging from a big hook in the breezeway shifted in the light wind.

A roar came from the lawn, and Danny rolled past the breezeway, bobbing on a green lawnmower. He was shirtless, in a pair of perfect, crisp jeans. He took a sip from a can of beer that had been resting between his thighs and stepped off the mower.

She was next to him. A baby somewhere was crying. Her baby. *Ethan.* He had her black hair and Danny's flat nose and red cheeks.

It wasn't possible. She hadn't seen Danny in—

BANG!

Charlie shot up erect. She was alone in her bedroom, the only light coming from the Wally Rabbit table lamp she had left on.

BANG!

At the window, Charlie glimpsed a face as it fell away.

"*Mark?*"

She ran out the front door, nearly swallowing a firefly. Below her bedroom window, Mark was panting, hands on his knees. "Can we just talk for a minute? Your contract's over now."

He was right, of course, but Charlie was still bound to keep silent. "I'm not supposed to have anyone over."

"You're going into the factory tomorrow, aren't you?"

How could he know that?

Mark took another heaving breath. "I know you think you can't talk to me," he said. "But your contract is over. I've seen it."

How was that possible?

"Don't you see?" he asked. "Lucy wants you for something."

Before Charlie could formulate which canned response she was going to give him, a whistling shadow swept overhead, skimming across the thin slice of moon. Dark leaves clicked like teeth in the trees.

"*What was that?*"

"Come on," Mark whispered. He caught her arm and pulled her across the lawn toward the darkened Big House. "It was going this way."

It would have been pitch-black if not for the lone security spotlight glowing at the base of the driveway. The wind whistled again—longer this time—and a hulking black shape drifted over the lawn less than twenty yards away.

Mark yanked Charlie down by the upper arm, pulling her behind a withering rosebush as a hot-air balloon holding an enclosed cab settled onto the lawn as quietly as a curtain falling.

"What—"

Mark squeezed her arm, a firm warning, and hushed her.

Within seconds, the balloon eased back up again, lifting the small cab with it. Crickets shrilled in its wake. Three dark shapes remained on the grass in front of the house, perfectly motionless. The whole scene pulsed in and out, expanding and contracting with the thudding of Charlie's heartbeat.

Wind whistled through the branches overhead, and the balloon vanished into the darkness almost immediately. When Charlie turned back toward the Big House, the shadow men were gone. Mark had crouched even lower, sinking into the mulch with a faint crunch.

"Where'd they go?" Charlie whispered.

The lights inside the compound's detached garage flared to life, bleaching the windows. All three overhead doors rattled upward. Two of Lucy's black Navigators rolled out and slipped through the main gate; the third eased to a stop at the apex of the driveway and cut its headlights.

Charlie watched, straining her eyes in the darkness, waiting to see if a shadow man got out … but none did.

"What's happening?" she whispered. "We need to …" She couldn't think of a way to finish her thought. She didn't know what they should do. What she should do.

Mark, on the other hand, seemed entirely unfazed.

"None of this surprises you?" she said. "How much do you know?"

"About the factory? Not much." Mark pulled her away, leading her back across the lawn towards the guest house. "But I know a lot about you," he said. "I know you're shopping for houses in Louisiana. I know you tear through trashy romance novels, and that your brother hooked you up with Lou ten years ago and got you this job. I know you were with a man named Dan—"

"I don't want to talk about him," she said.

"You don't have to," Mark said. "I've already spoken to him."

Charlie stopped dead. "*You what?*"

"What did you expect? In ten years, you've given us nothing."

"Nothing about what?" she said, heart pounding. "I don't have any idea what you're talking about. Who the hell are those people?"

Mark's face darkened for the first time. "Oh God. You really don't know anything, do you?"

"Anything about what?"

"The factory," he said. "No one alive has ever been inside it except Lucy."

"That's impossible."

"I can assure you, it is very possible. We don't have a clue what Lucy has in mind for those people she's bringing in there. Do you want to be responsible for what happens to them?"

"Can't you just stop the tour?"

Mark sighed. "No," he said, shaking his head. "I've been hoping you'd know something. I told Violet you had to. That I could talk some sense into you."

"No one's even left yet," Charlie said. "Just stop the tour."

"Corporate's not going to do that." By Corporate, Mark could only mean Roy and Violet Allen.

"Why not?"

"Because … Corporate assumes ownership of the factory within twenty-four hours of the tour's conclusion."

"But … the factory is the corporation."

"No, Charlie. It isn't." He took her arm. "You are going in there though, aren't you? I've got that much right."

Charlie nodded.

"And why is that? Your contract's up."

Charlie didn't answer, but Mark didn't need her to. "It's because you want to know what's in there. We do too."

" … You really can't do anything?"

"I didn't say that." Mark pulled a sliver of paper from his slacks and handed it over "Take it."

01001000010000010101000001010000010010010100110001011001001000000100010101010110010001010101001000100000001000001010001100101010001000101010010010

"It's a reboot code, we think. It's all we've been able to pull from the factory's computer. Though I'll be damned if I know where or how you would be able to enter it even if you needed to."

Charlie scanned the train of numbers. "I'll never be able to remember this."

"I doubt you'll have to, it's simple binary. The code translates to 'Happily Ever After'."

CHAPTER TEN

WELCOME TO THE DREAM FACTORY

At 7:00 am, the Navigator in Lucy's driveway started its ignition, blowing out gray wisps of exhaust. Precisely an hour later, Lucy emerged from the Big House. Charlie didn't know Lucy to smile or laugh much, but today the old woman was grinning ear to ear.

"Charlotte, good morning," she said. "I'm so glad you're coming."

Charlie had been having second, third, and fourth thoughts about going to the factory. But Mark had been right. She had to know.

Lucy tapped on the Navigator's hood. "I'm sure you've been wondering about our driver the last few months."

Charlie had never lied to Lucy, and she wasn't about to start. "I have."

"Well, now that your contract's over and we're just old friends, feel free to ask me anything."

"You'll answer all my questions?"

"In time, I will, dear. In time I will answer them all … but don't be afraid to ask."

The driver's door popped open, and a tall man in a purple tracksuit stepped out. He had a little boy's shiny face and shock white hair that grew over his ears. His eyes were open but lifeless, like holes cut in a mask. "Good morning, Ms. Cooper. My name is Japper. It is great to finally meet you in the flesh!"

"You've been … driving me?"

"Many times." Japper opened the SUV's rear door. "I'll be taking you both to the airfield."

Charlie followed Lucy into the backseat. "What is he?" she whispered.

Lucy grinned again. Two smiles in one day was an absolute record. "So you can tell?" she said.

"Tell what?"

"I shouldn't say just yet," Lucy said. "But I am so excited to show you."

• • •

Jaxon had slept in his room alone, but he had not slept well. So much of his excitement had burned out. In the middle of the night, he had snuck out of his room to find his parents' bedroom door locked. *And they never did that.*

He had not meant to start a fight with Dad, and of course he would share the money with his family. What could he even do with a million dollars? He still wanted to quit school and start a YouTube channel, but while lying in the black silence of his room, it had occurred to him that his parents would never allow him to quit school—even if he was a millionaire.

When Jaxon emerged from his room, the park people had already sent up coffee, cereal, custardy eggs, burnt bacon, and triangular toast. His family sat and ate in the living room, but no one spoke. Jaxon had eaten about half of his little box of Cheerios before breaking the silence. "So … I … I'm okay with sharing."

Dad nodded but didn't look away from the new phone the park people had given him. He said thank you, but did not sound thankful.

"That's wonderful, hunnie," Mom said, though she likewise did not sound like she thought it was wonderful. The factory wasn't going to be much fun if Mom wasn't in a good mood.

Oddly Becky seemed to be the only one who welcomed the news. "So you'll buy me a pony?"

"No one's getting a pony," Dad said.

"Why not?"

"You know why not, princess. It's not just a pony. It's food. It's a barn. It's medical bills. We don't live on a farm, and a million dollars isn't so much money that Jaxon can waste it."

Who was Dad to say if Jaxon would or would not buy a pony or a barn? Jaxon was contemplating how much such things would cost when the taps came—three sets of four jerky knocks on their suite's front door.

Becky darted from the living room, leaving behind a table coated in blackened bacon crumbs and greasy napkins. Jaxon made it to the door as his sister was opening it. The door knocker was a tall, sticklike man in a garish purple tracksuit and bright white sneakers.

"Hi, I'm Tapper!" His mouth split into a wide grin, near high enough to touch the bottoms of his drooping earlobes.

Tapper didn't exactly seem old, but he had bleached white hair that matched his shoestring eyebrows. "I'll be taking you all to the airfield. If you have any questions: just ask!"

Jaxon took a step backward, colliding with Dad's midsection.

Dad gripped Jaxon's shoulders. "You said your name was?"

"Tapper, Mr. Kinney. I'll be taking you all to the airfield."

"You're a *professional* driver?"

"Oh yes, sir. I'm one of Ms. Bixby's regular chauffeurs. We can contact her if you wish to have references provided?"

Tapper blinked in a strange, jerky pattern—three quick bursts.

"Alright," Dad said, fingers digging between Jaxon's shoulder blades. "Come on, kids … it's just a ride."

• • •

The Navigator drove through the airfield's empty parking lot and directly onto the desolate runway, rolling past a crop-duster plane, hazed over and covered in cobwebs.

A knot had formed in Don's stomach the moment Rosie had opened the door of their suite to reveal the bizarre man in the purple tracksuit. The knot had yet to go away. "Why we meeting way out here?"

Rosie jabbed him in the ribs.

Sapper rolled the car to a stop and unlocked the doors. "You both are going to have a wonderful time!"

Don and Rosie exited, but Sapper didn't budge.

"You're not coming?"

"No, Mr. Williams. Your air transportation should arrive in the next ninety-three seconds, but if you have any questions: just ask!"

Don looked to the sky. Nothing. "Ninety-three seconds?"

"Eighty-eight seconds now, sir."

Don had more questions, but Sapper had already started up the blacked-out divider screen, sealing off the front seat.

Don slapped shut the car door. There was nothing to do but wait.

The cracked runway stretched out ahead of them, painted in weeds, the old control tower nothing but a husk.

"I guess it's probably a helicopter," Don said.

"I hope it's a Sikorsky," Rosie said, bouncing on her toes. "Daddy flies in them all the time. They're so much fun."

If a helicopter was less than a minute away, it was a quiet one. Don strained his ears for the chop of blades but could hear nothing but the squawking of crows.

Wind sent a shudder over the abandoned hangars, rattling their loose and flaking steel panels and sending the panicked black birds into the sky. Whatever was coming … *it wasn't a helicopter.*

A massive balloon, red-and-gold, glided over top of the abandoned control tower. Instead of a basket, like in *The Wizard of Oz*, the colorful balloon was holding something like a gondola lift or cable car, large enough to hold a dozen people.

When the car touched down, resting on the runway, Rosie squealed and clapped. "This is so exciting!"

Don did not feel excited exactly. The windows of the little car were not tinted. No one seemed to be on board.

What the fuck? No pilot. Who was flying? Don pulled Rosie into him by the crook of her arm. "This shit weird though, right?"

"What?"

"What you think I mean? Who's flying that?"

"Have you never heard of drones?"

"Yeah, I heard a damned drones. But what about that *Children of the Corn* motherfucker that drove us here?"

"*Children of the Corn?*" Rosie said, confused. "You mean Sapper? I'm sure that's not his real name, goofball."

How could she not see how bizarre all of this was? Before Don could press further, a second Navigator rumbled onto the runway, parking alongside the other.

Lucy's assistant, Charlotte, slipped out first. Her eyes flicked up to the balloon, but, as was apparently her custom, she said nothing. Instead, she helped Lucy out of the car. "Oh good," Lucy said. "It's here."

Rosie burst forward and threw her arms around the old woman. "We are so excited to be here, Ms. Bixby! Are we going to get to ride on this?!"

"Of course," Lucy said. "I'm so glad you're excited. It's going to be an amazing day." She smiled, revealing dull gray teeth. "And this must be young Mr. Jaxon and his family."

Don watched as the third Navigator eased into place beside the other two. A preteen girl hopped out first, wearing jean shorts and a Princess Sakhaar t-shirt, her brown hair yanked into a high ponytail. Her parents climbed out after her, followed by a small, skinny boy in gym shorts and Crocs.

"Well, aren't you both the cutest?" Rosie said. She bent forward to meet the kids at eye level. "Are you both excited?"

The boy said nothing, but the girl nodded enthusiastically.

"This is Mr. and Mrs. Dave and Amy Kinney," Lucy said. "And their children, Jaxon and Becky."

"Which of you found the ticket?" Rosie asked in her little-girl voice.

Becky cocked her head towards her brother. "He did." Jaxon shrugged nervously and his eyes shifted to the ground.

Rosie slipped her arm around Don's waist and pulled him tight. "This is my friend, Donny. He found ours!"

Un-be-fucking-lievable.

Don had already corrected Rosie again during their ride from the Safari Lounge. He would have again right then too, but he didn't want to cause a scene. He had not read the contract he'd signed closely and didn't want to risk losing the money. He would have a real sit-down with Rosie after the tour though. A sit-down in which she would keep her clothes on.

"Well, dears," Lucy said, "now that we're all here, it's time to go." The old woman went to the box-shaped car sitting beneath the balloon and pulled open a thin metal door.

It was bigger inside than Don would have thought, large enough to carry his entire college team.

"It's a quick trip," Lucy said, buckling herself. "About three minutes."

Dave Kinney buckled in his son before checking his daughter's harness. "Is this thing safe?" he said. "Who's flying it?"

"All computers, Mr. Kinney," Lucy said. "It's the future, you know."

"But couldn't we have just taken one of the ferries?"

The car thrummed and shook.

"I'm afraid there's no dock or harbor on the island," Lucy said.

That sounded impossible. "Then how do you bring in supplies?" Don asked.

"By air, of course," Lucy said.

That notion sounded even more impossible. "But that's—"

"Donny," Rosie pleaded. "Would you stop asking so many questions?"

"I've told you to stop calling me that."

"Now, dears," Lucy said, "let's not fight." She pointed between Amy Kinney's legs. "Mrs. Kinney, could you grab and open up that box at your feet?"

Dave Kinney reached for the box before his wife could grab it, and opened it on his lap like a thick book. "What is it?" he said, before turning the opened box around so they could see. Inside was a piece of foam with vertical and horizontal slots cut into it.

"In accordance with your agreement," Lucy said. "This is the part where you all turn over your phones."

Gasps and groans came as the balloon shuddered and lifted off.

"You didn't say nothing about no phones," Don said.

Lucy pursed her raisined lips. "I'm afraid it was in the agreement you signed."

"I didn't see that either," Dave Kinney said. "I need the phone. I can't give it to you."

Lucy shrugged her shoulders. "Then you don't go in. Rules are rules, dears. No flash photography. But rest assured there are phones on the premises, and I can see that anyone who attempts to reach you at your respective resorts will be able to contact you."

Don pulled out his phone but cradled it into his chest. "I won't take no pictures."

Rosie's hand darted out like a viper and snatched the phone. "You're making everything so difficult." She unbuckled and leaned forward, sliding both of their phones into separate compartments.

Before Don could snap at her, Mr. and Mrs. Kinney reluctantly inserted their own phones. Dave Kinney started to shut the case when Lucy put up a withered hand and looked to her assistant. "You too, Charlotte."

. . .

Charlie was startled by the command. And there was no doubt it had been exactly that: a command. The phone technically belonged to

Lucy anyway, but Charlie had hoped to hold onto it until she could purchase one of her own.

Lucy leaned in and whispered, "It's alright. The phone's yours after the tour, though you'll have to get your own plan at the end of the month. It's the least I can do, but as I said, there's no photography in the Dream Factory. This is an exclusive event, and I cannot afford for there to be any leaks."

Charlie looked at the phone a final time before slipping it in the top corner of the safe box.

"I can see it!" Rosie squealed, pointing to the window.

Charlie had seen the factory only a few times during her decade-long employment. From Bixby Harbor, the Dream Factory had been distant and looked as if it stood on the water, but up close the factory rose abruptly from the small island's densely green canopy, its inactive smokestacks poking at the sky like extinguished birthday candles.

Becky spun towards the window and pressed her head against it, smudging the thin plexiglass. "How does it get power?"

"What a nice question," Lucy said.

Mrs. Kinney perked up proudly. "She loves science."

Jaxon rolled his big brown eyes, and Charlie thought that as annoying as Rosie was, she had been right about one thing. The Kinney children were adorable.

"Well, this should be a fun tour for her then," Lucy said. "The factory generates its own power." Before a follow-up question could be asked, Lucy said, "Hang on, everyone. We're beginning our descent."

The cabin jerked hard to the left.

"Where we supposed to land?" Don said.

"There's a small landing pad," Lucy said. The cabin jumped upward. "It's alright," she said. "Only wind shears."

"It's kind of fun," Rosie said. She had worn a ridiculously low-cut tanktop, and her boobs were bouncing wildly as the balloon descended.

Outside, the foliage filled the window, stretching towards the cabin. Another jerk brought a collective inhale of breath before the little metal car rocked down.

"Can we do it again?" Becky asked.

Outside, someone was jogging towards them. When Charlie saw who it was, her mind started to race. *He couldn't have made it here ahead of us.*

Japper pulled open the little metal door, his cheeks contorting to form his grotesquely wide smile. "I'm so excited to meet you all. My name is Clapper. If you'll—"

"Clapper?" Dave Kinney said. "Are you Tapper's twin?"

Don's dark complexion had gone ghost white. "I thought his name was Sapper."

Charlie said nothing.

● ● ●

There were bugs back home, big ones, but Jaxon had never seen any like these: huge, fat ones with hummingbird wings. He'd swatted three of them on the short walk down the twisting dirt path. Even Becky's façade of the perfect daughter was cracking further with each bug's kamikaze dive at her head.

Rosie batted them away from her smooth thighs with grace. She was the most beautiful person Jaxon had ever seen in real life—perfect lips and hair, and skin that Jaxon imagined melting into. She'd have been consuming all his thoughts if not for Tapper's strange twin leading them to the factory.

"It's just up here, folks," Clapper said, swishing forward in his tracksuit. Tapper had been terrifying enough when he was the only one. Now there was apparently a whole army of the freaks.

The front door was a simple metal panel painted a dull green, with bits of brown mud splattered across its base. Clapper skipped to the door and announced his name. In a moment, a red light ran over his face, and a digitized voice announced: "*Approved.*"

The green door shot upwards. Instead of a factory full of bright lights and happy music, it opened on a shifting and swirling void. Clapper looked back to the others and waved before stepping forward and disappearing into the black fog.

"What is that?" Don said. "I don't want to get x-rayed. I *know* that wasn't in that paperwork we signed."

"I'm afraid it was, Mr. Williams," Lucy said. "But not to worry. This is just a bit of pyrotechnics. I promise, nothing here will hurt you. There's no reason to be scared."

"I ain't scared."

Lucy grinned. "Then after you, Mr. Williams."

Jaxon felt his mom and dad hunker closer to him, hovering over him. Dad grabbed hold of his shoulders.

"Go on, Donny!" Rosie said.

Don shot her an angry look, but took a tentative step forward towards the swirling black fog.

The red light washed over him.

"*Approved.*"

Don blew out a bit of air and went through.

Rosie, who went through next, was not nearly as tentative, bouncing rhythmically on her toes as the red light passed over her body.

"*Approved.*"

Rosie smiled and waved to the group before disappearing into the black fog.

Becky slapped away a bug and pulled Jaxon towards the void. "Come on, Jax. I'm getting eaten alive out here."

Dad pulled them both back in place. "Hold on a sec there, both of you," he said. "Ms. Bixby … what is that?"

"I understand your concern, Mr. Kinney." Lucy pinched her thumb and finger close together. "But won't you allow an old woman a drop of mystique? I promise all will be explained shortly."

Dad bit the inside of his cheek.

"My assistant will go next," Lucy said. "Charlotte?"

Jaxon looked over in time to see a flicker of doubt cross Ms. Charlotte's face. Unlike most of the park people Jaxon had seen, she did not have a perfect park smile and wasn't particularly pretty. Still instead of turning and running, she said, "Yes, Lucy."

She stepped forward for her scan, pushing a lock of black hair away from her ear to reveal a tiny spiral of green. Jaxon was sure he hadn't seen any other park people with a tattoo, and the sight of it was bizarre.

After Ms. Charlotte's approval, she hesitated only a moment before disappearing through the void.

"Daddy, I want to go in," Becky whined.

Dad bit his cheek again. "No," he said, slowly. "I think I'll go next."

After Dad had stepped through, Becky tried to chase after him, but Mom had hold of her arm. "Wait a sec."

Dad's head and shoulders backed out of the mist. He was smiling. "Pretty neat." After he'd gone back inside, Becky tripped over her feet, scrambling to the landing for her scan.

"*Approved.*"

Mom's hand was on Jaxon's neck, pulsing slightly. "Alright, Jax," she said. "You're up."

Jaxon's toes curled, digging into the navy-blue rubber of his Crocs. He took a delicate step towards the portal: swirling cyclones of black.

The red light flashed, igniting floating dust motes.

"*Approved.*"

The black cyclones spun. The air buzzed with the thrum of wings and chirps.

"Go ahead, Jax," Mom called. "I'm right behind you."

Jaxon took a breath and stepped through the void. When his Crocs hit white marble tiles, he looked up and was in a palace. The swirling void was behind him now, framed in wood carved with butterflies and five-pointed stars.

Ahead, the glossy floor stretched out beneath a crystalline chandelier. At the far side of the foyer, the others were gathered between twin bases of an imperial staircase. Each side was blocked with a pair of drooping red velvet ropes attached to golden stands.

Mom came through, breaking into an immediate smile. "Wow," she whispered, taking Jaxon's hand. "Isn't it amazing?"

It was nice, but it didn't look much nicer than the lobby at the Grand Victorian. "I don't like the twins," Jaxon whispered. "They're creepy."

Mom shushed him before whispering, "Me either."

Lucy tottered through last, looking as if she might topple over at any moment. "We're all here," she croaked, starting for the stairs. "Our guide will be arriving any mom—" Lucy's mouth twisted in annoyance as she produced a vibrating flip phone from her purse.

She whipped it open and put it to her ear. "I see," she said. "I'll let him know."

"What is it?" Dad said.

"Phone call," Lucy said, putting the little phone to her chest. "For you actually, Mr. Kinney. A man named Joe would like to speak with you. I have a room where you can take your call. Clapper will show you."

The freakish twin's tracksuit swished as he padded across the reflective floor. "Follow me, Mr. Kinney!" He opened a small door to the left of the stairs. Inside, Jaxon could only see stark white walls. "Right through here, sir!"

Dad turned back to Mom and winked. "Be back in a minute." He slipped around Clapper into the blindingly white room. The door slapped shut, and Jaxon's stomach felt as if it were flipping end-over-end in painful somersaults.

Rosie giggled. "This sure is fun, isn't it?"

"I guess so." The truth was Jaxon had an itching bug bite above his elbow that was beginning to swell, and while the foyer looked fancy, there didn't seem to be much to do. To this point, the Dream Factory was proving to be less than magical.

"Who's your favorite Bixby character?" Rosie asked.

No matter how many times Jaxon had heard the insipid question, it never really grew less annoying, but he was happy for a chance to speak with Rosie.

"He doesn't really like this kind of stuff," Becky said.

Rosie pouted out her glossy lips, and Jaxon immediately forgot about how stupid Bixby shows and movies were. "I do so like it!"

Lucy's phone vibrated again. She picked it up. "Of course," the old woman said. "She's right here." Lucy put the little phone to her chest again. "Mrs. Kinney," she said. "Mr. Kinney would like to speak with you in the back."

Mom's hand disappeared from Jaxon's neck. "What?"

"He's on the phone here." Lucy held up the cell. "Would you like to speak with him?"

Mom stormed over and took the phone. "Dave?"

Jaxon couldn't hear what was being said, but recognized Dad's voice on the other side of the line. Mom handed Lucy back the phone and looked to the little door. "It's right through there?"

"Yes, Mrs. Kinney."

The door opened, and Clapper—at least it looked like Clapper—reemerged. Mom made the kind of face she often did when Dad had asked her to do something that she didn't want to do.

"We'll keep an eye on them for you," Rosie said.

Don nodded. "Yeah," he said. "I teach gym. These two look easier to handle than most of the kids I'm used to."

"Thank you," Mom said, starting away. "It won't be a moment."

Mom had almost stepped through the door when Lucy's assistant said, "What is it?" Her voice was startling in its crispness.

"Something that apparently only I can solve," Mom said. "I'll be just two minutes." She disappeared into the little white room, and when the door slammed shut, Becky was next to Jaxon, taking wheezing breaths.

Rosie bent closer to the pair of them, smelling faintly of strawberries. "Who do you think our tour guide will be?"

Jaxon wanted to give an answer that Rosie would want to hear. An answer that would make her happy. But he couldn't think of any answer at all. He couldn't think of anyone that might excite her. "I don't know."

"I bet it's someone amazing," Rosie said.

Don chuckled. "After all this bull, this tour better be."

The sound of clacking heels came above them. A man wearing a white hat with a thick, black band leaned far over the banister.

Jaxon's blood went cold.

"This can't be real," Becky whispered.

She was right. It couldn't be. But it sure seemed to be.

Max Bixby pulled off his hat and took a sweeping bow. "My friends," he said, "welcome to the Dream Factory!"

INTERLUDE

Last Will and Testament of Maximillian Bixby
Page 12 of 1124

…and I remember the day of Violet's marriage to Roy Allen and how it hardened my heart to know that I had lost her to such a gloriously successful, ruggedly handsome, diabolical bastard.

To you my sweet and beautiful Violet I leave your mother's emerald bracelet $_{D3-C}$, complete ownership of Bixby Ranch in Fort Worth $_{C2-1}$, and a forty percent share of my personal Bixby stock $_{B9-5}$.

Oh, how excitingly terrifying this must be for the rest of you. You're thinking: '*That's a lot of stock for one person. What about my stock?*'

How I wish I was there to see all of your faces. Especially yours, Future Larry. Are you throwing things? I hope not. The value of anything you break in this room will be deducted from the shares I'm leaving you. $_{E12-1}$.

That's right, Larry.

Of course, I have some stock for you too. I wouldn't forget about you. Five percent. $_{C1-B}$. You have earned every bit of it. But unfortunately for you, not a bit more. Don't blame the kids.

At least don't blame them yet. I'm also naming you CEO of the Bixby Company until such time as Roy Allen can pry it away from you [B2-5]. I give that about two years.

Let's see, who is next?

Joseph.

You have become such a dashing man. Just this past week, I saw your headline in *Picture Weekly*: All Hail the Coming King! You know I wouldn't dare disappoint the paying public, my boy. For you, I am leaving my estate on Treasure Circle, along with all its assets [C5-D thru G], and … there should be drums playing. If there are not drums playing, Willis and Burley's fee is to be reduced by half [A1-1] … I leave you, Joseph, a fifty-five percent share of my stock [C1-2].

Oh boy-o. That was a big one, wasn't it?!

Now, let's see … who else is in the room? Ah. Yes. Roy Allen. You're here, I'm sure. What do I have for you … ? Oh, that's right. Nothing. I already gave you Violet, and Violet is more than enough for anyone.

Now … who else? Let me see. If drums are not playing for this one, Willis and Burley's fee is to be cut down another twenty-five percent, and the firm must be dissolved and reformed as Crooks, Incompetents, and Louts LLP. [A1-2].

My sweet Lucille.

I wouldn't forget about you, Lucy. For you, I give the greatest gift of all: I give you the Dream Factory and all its associated assets, including the island $_{B1-1}$.

But more than that, I give you its secrets. The others don't think they care much about the factory now: *but believe you me, they will.* You don't need any more stock, sugar. You've got plenty of stock. No doubt, everyone in this room has lots and lots of stock. But only you get the secrets.

I present to you … the key! I hope the key is on a blue satin pillow. It doesn't have to be, but I think Willis and Burley will do that for me. I've always liked those boys.

Take the key to First National Bank at 54 Beachside Road. Present it to the bank's manager, Jonathan Scott Robinson. He will be waiting for you. Go today. If you go today, the others will not follow you. If they do, they'll need to read sections D-51 through D-102 to find out what happens to the shares I just left them. It's all quite tedious, but I can assure you they won't like it.

After you know the truth, you can tell your brother and sister or anyone else whatever you like, but it will be up to you. They'll pressure you. They'll beg you for the secrets of the factory. They'll try to find ways to get at them. I know you won't give them away though … which is why I'm giving them to you.

PART TWO:

THE DREAM FACTORY

CHAPTER ELEVEN:

FOLLOW ME

Becky's hand clamped hard enough around Jaxon's wrist to cut off circulation.

It couldn't be true. Yet it sure seemed to be.

Max Bixby was very clearly not dead and didn't even look particularly old. He skipped down the right side of the horseshoed stairs with ease and grace, despite his snug-looking Southern leisure suit. "Welcome, my friends. Welcome." The dead man grinned and spun his signature cane like a propellor.

It's impossible. Santa couldn't even bring back the dead. Jaxon had asked.

"I've been waiting for this for so long, I can't tell you all. It's going to be such an exciting day!"

Rosie squealed and clapped, but Don's formerly rigid jaw had collapsed into shock. "*The hell …*"

Bixby waved his cane. "Form a line now, folks! That's the only way to do it! Come on, everyone: follow me!"

"It's a fake," Don whispered. "A double."

Lucy's assistant was squeezing her hands into pinkish fists when Lucy said, "Daddy, I think I'd better go collect Mr. and Mrs. Kinney. They're already missing so much of the fun. You all best go on ahead."

"You're absolutely right, sugar." Bixby unclasped the velvet rope at the base of the stairs. "So much to see and so little time. Line up everyone. Come on now."

The idea that the old woman could be the daughter of the twitching man on the stairs was absurd, though the two did have oddly similar noses—elongated and slightly hooked.

Becky squeezed Jaxon's hand harder, digging into the fleshy pit at the base of his thumb.

"Charlotte," Lucy said, heading for the little side door, "will you help take charge of these youngsters for a few minutes?"

"Yes, Lucy."

Jaxon's hand was throbbing now. Becky was squeezing down so hard it was driving blood to the tips of Jaxon's fingers.

"Ms. Lucy," Jaxon said. "Can we come with you?"

Lucy chuckled as if it were the silliest idea in the world. "Why would you want to do that? You'd miss the first part of the show. You don't want to miss out on that. It's one of the best parts."

"It's okay," Ms. Lucy's assistant whispered. "My name's Charlie. It's all part of the show. Just stick close to me until we see your mom and dad again."

Jaxon hoped that wouldn't be too long.

"Come along, come along," Bixby called, waving the group to the stairs with his cane. "We're on a tight schedule. All will be explained on the tour."

Lucy disappeared through the side door, and Becky shivered when it slammed shut. "Do you think it's really him?" she whispered.

Jaxon watched Bixby carefully as he directed Don and Rosie up the curling stairs. He had only seen Max Bixby a few times in black-and-white, and never in the full color of real life, but … *it sure looked like him.*

Charlie stopped at the base of the stairs. "Who are you?"

Bixby rolled his eyes towards her. "Isn't it obvious?"

Jaxon started to take a step before realizing Becky's hand was anchoring him in place. Charlie had still not followed the others up the stairs. She was waiting for them.

"Come on," Jaxon whispered. He had to know if it was true. If it really was Max Bixby skipping up the stairs … who else could be brought back?

"Mom and Dad will meet us inside," he said.

Becky's heavy feet and locked knees loosened enough to allow Jaxon to pull her after the others.

A line had formed at the top of the stairs, but no one except Bixby had stepped onto the landing. Bixby's hands were swimming through an open coat rack stuffed with puffy banana-yellow jackets fastened with ginormous white snap buttons shaped like snowflakes. He pulled two coats free and skipped back to the top of the steps.

He held the pair of coats up to Don's and Rosie's shoulders. They ran oddly long for thermal coats, extending down to their shins.

"Yes," Bixby said. "These look like they'll fit you each perfectly. I'm afraid it can get a little chilly in there."

"What we need them jackets for?" Don said.

Bixby grinned and pressed the coat into his chest. "You must be Mr. Williams," Bixby said. "My princess has told me that you're an inquisitive little one."

Jaxon didn't think there was anything particularly *little* about Don. He was at least as tall as Dad and in way better shape.

Don did not appear to agree with the assessment either, though Bixby himself showed no signs of noticing his reaction. "And this must be your significant other, Ms. Rosie," he said. "Quite a catch, sir. Quite a catch, indeed. I can assure you both that all will be explained shortly."

"Yeah," Don said, pulling on the coat and snapping the snowflake buttons. "I keep hearing that."

Bixby skipped back onto the landing. Besides the coat rack, there was very little else at the top of the stairs. Only four humongous portraits of Wally Rabbit, Canyon Jane, Regina Rat, and Shykker the Cat, and a simple flat-paneled door. Bixby tapped the tip of his cane against its frame, and the door popped inward.

"Straight through here, Mr. Williams. I promise you, you're going to love this. Just love it."

After Don and Rosie stepped through, Bixby handed Charlie a coat. "My princess has had nothing but good things to say about you, Ms. Cooper."

Charlie said nothing, but pulled the coat on.

"Don't talk much though, do you?"

"No."

Bixby's shoulders twitched. "Oh well." He took another pair of coats and lowered himself to his haunches, close enough for Jaxon to smell his peppermint aftershave.

"A coat for you, Ms. Becky. There you are … and this must be Mr. Jaxon!" Bixby's eyes widened—piercing and alive. "I'm so happy to show you what I have planned," he said. "So very … Oh no." He was looking at Jaxon's feet. "Those shoes you're wearing won't do. Won't do at all."

Jaxon's Crocs were the only footwear he wore outside of school.

Bixby put up a waiting finger and went back to the rack. When he returned, he had a pair of yellow boots the same shade as the coats.

"Here you are," he said. "You should be able to slip your whole foot in, even with those ghastly shoes of yours still on."

Bixby was right. Jaxon's feet slipped into the boots easily. They fit so perfectly that his toes immediately began to sweat.

"Why do we need these?" Becky said, pulling on her coat. "It's not even cold in here."

"It's not now," Bixby said. "But you never can tell what the future may have in store." He spun his cane and started through the open door. "Come along now. Follow me. Much to do."

"But Mr. Bixby," Jaxon said, "shouldn't you have a coat too?"

"Yeah," Don said, peeking his head back out onto the landing. "Why don't you got a coat?"

Bixby held up his hands innocently. "Nothing left that fits, I'm afraid. But not to worry. I've always been rather warm-blooded." He snaked around Don and through the door.

The new room didn't feel any colder than the previous one, though it was far less fancy: a windowless corridor curling around a bend.

It looked like the building where Dad went to pay for his speeding tickets.

Bixby spun his cane and skipped to the head of the group, curling past door after door that lined the hall. "Right up here, folks!"

"It's fine, Becky," Jaxon whispered. It felt as if his sister were steadily gaining weight as they slipped down the hall.

"Like heck it is," she said. "Something's wrong."

Ahead of them, Rosie was giggling and skipping close to Bixby's heels. She didn't seem nervous. Still, Jaxon felt a sudden and urgent need to pee. "What are all these rooms?" he said.

"Oh … bits and bobs," Bixby said. "This and that." It was hardly the answer Jaxon was hoping for. But before he could make his intensifying need to piss clearer, Bixby announced, "Ah … here we are."

At the end of the hall, Bixby pulled open a pair of gilded double doors. The group was suddenly staring back at themselves, shattered and split.

"It's a mirror maze," Rosie squealed.

Bixby stepped into the bottomless fathoms of cutting reflections. "Don't be shy. Step right up."

"Where does it go?" Don said.

"It goes everywhere, Mr. Williams," Bixby called, disappearing amongst the shards. "Now please hurry along, everyone. There's much to see, and we have so very little time together."

Becky looked back at the snaking corridor behind them. "I don't want to go in there, Jax."

He checked the nearest side door. Locked. He needed to hurry. "It's just a ride," he said.

"Keep moving forward," Bixby called. "Got to go forward to get back. One foot in front of the other now."

"Come on," Jaxon said. Not only did he have to go to the bathroom, but he was starting to cook inside his coat and boots. "It's the only way."

He pulled Becky closer. As he did, the air grew blissfully colder. By the time the sharp glass had filled his field of vision, the endless reflections hummed and buzzed like insects. The wispy hair on Jaxon's forearms sizzled upward on end.

"Jax …" Becky squeezed, pinching a joint.

"Ow!" Jaxon tore his hand free.

"Jax!"

The light reflecting against the shards flashed, and echoing screams seemed to bounce against each other.

"Hey!" Don shouted. "What the shit is this, man?"

Bixby's high voice came from a deep nowhere. "*All that we see or seem to see, is but a dream within a dream. I stand amid the roar, of a surf-tormented shore …*"

"Enough, man!"

"*And I hold within my hand, grains of the golden sand … how few … yet how they creep. Through my fingers to the deep, While I weep! While I weep!*"

Jaxon spun and saw Becky, her eyes darting and terrified. He reached out, banging against freezing glass. "Becky, where are you?"

"Jax," she said, barely audible over the roaring buzz. "I'm over here. I'm scared."

"*Oh God, can I not grasp them with a tighter clasp? Oh God, can I not save one from the pitiless wave? Is all that we see or seem but a dream within a dream?!*"

Jaxon spun towards another Becky.

Glass.

"Forward, please!" Bixby called. "Keep moving forward!"

Frigid bumps spread across the back of Jaxon's neck. "Keep moving, Becky," he called. "It's fine. It's a ride."

He found another Becky.

And more glass.

The image of her whimpered and cried. "I want to get out of here. Now, Jax!" Jaxon spun and found another Becky and felt the heat of her before taking her arm.

"Jax!"

"Come on," he said. "It's right through here." Jaxon had said it as much to convince himself, but in a flash, a hand of black ice flew at them from empty space. It seized Jaxon's arm above the elbow, hauling him out of the intersecting reflections.

Don blew out a frosty plume of air. "You kids alright?"

"No," Becky said, pulling herself free of Don's other hand. "That was an awful place."

"But this isn't," Rosie said, her eyes twinkling and her cheeks flushed.

It was impossible.

The lawn ahead of them was as white and smooth as vanilla frosting, and bathed in the light of the biggest and brightest full moon Jaxon had ever seen. A streetlamp-lined walkway led to a distant twinkling town of red and green lights.

It was so far. They couldn't still be inside the factory.

A drop of snow touched Jaxon's nose. Then another.

"It's snowing!" Rosie whipped her arms around, twirling in the falling white flakes.

"How?" Don said, barely able to choke out the word. "How is this possible?"

"Magic, Mr. Williams," Bixby said. "Real magic."

Don spun back towards the mirror maze. It had been cut right into reality alongside the frozen landscape and glittering stars. Don swept his hands over the night sky as if miming a window.

"Oh now, Mr. Williams." Bixby nodded the tip of his cane. "You're going to spoil the fun for the others."

Don pressed his hand flat against the stars. "It's some kind of illusion."

Jaxon released a flash of air he hadn't realized he had been holding. *Of course it's an illusion*, he thought. *How could it be anything else?* God, he really needed to pee. "Mr. Bixby," he said, "is there a bathroom?"

Bixby crunched across the snow, leaving behind a trail of shallow footsteps. "Bathroom's in the village. It's not as far as it looks. Come along, everyone."

"No," Charlie said, her tone whiplike. "I'm sorry, Mr. Bixby, or whoever you are. But no. We're done here."

"I'm sorry," Bixby said. "Is there a problem?"

"No," Charlie said. "There's no problem. But I've had enough of this ride. Where is Lucy?"

"Had it with the ride? Oh, dear."

Rosie muttered, "Ridiculous," before taking Don's wrist and dragging him to the path.

"My friends," Bixby said, "we really must stay together."

Don nodded. "He's right. It's an optical illusion. If we split up it probably won't work."

Becky edged closer to Charlie. "I don't want to go down there either, Jax. I want to go home."

"I'm taking these kids back to their parents," Charlie said. "Where are they?"

Bixby frowned at her. "Being Lucy's assistant, I'm sure you're aware of the rules with regard to our special present? If Mr. Jaxon were to leave the tour, he would become ineligible for his prize."

Charlie seemed not to hear him. "I'm not kidding," she said.

Bixby spun his cane lazily and trudged back across the snow, towards the mirror maze. "As you wish."

He traced the tip of his cane along the impossible wall. "Ah yes … here it is." He tapped the tip of his cane against the starry sky, and a passage swung open.

Inside was a dimly lit stairwell. The number two was spray-painted on a dirty cinderblock wall. "Right through here," he said. "It is too bad for Mr. Jaxon … that he has to surrender such a gift. Oh well. I'll have Mr. and Mrs. Kinney meet you all downstairs. Clapper will take you back to the mainland."

"Let's go, Jax." Becky tugged hard on Jaxon's coat, before he ripped it free.

"You go," Jaxon said. "I need to go to the bathroom."

She stared at him. "What?"

Even if Jaxon hadn't needed to use the bathroom, he still wanted to keep going. Dad would be angry if he lost all of the money, but more than that, Jaxon still wanted to know if this man really was Max Bixby.

"It's just a ride," Jaxon said. "Mom and Dad are meeting us in the village."

"You'd leave me?"

"I'm not leaving you. You're leaving me."

Charlie looked horrified, but Bixby was smiling and flipping his cane idly, watching the drama unfold.

Jaxon held out his hand to Becky. "Come on," he said. "It'll be fine."

Becky waited a long moment before taking it and walking with him to the path.

Bixby looked around theatrically. "So no one is leaving then?" He held a moment on Charlie, who shook her head.

"Excellent." Bixby tapped the sky next to the stairwell with his cane, and the door swung seamlessly back into place, disappearing into the stars as if it were never there. "Follow me, my friends. Follow me."

CHAPTER TWELVE:

SHOW HIM WHAT YOU'VE GOT

Don had seen snow once before while travelling to North Carolina for an away game. He had heard another player call it a dusting, but there hadn't been anything dusty about the slushy mess. In under forty-eight hours, most of the snow had melted away, leaving behind only the occasional sloppy, black puddle.

The snow in the Dream Factory was something else entirely. This snow was more like something out of a Christmas movie. During the walk, Don had scooped up a handful of the snow and compacted it, forming it into a tight ball. It wasn't as cold as he would have expected and was oddly pliable, like sand for the perfect sandcastle. Wet but not too wet.

Rosie cuddled against him as they walked past the first cottage, a single-story European-style house with a snow-covered roof. There was an orange glow behind the windows, but the glazing had been frosted over, making it impossible to see inside.

"It's so pretty here," Rosie said. "Do you think we could build a snowman? I haven't built one since I was a girl in Vermont." The cool air had brought a sweet redness to her cheeks, but Don could scarcely focus on it.

Something had been eating at him for the entire walk. It was not the snow or even the village that should have been impossibly far away but was now closing in all around them. Don had convinced himself that all of those things could have been engineered with enough time and money. Almost anything could.

What was eating at him more than that was Bixby himself. He had tried telling himself it was silly, that he barely knew what Bixby looked like. Except that wasn't true. Don knew exactly what Max Bixby looked like.

Twenty years earlier, during the summer he'd spent in Franklin Parish, his Aunt Nicole had refused to let him outside to play in the neighborhood, saying, "The only playing these boys is doing you sure enough don't want to be a part of."

It had been the most boring summer of his life. Aunt Nicole didn't read or have cable, so the only thing for him to do was watch through her collection of mislabeled VHS tapes. They were mostly 90s sitcoms that had been taped with the commercials, but after his first miserable week in Franklin Parish, Aunt Nicole had purchased a complete set of *Bixby Fun House* tapes at a yard sale.

The show was a hodgepodge of cartoon shorts for children, featuring the regular lineup of Bixby characters. In this original version, Bixby himself had hosted the program, bringing the audience into and out of the commercial breaks.

The resemblance of the man leading the group through the snow in Southern Texas was striking and uncanny. It wasn't only the face and the outfit that were so unnerving. It was the little things like the practiced and confident way he swung his cane, and his high, flutey voice that was inescapably perfect.

It was him. *But it couldn't be him.*

The street opened on a square, the glowing buildings horseshoeing around a tall, twinkling Christmas tree. "Here we are, my friends," Bixby said. "You know what they say about Christmas. Every year it shows up earlier and earlier."

A door clicked shut to their left. Lucy Bixby, now wearing one of the long and puffy banana coats, hobbled down the short landing of the nearest cottage, holding a steaming mug between cotton gloves. "I hope you don't mind I took a shortcut," she said. "All this walking is terrible on my knees. Getting old's a curse. How are you all liking it so far?"

Don was too terrified to enjoy the ride, but Rosie spoke first. "Oh. My. God," she said. "So amazing."

Lucy's assistant spoke next, looking relieved to see the old woman. "Lucy," Charlie said. "Where are the Kinneys?"

Don had been wondering about that too. It was unnerving that they had disappeared only moments before Max Bixby's doppelganger had shown up.

Lucy made a little wave to the cottage she had emerged from, and the door opened. Mrs. Kinney was inside holding out her arms.

"Mom!" Becky crunched through the snow, running for her mother. Jaxon wasn't far behind.

Don was relieved to see Mrs. Kinney, but it was nuts that Charlie seemed as in the dark about what was going on as the rest of them were. Even now that Mrs. Kinney had turned up, Lucy's assistant still looked on edge.

Don supposed she could have been faking it. That she was part of the show. If she was, she was a tremendous actress, though he guessed Bixby Park was full of those.

Lucy took a tentative sip from her mug and licked a pruned upper lip. "You look positively spent, Charlotte. Would you like some coffee?"

Charlie shook her head, but said nothing, and instead watched the Kinney children disappear inside the cottage.

"They are so adorable," Rosie said. "I could just eat the both of them up."

"Me too," Lucy said, turning to … *whoever the fuck he was.* "You don't mind stopping here for a minute, Daddy?"

"Course not, sugar," Bixby said. "I'd say this is just about the most perfect place we could have stopped at. There's something for everyone here in the village. If you want to take your lovely assistant around, I can take charge of Mr. Williams and Ms. Rosie here."

"Of course," Lucy said. "Follow me, Charlotte. I'm sure you're full of questions."

She wasn't the only one.

Don did not want to be left with only Bixby and Rosie, but he couldn't think of a dignified objection before Charlie was following Lucy back up the snow-blown path.

"Well now," Bixby said. "What to do while we wait? We're very near the gymnasium." He mimed dribbling a ball. "What do you say, Mr. Williams? A little one on one?"

A gymnasium?

The cottages hardly looked big enough for a couple of bedrooms and a kitchen. It didn't make sense, but the idea of the game brought Don a familiar and immediate comfort. "You want to play basketball?" he asked.

"Oh," Bixby said, twirling his cane. "I wouldn't stand much of a chance against someone like you, and it wouldn't be much fun for Ms. Rosie to watch you run circles around little old me. I'll have to choose a champion to play for myself, of course."

Bixby crunched across the snow, skipping to the next cottage. He waved for Don and Rosie to follow. "Come on," he said. "You both are going to especially love this."

He opened the groaning door of the cottage, revealing the impossible again: a full-court arena with thousands of empty seats.

Don followed him inside the warm building, slack-jawed, as Rosie released an elongated squeal that reverberated throughout the arena. Don clamped shut his eyes, but the brightness of the jumbotron and the overhead floodlights shone through his eyelids like they were made of mesh polyester.

When he reluctantly opened his eyes, the arena was still there. It was at least three times the size of the one he had played in during his college years.

Bixby stepped gingerly around the puddles of water pooling on the hardwood. "Well, this won't do at all," he said, helping Rosie out of her jacket. "Let me take those."

Don handed Bixby his dripping coat, and the dead man said, "We have some gym shorts and shoes that should fit you fine in the locker room. It's right over there." Bixby pointed to the center left tunnel as something emerged. It was as big as a man but had long floppy ears. Don's heart hammered faster as it stepped out of the shadows, fully under the lights.

Rosie broke out into an excited fit of laughter. "It's him! Oh my God! It's him!"

Don's tongue was numb. "… *The fuck is that* …"

Wally Rabbit walked to center court, basketball pinned to his hip. This was not a man in makeup or a bulky costume. Wally's fat, fluffy cheeks enlarged as his mouth split into a toothy grin beneath a nickel-sized pink nose.

Don's left leg twitched.

"Hey-ya, folks," Wally said. "I heard someone's in the mood for a game." The cartoon rabbit dribbled the ball between his unnaturally thin humanoid legs before firing it across the court at Don's chest with shocking force.

Don ran his thumb over the ball. It felt brand-new: slightly slick, with a strong rubbery scent.

"What do ya say?" Wally asked, sneakers squeaking as he stepped closer. "How 'bout a game?"

Don threw back the ball, and Wally made a smooth catch with his pair of four-fingered paws the size of oven-mitts.

Rosie leaned into Don. "Come on, baby," she whispered, near breathless. "Show him what you've got."

CHAPTER THIRTEEN:

HAVING WAS WAY BETTER THAN WANTING

It was easy for Amy Kinney to imagine why the Dream Factory would be open only for a short time and to a limited number of special guests. The entire operation had to cost a fortune to run, yet behind the scenes, the Dream Factory looked remarkably ordinary, almost mundane.

Amy had been so nervous that morning. She had never seen a hot-air balloon before, and she hadn't been sure how safe they were. On top of all that, Tapper and Clapper had been terrifying. Now all of that worry seemed so silly.

The lobby of The Dream Factory had had nice enough production value, but as soon as Lucy had led Amy from the room, the old woman had immediately begun making excuses. "Terrible that you're going to see all of this behind-the-scenes sausage-making, dear. I'm so sorry to spoil so much of the magic for you, but we are tight on time, and Mr. Kinney was quite insistent."

They walked through a slithering steel hallway with flickering pendant lights and more than the occasional exposed electrical panel.

Beyond the thin walls, Amy could hear Dave's voice but couldn't make out what he was saying.

Lucy came up short at a glossy red sliding door, that was split right down the center. "Oh dear." She placed a withered palm on either side of the seam. "I've forgotten that this door is really just for looks," she said, struggling to pull the panels apart.

Amy rushed to help. She had expected the door would be metal, but when she pushed the panels apart, she could feel slight imperfections in the painted wood.

On the other side of the door, Amy recognized the bridge of the starship *Resistance* from the 70s TV show *Space Troop*. Dave loved this show and often had it on in the background when he was working around the house on the weekend.

Amy guessed her husband was having an absolute ball in here. He was lounging in an uncomfortable-looking command chair at the center of the bridge, talking directly to the armrest.

"Alright, Joey," he said into the command chair. "I gotta go. Good work."

Lucy was already going back the way she had come, towards the maintenance hall. "If you wouldn't mind closing this door behind me." Lucy pointed a finger at the red door on the adjacent side of the bridge. "The tour will be coming through there in a few minutes. No sense you following me, trying to run them down."

After Dave shut the stiff door behind the old woman and turned back, he was smiling near as wide as Tapper or Clapper. "Can you believe this place?"

"Seems pretty cheap to me."

"Well, the show came out in the 70s, but this is about as accurate a re-creation as you can have."

Amy thunked across a thin layer of carpeting and sat at an empty station with blinking lights and switches. She flipped a few of them, clicking them back and forth. "What do all these switches do?"

"Sweetheart, it was a television show. They don't do anything."

"What was so urgent? You realize I had to leave our children with three complete strangers."

"Oh," Dave said, remembering. "I was trying to find Jaxon's social security card. The bank needed it."

"It's in the safe."

"Hmm … I guess I should have thought of that," he said. "But luckily Joey was actually able to find a copy of it in the office just before you showed up."

That didn't sound right. "Where in the office?"

"I don't know where exactly," Dave said. "He was fumbling around your desk and found a copy of it."

Why would there be a copy there? Before Amy could ask a follow-up question, the bridge's adjacent door hissed apart. Jaxon and Becky burst onto the deck with uncommon gusto, and Amy's thoughts slipped away.

"What do you think, guys?" she said, smiling. "Isn't this place amazing?"

●　●　●

Charlie had not wanted to let the children go, but they had disappeared before she could think of a word to say.

Their mother had seemed far too relaxed. Too happy. Mrs. Kinney would not have been so casual if she had seen what Charlie had seen. How could she?

But Lucy was already tottering away down the snow-blown path towards another cottage. As much as Charlie wanted to follow the children, she didn't want to let Lucy out of her sight again. She was the key to everything here.

Lucy took a pained and wobbly step onto the building's small landing. Charlie took her arm, steadying her. She could not recall a time she had seen Lucy walk this much.

"Thank you for taking charge of the Kinney children earlier."

"Where did they go?"

"You saw," Lucy said. "They're with their parents." She reached for the cottage's brass knob. "You like children, don't you?"

Before Charlie could answer, the door opened, expelling a warm rush of air tinged with sweet-smelling swamp lilies and honeysuckle. The hair on Charlie's neck tingled. "What is this?"

Lucy stepped inside the cottage and set down her coffee on a little wicker table. Charlie followed her in, and Lucy eased shut the door. They were not inside a cottage, but outside, standing on a shade-covered porch. It was no longer snowing. Quite the opposite. The air was warm and pleasant.

"Do you recognize it?" Lucy asked.

Charlie did.

They were standing in the breezeway of the house she had planned to visit in Deridder that weekend. No ... not quite the same. The view wasn't right. A hundred yards off the breezeway should have been a neighboring home, but instead there was an endless field of blowing cornstalks.

Charlie stumbled forward, lightheaded. She gripped one of the porch's warm wooden columns. "Lucy," she said, hacking out queasy breaths, "how are you doing this?"

Lucy struggled out of her yellow coat and let it drop to the pavers with a splat. "I can't take credit for it," she said. "Daddy did it."

Charlie pushed herself away from the column and went to the hammock of her dreams, letting her fingers run over the fraying fibers as it shifted gently in the breeze. "It's not possible," she said. "None of this is." Lucy couldn't have known about this particular house. It didn't exist. Charlie had only seen this full picture in her dreams.

"Yet here we are."

No, Charlie thought. She had been using her company-issued phone. Lucy would have access to everything on it. This was a trick.

"Who was that man?"

Lucy chuckled. "I thought that was obvious."

"Your father is dead."

Lucy shivered, shaking the thought away, and Charlie felt an immediate pang of remorse. She had not intended to be so direct, but it was the truth. Max Bixby was dead, and not a thing in Heaven or on Earth could change the fact.

"Where are we really?" Charlie said.

"Where dreams come true."

One of the freakish men in purple tracksuits pulled open a glass slider connected to the kitchen and stepped into the breeze-way. He was holding a tray loaded with garlicky-smelling baked oysters.

"Have you eaten, Ms. Cooper?" he said, happily. "It's not quite lunch yet, but you look as though you may have skipped breakfast."

Charlie peered at the cracked-open oysters, sprinkled with burnt breadcrumbs. They looked as delicious as they smelled.

"I don't know if they are as good as the ones you make at home," Lucy said. "But they aren't too bad." She pried an oyster free of its shell with a little fork and offered it to Charlie.

It looked good and smelled better, but Charlie did not think she wanted to eat it.

"I did not bring you here to hurt you," Lucy said. "I brought you here to give you a gift." Lucy ate the oyster and pulled loose another. "You see? They're not poisoned." She extended the dripping fork. "Try it. Please."

Charlie ate the oyster. Tangy. Creamy. "Is that pimento?"

Lucy pinched her fingers close together. "Just a little."

"I'm sorry, Lucy," Charlie said. "It's just … I don't understand." She looked at the strange man still holding the tray, and examined his flawless, waxy skin.

"What are you?" Charlie said.

The man seemed pleasantly unbothered. "I am Rapper."

"That's not what I asked."

Lucy wiped the corners of her mouth with a square napkin. "We call them assistants."

Rapper grinned and nodded, but his eyes were hollow and dead.

"Are you a robot?" Charlie asked.

Rapper's grin widened. "I am an assistant. I'm here to help."

"Help with what?"

"Whatever you need, of course."

"They protect the factory," Lucy said, looking obscenely serene. "But they are quite harmless, I assure you."

I don't know you at all, Charlie thought.

And of course she didn't. She scheduled Lucy's appointments. She sometimes drove one of the Navigators. She prepared Lucy's meals. She cleaned the house and answered the phone. But before today she had never asked questions.

"I'm sorry," Charlie said. "I just don't understand. I'm worried about the others ... and you too."

"Goodness, Charlotte. You act as if I'm some knife-wielding maniac."

"Why are they all here? You picked them specifically."

Lucy shook her head. "I didn't pick them. Daddy did."

"That's ridiculous, Lucy. I don't know who that man was, but your father is dead. He has to be."

"And yet he's here."

It was a contradiction that Charlie was coming no closer to squaring. "Who else knows about this place?"

"No one," Lucy said. "It wasn't my secret to give away. It was his. I told you—it's an amazing gift to see this place. To know it and experience it. Even if for only an afternoon."

"You've been coming here alone?"

"Not alone, dear. Never alone." Lucy grimaced and looked to the assistant. "Mr. Rapper, is our little presentation ready?"

"Yes, Ms. Lucy. In the media room."

"Excellent. Come along, Charlotte. My father and I have something special to offer you."

• • •

Jaxon's senses still had not quite become accustomed to seeing the impossible. Once he and Becky had followed Mom into the cottage, everything had changed again.

They had stepped inside a little building, but through its dusty windows, night had somehow flipped back into day, bright and harsh. The air had changed too—from crisp and cold to muggy and thick, stinking faintly of poop like the indoor arena where Becky rode horses. Jaxon wrinkled his nose. The building's rough-sawn floorboards groaned beneath them, and outside a rooster cackled.

Becky peeled off her dripping yellow coat and draped it over a wooden chair whose legs didn't match. "It's a saloon."

Ahead of them, a bartender with shiny slicked hair and a string tie was methodically wiping out cloudy glasses with a little rag, stacking them on a shelf behind the bar. The smell of whiskey and dust hung around him like a cloud.

To the left, Dad sat at a round table with a handful of clean-looking cowboys, like they'd just come out of a box. Their boots didn't have a single scuff.

Dad lifted a fan of cards and grinned when he saw them. "Hey-ya, kids," he said, waving them over.

Jaxon stepped out of his yellow boots, and Mom helped him slide out of his coat.

"I don't like this place, Mom," Becky said, crossing her arms. "I want to leave."

Mom's face pinched. "We can't leave right now, sweetie. Why don't you guys grab yourselves a pop from the bar?"

It struck Jaxon as an odd thing for his mother to say. The family didn't drink much soda, and Mom in particular thought the drink was essentially carbonated poison.

The last time Jaxon had had any soda at all had been with Pops in Florida, ages ago. The pair of them had drunk fizzy Coke straight from glass bottles at the kitchen counter.

The barman sat a pair of glass mugs on the counter and pulled down a dispenser, expelling black and foaming soda that sent Jaxon's bladder into knots.

"Mom," Jaxon said. "I gotta go."

"Not you too."

"No … I mean to the bathroom."

The barman chuckled and pointed to the back of the saloon. "Back that way, Mr. Jaxon. First door on yer right. But we got an outhouse too, if yer looking for that more authentic experience."

Jaxon was most certainly not looking for that, and he was relieved when the saloon's bathroom turned out to be an oddly modern one with prison-green ceramic tiles and bright-red stalls. He would have been nervous to have been left alone, but he could hear Becky whining beyond the bathroom door.

"Dad, please," she said. "There was a mirror maze … and … Max Bixby is here! And those men creep me out."

"*What men?*"

"Those … *apperbots.*"

Jaxon began going. The sound of urine echoing in the toilet drowned out Dad's hacking laughter. Jaxon didn't see what was so hilarious. The name apperbots seemed as apt as anything he could think of, and before now, Mom and Dad both had seemed as unnerved by the twins in tracksuits as he and Becky were.

When Jaxon returned to the saloon, Dad was raking a pile of crumpled-up bills towards a heap of winnings as the cowboys grunted and spit in little cans. Mom and Becky were gone.

"Where's Mom?"

Dad tossed a thumb to the dusty window behind him and peeked at his freshly dealt cards. "Riding horses with your sister," he said. "They'll be right back. You want to pull up a chair and play a few hands? My friends here won't mind, will you, guys?"

The cowboys laughed in unison and smiled the perfect park-people smile. "No, we ain't gonna mind," one of the clean and grinning cowboys said.

"Are they coming back?" Jaxon asked.

"Of course," Dad said, tossing some brown coins to the center of the table. "You're not worried, are you? You know this is only a ride, right?"

"Yeah, Dad. I know. But I'm really the only one that needs to stay. If Becky wants to leave, why not just let her?"

Dad shook his head. "No. We're all staying. Now go grab yourself a drink if you want one, and sit down and play a few hands. I hear from these fine folks that the root beer they have here is the best."

Jaxon had never had root beer, and he wondered if it tasted like the yeasty-smelling kind that the grownups drank. He decided he would try some regardless and took a seat at the nearest wooden barstool.

The barman slid over a filled mug, the layer of bubbly foam at least an inch thick. "We make it in house," he said. "Nothing like it any place else."

It smelled more like coke than beer, so Jaxon took a tentative sip. It was creamy and spicy and not too sweet. He licked foam from his upper lip.

"I told you," the barman said. "Not bad, right?"

Jaxon took a deeper gulp. "You're not one of the twins."

"No," the barman said. "Those boys are a special breed. Do you like them?"

"I guess so." Jaxon did not like them at all, but he didn't want to be rude. "There's just a lot of them. How many kids did their mom have?"

The barman shook his head and lowered his voice. "I am afraid, strictly speaking, that they do not have a mother."

"But everyone's got a mother …"

"Not them," the barman whispered. "But do not be frightened of them. They're here to help."

That was what they had kept saying. "What's your name?" Jaxon said.

"Gus," the barman said. "But I'm not here to tell you my troubles. I'm here to hear yours."

"Hear my troubles?"

Gus nodded. "That is what grownups do at the bar after all, and you yourself are not so small. Nine years old—you are practically a grownup already. So tell me, what's the scuttlebutt? How's it hanging?"

Jaxon wasn't sure how to answer either question. "What's a scuttle butt?"

"On old sailing ships, the men would gather around a cask called a butt with a hole or scuttle cut into it. When they did this, they'd talk about news and gossip and the various goings-on around the ship. Sort of like when you meet your friends at the water fountain."

How did he know about that?

"So, Mr. Jaxon, what's the news?"

"I thought Mr. Bixby was dead, but he looks like he's alive."

"Oh he's alive alright.," Gus said. "One thing you should never doubt are your own eyes and ears."

"But how can he be? He'd be like two hundred."

"Mr. Bixby is barely a hundred and twenty."

"But he doesn't look a hundred and twenty. He looks like he's my dad's age."

Gus nodded. "Mr. Bixby can do some amazing things, it's true. But you haven't seen half of what he has up his sleeve. I bet you would like to see though."

Jaxon peeked over his shoulder. Dad was laughing and raking in more coins and wads of squished-up cash. He didn't look like he was ready to leave.

"See what?" Jaxon said. *What else could Mr. Bixby possibly do?*

Gus leaned forward, knocking an elbow on the bar. "Do you know why opening your presents on Christmas is not half as fun as wondering beforehand what Santa will leave for you?"

That didn't make sense. "But opening presents *is* fun," Jaxon said.

"Is it now? What did you get last year?"

Jaxon thought about what he had opened last Christmas. There had been lots of presents, but nothing specific was coming to mind.

"What I'm trying to tell you, Mr. Jaxon, is that having something is not nearly as much fun as wanting something."

"That doesn't make any sense."

"I guess we'll see." Gus flipped up a wooden gate and slipped around the bar. "Mr. Kinney," he called towards the poker table. "Could I show young Mr. Jaxon something he'll enjoy?"

Jaxon expected Dad to refuse, but he didn't. "Sure," Dad said, without looking up from his cards. "Me and the girls will catch up as soon as they're back."

"Excellent, sir." Gus already had a hold of Jaxon's shoulders and was leading him to the back of the saloon. "It's just this way."

It seemed an impossible idea that anything more amazing could possibly happen. Only one thing came to mind.

"Here we are," Gus said, pulling open a sliding wood door large enough to admit a horse.

It was too dark inside for Jaxon to see anything at first, but a dim light grew as he stepped forward. And then Jaxon was in Florida. In the condo's living room, everything like it always was.

Pops pushed himself up and out of his weathered recliner. His bushy white mustache puffed out like a dusting brush as he grinned and opened his arms wide. "There's my boy."

"*Pops ...*"

The old man grinned. "What's the matter?" he said, waving Jaxon over. "Come on. Get over here."

Jaxon barreled into him. He was sobbing, but worse than that ... he couldn't think of a thing to say.

Pops laughed and clapped him on the shoulder. "It's good to see you too."

The voice was surreal. Jaxon hadn't heard it in what seemed like forever, but he knew it belonged to Pops. No one else smelled like him either: salted peanuts and coffee.

Gus had been wrong. Having was way better than wanting.

CHAPTER FOURTEEN:

JUST A TEST DRIVE

The locker room didn't smell like any locker room Don had ever been inside of. It had luxurious carpeting that ran to the edge of the shower stalls, and it was clean to the point that it smelled antiseptic, like a doctor's office.

A red locker affixed with a nameplate reading 'Don Williams' was nestled between the lockers assigned to Shykker the Cat and Benny Coyote. The jersey and shorts inside were white with red-and-blue striping along the edges, 'Bixby Ballers' emblazoned on the front in a fat, bubbly font. On the back was Don's number: 26.

Of course they would know his number. It wasn't a secret. Don had never worn any other. His father had worn number 13 in high school, and Don had always thought he was at least twice the man.

Don found a pair of black sneakers at the bottom of the locker and ran his thumb around the ankle collar. There were no tags, so he wasn't sure of the size at first, but when he put them on, they were near tight enough to cut off circulation to his feet. Exactly the fit he liked when he played.

The park's intimate knowledge of him was frightening, but not nearly as terrifying as the cartoon rabbit that had come to life. Don found Wally outside the locker room at the near court, nestled next to Rosie in plushy floor seats. She was tugging at a loose bit of fur on his forearm.

Don had been playing the events that led him here over again in his mind. All the crazy shit had started at almost the moment he had met Rosie. Maybe she was part of this somehow. But even if she was … it would not have explained the rabbit.

It waved to him and shouted, "Hey-ya, Donny!"

"It's Don!" he yelled. "*D-O-Motherfucking-N.*"

Rosie shot back rigid in her chair, horrified.

Wally only smiled, exposing his massive buck-teeth. "Hokie-dokie. Sure thing, Don."

A whistle screeched as Max Bixby emerged from the visitor tunnel, now in slacks and a black-and-white-striped shirt. He spat out his metal whistle, letting it bounce around his neck as he jogged towards center court. "Players," he called, waving them in. "Approach."

Wally hopped up and grabbed a ball, spinning it perfectly on one of his paw's unnaturally long digits as he made his way below the jumbotron. When he met Don at the opposite side of the Bixby Baller logo that had been stenciled across the hardwood, he sent the ball into Bixby's hands with a perfect bounce pass.

"Well, gentlemen," Bixby said, "what are we going to be playing for?"

Don could only think of one thing he wanted. "You tell me what the hell is going on around here," he said. "Really tell me. No bullshit."

"I'm going to tell you that regardless, Mr. Williams," Bixby said. "Is there anything else you might like?"

There absolutely was. "You could give me my prize money now and have that balloon fly me home."

"Now," Bixby said, smiling sadistically. "*That* is more like it." He looked to the rabbit. "How 'bout you, Wally? What would you like?"

"Well gee, Mr. Bixby … I wouldn't mind getting to know Don's lady friend better. She seems swell. But I wouldn't want there to be any hard feelings or anything."

"Deal," Don said, instantly.

"So quick," Bixby said. "Are you sure? She's quite a fetching young lady."

"I'm beginning to think I'm not quite her type," Don said. "Let's play." He didn't trust Rosie, and he was tired of her fascination with cartoon rabbits and rats.

"Very well," Bixby said. "You'll be playing half-court one-on-one starting from the top of the key. As our distinguished guest, you Mr. Williams will go first."

"Well gee, Mr. Bixby," Wally said, "do you think that's fair?"

"Now Wally, Mr. Williams is our guest. It's perfectly fair. First player to eleven points wins. Shots outside the three-point line will count for two points. A scoring player will maintain possession. A missed shot, foul, or lost ball will count as a turnover. A defensive foul will result in a point for the offensive player, save for the game point. In which case, the player will take his free shot from the free throw line."

"I take it you'll be calling the fouls," Don said.

Bixby put a hand on an imagined Bible. "Why, good sir, I pledge to call an honest and fair contest. Would you question my honor?"

"Never."

Bixby smirked and shot the ball into Don's chest. It hadn't been broken in, much like the ball he had held earlier. Don guessed it was the same one, but in this place anything was possible. He took a few practice dribbles between his legs before trailing after Bixby to the apex of the three-point line.

"Wait for my whistle," Bixby said, jogging to a position beneath the net. "Oh, and I forgot to mention—there's a three-dribble maximum, Mr. Williams. Can't have you out here dribbling all day, can we? There's too much more to see."

Don wasn't planning on dribbling much at all. "Fine," he said. Across from him, Wally was opening his stance into a defensive position. As freakish as the rabbit appeared up close, he was still at least a foot shorter than Don. If Wally wasn't quick, there was a chance this could be easy.

The whistle screeched.

Don hopped and fired, sending an arcing shot over an outstretched paw. As soon as the ball knocked off the backboard and through the hoop, Don felt a familiar, victorious heat running up his neck and across his chest. The hardest points to get were always the first ones, and now Don had them. He didn't see any reason to give the rabbit any chance with the ball.

"Two-nothing," Bixby called, sending the ball back. Don repeated the process again. *And again.*

"Six-nothing!"

If there was any doubt as to where Rosie's loyalty lay, it was over now. She had offered only a half-hearted clap after Don sank his first basket and had not even pretended to be excited after that.

"Wow," Wally said, wheezing through his pink nose. "You're pretty good, Don."

"I've played a little bit."

The whistle blew, and Don sent up another shot that popped off the top of the rim before rolling in. Don looked to the floor seats in time to see Rosie's lower lip fold over.

Bixby sent the ball back to Don. "Eight-nothing," he said, starting to put the whistle to his lips. "You know," he said, putting up a finger. "Something is missing … ahh … that's right. How could I have forgotten?"

Bixby snapped his fingers, and the empty arena was full.

Rosie screamed with delight as Regina Rat and Canyon Jane popped into existence in the seats on either side of her. Throughout the deafening arena, the people looked real—but they couldn't be.

A heavyset man in a vintage Knicks jersey pounded a drum on his knee. A woman with a sequined foam finger waved a **GO BALLERS** sign. A teen with his face painted half blue and half white spilled popcorn as he jumped to his feet.

They've got to be optical illusions or … something.

But they weren't. Don could feel the heat of them in the air, sucking up his oxygen. The hardwood and the bright lights were blurring together.

A warm paw took his arm. "Whoa there, Don," Wally shouted over the murmuring crowd. "You look a little green around the gills!"

Don ripped his arm free. "I'm fine."

The crowd of what could have been thousands, and Rosie too, were now watching him silently.

He's trying to get into your head. You're only a few baskets away …

'Come on, Williams.'

'If you don't want to run, you can get the fuck off my team. Shooting don't mean shit, 'round here if you can't run. My teenage girl can fucking shoot. Got her one of those little bitty playmate motherfuckers last Christmas … but she can't run for shit.'

'Run, Williams.'

Run!

This wasn't mirrors, or sleight of hand, or doubles.

I gotta get out of here.

"Ready, Mr. Williams?" Bixby called from beneath the net.

Don nodded. He was as ready as he was ever going to be. Bixby grinned, put the whistle to his lips, and blew.

Wally's paw shot out, knocking the ball away. The crowd erupted. Don couldn't hear Rosie, but he could see her, clapping and pointing.

"Gee, Don," Wally said, over the dying roar of the crowd. "Guess it's my ball."

Bixby sent the ball underhand across the court, and Don caught it with the toe of his noose-tight sneaker. He picked it up and thrust it into Wally's midsection. He still had the lead. The rabbit wasn't going to be able to get enough height to shoot the ball over him.

The two circled around each other, changing positions.

"Wow, Don," Wally said, dribbling between his furry, twigish legs. "You sure are tall."

Don spread his arms and hunkered down. "Take your shot, rabbit."

The whistle screeched.

Wally spun, switching to his off paw as Don swung at him, toppling forward. He didn't see the shot, but the arena had erupted again.

Don scrambled upright just in time to see Wally step over him, smirking, and pointing at the jumbotron.

Don watched himself tripping over his own feet and landing flat on his ass. The rabbit had outplayed him in an instant, and Don was just sitting there, like a jackass.

"Come on, Don," Wally said, stepping back to the three-point line, his buck-toothed grin filling his furry face. "I'm sure you'll get the next one."

● ● ●

Lucy signaled for Rapper to push open the red leather double doors. The assistant came forward and pushed them open, expelling a plume of chilled popcorn scented air.

It was a movie theater, dark save for the clicking beam of light that caught flittering bits of dust above the center aisle.

"Sit wherever you like," Lucy said, tottering ahead and holding Rapper's arm.

Charlie followed her down an aisle of burgundy and black carpet squares separating blocks of theater seats. She guessed there were at least a hundred of them.

On the movie screen, a looping black-and-white image flickered: Wally Rabbit's head, vintage and grainy, winking and bobbing beneath an oversized train-engineer's cap.

"None of this is real."

"Of course it isn't," Lucy said. "But what I want to show you is." Rapper led Lucy down a row of seats in the middle of the theater.

Charlie didn't want to keep following Lucy through any more of this maze, but she didn't see that she had many options. She had been trying to keep careful track of her path through the factory, but she was beginning to doubt that it would matter much. Things in the factory seemed to change at will.

Charlie edged around Lucy's legs in a daze and sat beside her in one of the theater seats, splintered with cracks. "I don't understand what's happening," she said. "How did any of this stuff get here?"

"They didn't *get here* exactly."

"But they are here," Charlie said, running a thumb along a splitting edge of leather. "Everything's real."

"You keep using that word. I don't think you know what it means."

Of course Charlie knew what it meant. "I don't understand."

"I know you don't," Lucy said. "Let's watch."

A black-and-white cartoon chemistry lab came into focus. The classic version of Wally Rabbit, with his floppy clipped ears, strolled onscreen wearing an open white lab-coat, exposing a fluffy tuft of fur on his chest. "Hi-ya there, folks. I hope you're all enjoying your time here in the Dream Factory. I'm currently standing in the factory's nerve center: the Imaginarium. This is where Mr. Bixby brings all of the magical creations in the factory to life!"

A window pulled open from the bottom corner of the screen: a robot dog wearing a headset, smiling and showing off a zig-zag alignment of metal teeth. "That's right, Wally," it said. "I'm Spark, your AI-powered assistant, and I'll be helping explain everything to you today. We've got a lot to talk about, so let's get started!"

The cartoon lab faded out, and Wally and Spark appeared in open black space. "Whoa, Spark!" Wally said, pinwheeling his arms. "What happened?"

"This is the neutral state," Spark said. "Think of this place as the canvas. The fun starts when you tell me what to paint."

"Gee," Wally said. "So it's like a green screen like they use in movies?"

Spark raced around Wally's narrow legs, barking robotically. "Of course they're not green screens!" Spark said. "A green screen just replaces what you can see. *The Imaginarium builds the environment inside the Dream Factory!*"

"How?"

"Out of three main components," Spark said. "First: matter replication. The Imaginarium takes raw energy from the Earth's core and rearranges it into actual physical objects—rocks, trees, furniture, a coffee cup, you name it!"

Harsh red dots flashed all around Wally and Spark, so bright Charlie had to shield her eyes as the light took over the formerly monochrome screen.

"Whoa," Wally said. "What's happening?"

A real world appeared around them. They were standing in a ballroom, real-life dancers twirled around them in a waltz.

"Second," Spark said, "is force fields. These are used for things that don't require permanent matter. Things like wind, waves … or the feeling of a horse galloping beneath you. These fields are what makes the environment inside the factory seem endless. Step forward, and the Imaginarium will shift force-field 'zones' so you never hit a wall. You just keep walking, and the Imaginarium keeps moving the simulated world around you seamlessly."

Charlie gripped the wood of her armrest, rubbing her thumb across the grains.

"Third," Spark said, "is holographic projection. That's the visible surface—the light patterns that make a mountain look like a mountain instead of a black wall. It's synchronized with the force fields so your eyes and your sense of touch match perfectly. Add in a full environmental control system for air composition, temperature, humidity, and scent molecules, and you've got something your senses will read as completely real!"

Charlie couldn't breathe. "This isn't …"

Lucy pointed to the screen as it faded away from the lab. "You still haven't seen Daddy's best trick."

It was obscene that Lucy was still calling that man her father. Even if what Charlie had just learned was true, Max Bixby was still long dead.

"But," Spark said, "we've been able to do this particular trick for years at the Dream Factory. What's really going to knock your socks off is our newest attraction."

"This is the gift," Lucy whispered.

Max Bixby passed through a pair of dancers as if they didn't exist and stepped into the foreground. It was the same man Charlie had met earlier. "Hello, Wally," Bixby said. "I've invited you here because I've made a very special discovery."

"More special than the Dream Factory, Mr. Bixby?"

"Oh yes," Bixby said. "Up until now, scientists have only been able to upload information into computers—like pictures, facts, and videos. But I've discovered a way to do something much more amazing!"

"What's that, Mr. Bixby?"

"I've discovered how to transfer consciousness—the very thoughts and feelings inside a person's mind—into a computer!"

Charlie's breath caught sharply in her throat.

"Are you alright, dear? Do you need Rapper to fetch you some water?"

Charlie shook her head and watched.

"Wait," Wally said. "You mean that a person's mind can actually live inside a computer?"

"Exactly," Bixby said. "Imagine being able to upload your memories, your thoughts, and even your dreams into a computer, where they can live on indefinitely! It's like you could 'transfer' yourself to another place, or even a robot! The possibilities are endless!"

"Gee, Mr. Bixby," Wally said, amazed. "So if someone's mind is transferred, they could control a robot or even *visit a different world*?!"

"That's right," Bixby said. "People could explore places they could never go before, like deep underwater or even space. Or they could live on after their bodies stop working or get sick—like having a second chance to keep learning and growing!"

"So does that mean I could live forever in a robot body?"

"Forever is a long time, Wally," Bixby said, chuckling. "But yes … you could live a very, very long time. But I wouldn't call what I want to show you a robot. It's not that at all."

Bixby spun his cane, faster and faster, until it became a whirring cyclone that enveloped the screen. When the tornado fizzled out, Wally and Bixby were in another lab, with a pair of large cylinders connected with a thick and sagging black cable.

Though each cylinder was large enough to hold a gorilla, only one of them was occupied, and that occupant was a small sleeping dog with ringlets of brown hair, its head resting on its front paws.

Bixby leaned against the empty tube. "Have you ever thought about what it might be like to be a dog?"

"You mean like Spark?"

"No, Wally," Bixby said. "Not like Spark." He opened the glass door of the empty tube. "Step inside and find out."

Wally tiptoed carefully into the tube, wearing a sheepish grin.

"Now this is very important, Wally. You must open yourself up to the transfer."

"Well gee, Mr. Bixby … what do you mean?"

"For the transfer to work, you must *want* it to work. The mind has a hard time letting go of a body, so you must relax yourself totally. It's not that hard. It's best to sing yourself a little song in your head."

"Okay," Wally said. "I'm super-excited. I definitely want to try."

"Good." Bixby eased shut the door. "Try to relax and think happy thoughts."

Wally closed his eyes and began to sing:

> *So come on, friend, don't hesitate,*
> *The fun's waiting for us—let's celebrate!*
> *Be our friend, let's laugh and sing …*

Bixby flipped down a switch with a thumb. The connecting wire between the tubes sparked and glowed. Wally's voice trailed away. "… together forever … that's the …"

The labradoodle burst from the second tube, bounding into the lab. "WAYYYYYYYY!"

The dog ran around Bixby in wild circles. "Holy wilickers," the dog said in Wally's high, squeaky voice. "It worked!"

Charlie was dizzy, near enough to be sick. "It's not possible."

Bixby turned away from the little dog and looked through the screen as if it were a window. "No … *it is possible*, Ms. Cooper. Though it is very expensive."

The world contorted around Charlie, before disappearing entirely and leaving only the clicking of the projector, until even that was gone.

● ● ●

Jaxon wasn't sure what to think of the show Pops had put on the TV.

Pops had poured each of them a Coke over ice and garnished the glasses with fat ruby-red cherries. They had watched the black-and-white show in silence as Wally Rabbit and his robot dog explained the body-switching procedure.

Pops licked soda off his mustache with a pale tongue. "So you wouldn't have to worry about being too short for rides anymore."

Or about Becky holding me down and fricking spitting on me.

"It would still be me?" Jaxon asked. He didn't like the idea of being a dog … but a taller and stronger version of himself?

"Of course it would be," Pops said, easing back in his old recliner. "These bodies … they're just shells." He tapped the side of his head. "Remember … it's what's inside that counts."

"So it would be sort of like … getting upgraded?"

"Now that's a good word for it," Pops said. "Upgraded. You'll still be like you are now—but better. There's nothing that old Bixby can't do. I think you've seen enough to know that."

"… I don't know."

"With this new body," Pops said, "you'll be able to live a long time, Jax. A very long time."

For the first time since the funeral, Jaxon thought about Pops's casket and the clacking lift lowering it into the ground, while a very sweaty graveyard man read some words off a notecard.

Jaxon had blocked the whole day out almost immediately. It had been easy. At home, there were pictures of his parents and grandparents at weddings and holidays, but no one had taken any pictures at the funeral.

It was only now that Jaxon realized he hadn't remembered what Pops sounded like or what he smelled like. Jaxon hadn't remembered him at all. Not really. Not enough.

"Pops," Jaxon said. "How can you be here? I saw them ..."

"Do you remember that mirror maze?"

Jaxon didn't think he could ever forget it. "You know about the maze?"

Pops nodded. "It wasn't just a ride. It was a genetic mapping scanner."

"It scanned me?"

"It scanned all of you. And not just the outside." Pops rocked himself forward in his big chair and pressed a finger against Jaxon's forehead. "It's where I came from. Bixby took me from your mind and built me."

"Then ... you're not ... you're not really ..."

Pops shook his head. "No," he said, taking a swig of his Coke. "I'm the best of him though. I'm all the parts you remembered."

"You're a robot?"

"Do I look like a robot?"

Pops didn't look like a robot exactly, but Jaxon couldn't keep himself from thinking about the apperbots. "What about—" Jaxon mimicked the creepy smile of the freakish twins in tracksuits.

"Oh ... them," Pops said. "It won't be like that. The assistants are different. They ain't got what you've got. Trust me. It'll still be you, but better, and once it's done I'll bet you could even show that old man of yours a thing or two."

Jaxon thought about the possibility for another beautiful moment, before sighing. "Mom will get mad."

"Yeah," Pops said laughing. "She always had your dad wrapped around her finger too. But she can't be mad that you're healthier and stronger, can she? You know that she wants you to live a long time, don't you?"

Jaxon supposed that *would* make Mom happy.

"It would only have to be a test drive," Pops said. "You can take a new body out and just give her the old spin around the block. If you like it, great. If not, old Bixby can whip you up almost anything you could want. Or nothing at all. No pressure. You've got to want it or it doesn't work."

Jaxon wasn't sure what to do. His parents would definitely want to know what was going on.

"I know it's awful being so young," Pops said. "Always at the mercy of everyone and everything."

Jaxon wasn't at the mercy of anyone or anything right now. He could do whatever he wanted. "So I'd be able to come back?"

Pops plucked the cherry out of his drink and ripped it off the stem with his teeth. "Of course," he said, chewing. "Like I said, just a test drive."

CHAPTER FIFTEEN:

MAKE A MAGICAL WISH

Don had spent many hours of his life playing basketball. In high school, he had always been the best player, and he had absolutely earned his scholarship to Sam Houston.

In college, things had been tougher. Don's coach had primarily used him as a three-point specialist, but Don had always thought his defense was underrated. During his junior season for the Bearkats he had knocked an errant dribble away from Wyatt Tillerson, who was currently the starting shooting guard for the Philadelphia 76ers.

Don knew in his guts he could play with some of the best players in the world because he had already done it. Even now, he regularly shot around with Ziaire, and Don felt that he would have been nearly as good as him if he only had a longer wingspan.

At least that was what he had always thought. The rabbit had not needed any additional height to humiliate Don in front of the type of packed arena he had always dreamed of playing in.

On the game shot, Don had charged at the rabbit a step before the whistle, and still he had not been able to hit Wally. His fingers instead passing through a cloud of fur.

Swish.

Rosie had run onto the court and thrown herself into Wally's arms. Afterwards, she had rode him rabbitback along the perimeter of the arena, each of them waving to the ecstatic crowd.

Don only watched a few seconds of it before trudging back to the locker room. He wasn't going to leave a million dollars on the table, but he was finished pretending that this shit was normal.

He threw the Bixby jersey in a ball on the floor, then fired each of his sneakers into separate urinals.

Splish splash, motherfuckers.

Don was done being nice. If they wanted to make him finish this tour, they were going to have to put up with him.

He changed back into his clothes and pulled on his wristwatch—ten minutes to noon. It was lunchtime, but whatever the Bixby Corporation was serving, he was certain he didn't want to eat it.

Bixby's flutey voice came from behind him. "I am beginning to worry that I may have gotten off on a poor foot with you, my boy."

Don slapped shut the locker. "I ain't your boy."

Bixby was back in his regular clothes, swinging his cane. "Yes, I know," he said. "But please, sir, I would very much like to be friends. Won't you let me try?"

"I don't want shit from you but my money."

"So you're not upset about Ms. Rosie?"

"If she wants to fuck that rabbit she can go ahead and get on with it."

Bixby shrugged. "Well now," he said, tucking the tip of his cane into the throat of one of Don's sneakers. He lifted it out of the urinal. "Did they not fit?"

"They fit perfect, motherfucker. Everything here is perfect. Okay?"

"See, this is what I mean. You sound angry. I have a gift for being able to detect these things." Bixby let the sneaker slip off his cane and clunk back into the urinal. "I can see you do not understand me at all. The only thing I have ever wanted is to put smiles on people's faces. It's my drug. I'm positively addicted. But you, my friend, have been a tough nut to crack."

"If you been trying to put a smile on my face, you been doing a piss-poor job of it. If you want smiles and giggles, you can go get that shit from Rosie."

Bixby smiled to himself. "Yes, I know," he said. "She's a child. The kiddos are always easier."

"Easier?"

"To amuse, of course," Bixby said. "Don't you see? *This is all for fun.*"

"*Does it look like I'm having motherfucking fun?*"

"Oh, please … in fairness, Mr. Williams, let me try one more time to impress you. I won't be able to bear it if you were to leave the factory unsatisfied."

Don coughed out a hoarse laugh. "Yeah, that ain't going to be happening. This place is getting a shit review from me."

Bixby prodded at him with his still-dripping cane. "You certainly are an ornery fellow … but I know exactly what you want."

"I've already told you what I want. I've done told your ass over and over again. You ain't listening."

Bixby bit his lower lip. "Very well," he said. "If you'll agree to give my proposal a full hearing, I will escort you back to the balloon myself with your check in hand and my best wishes besides."

"I'll listen to any proposal you got right here. Right now."

Bixby's head rocked, metronome-like. "Very well," he said. "Lift up your arms please. Out to your side, like a T."

Don blew out a breath and held out his arms, but only for a moment. "What's this shit got to do with a proposal? If you want to offer me something, spill it."

Bixby shook his head and clucked his tongue. "Seventy-inch wing-span. That's much too short."

"Fuck you."

"Are you quite sure there's nothing I can do for you?"

Don rolled his eyes. "You expect me to believe you can make me taller in an afternoon?"

"Well, it really is going to have to be this afternoon," Bixby said. "My factory is consuming a great deal of power. We need this all wrapped up today."

"It's impossible."

"Yes, I know," Bixby said. "But at this point why would you think there's anything I can't do?"

Don couldn't think of an answer.

• • •

"Mademoiselle?"

Charlie's head was swimming. She had been having the most bizarre dream.

In a flash, she shot up rigid in bed, heart hammering. She was not in Lucy's guest house.

She had been sleeping in an oversized bed draped with a thick gauze curtain. She checked her clothes—the same as her dream.

"Ma chere mademoiselle, are you feeling better?"

"Who is that?" she whispered, squinting through the fluttering curtain. She slapped it aside and placed her bare feet on cool marble tiles next to her sneakers, which had been stuffed with her socks.

An impossibly large full moon was shining bright and clear through the elaborately decorated room's towering French doors.

"Where am I?" she said, her eyes darting.

The room seemed oddly familiar, but Charlie couldn't place where she might have seen it. There were elaborate portraits decorating the stone walls and an oversized bust, black as a sunbaked rock, sitting on the mantle above a crackling fireplace.

"My name is Baron Sébastien du Clairval." The voice was deep and guttural, with a thick French accent. "You are currently residing in the guest quarters of the Chateau des Cyprès."

A shadow flickered above the fireplace. No, not a shadow. The bust's lips were moving.

"Pardonnez-moi," the talking head said, "but if you had been snoring any louder, they would have heard you clear down to Bourbon Street."

Charlie stumbled closer. The bust was Bixby, but with a marbled stone wig.

"You," Charlie whispered, gripping the mantel as the floor seemed to roll beneath her feet.

"Oh my, not again," the bust Bixby said. "This won't do." The bust's chin dipped, indicating the bright moon shining through the glass doors. "I'd suggest some air."

Charlie stumbled ahead and pushed open the doors, spilling onto the balcony a step ahead of the rippling curtains.

She took a heaving breath, and for a moment it was quiet, save for the buzzing of insects and the croaking of distant bullfrogs.

The air was warm and tasted like home.

But Charlie knew she wasn't anywhere, even close to home. She recognized now the room she'd been sleeping in. "This is the Chateau of the Moon," she said, disbelieving. "I saw the cartoon when I was a girl."

"Well," Bixby said, still wearing a powdered wig, but now standing on the balcony, "live action remakes are all the rage these days."

"You're not Max Bixby."

"Wee-wee," he said, grinning. "I know. I am Baron Sébastien du Clairval, heir to the sugar fields of—"

"Save it." Charlie flipped her elbows onto the railing and lolled her head, watching fireflies twitter beneath her. "You're not him either."

Bixby, back in his original form, rested his backside on the railing. "I think you can appreciate my little buildup to this point, but we are going to soon be late for lunch, and it's a tight schedule we're to keep. I'm sure you understand. Your episode in the theater has left us scrambling."

Charlie rested her chin on her hands and breathed in the honeysuckle that couldn't be there. "I'm sure lunch is going to be perfect."

"Yes indeed it is, but as I said, the trouble is that there really is an order to things as far as our tour. One thing and then the next. This then that, as it were."

"Where are the others?"

Bixby's eyebrows arched upwards. "Exactly where they want to be, of course. You all are."

"I *don't* want to be here."

Bixby smirked. "Sure you don't."

A gentle wheezing came from the darkened room. Charlie was sure it had been empty. "What's that?"

Bixby held back the room's billowing curtains. "Go and see."

There was a hump in the bed now, rising and lowering. Charlie crept back into the suite and sat numbly on the edge of the mattress.

It was a boy.

Charlie's fingers grazed his silk pajamas at the shoulder. His angelic sleeping face, immensely soothing. It seemed wrong to wake him. Charlie pulled her hand back, and the boy's eyes fluttered open. "Mommy."

She recognized the boy's eyes as Danny's and the delicate point of his nose as her own.

"Mommy?" Charlie said to herself. "I'm Mommy."

"You're acting funny," the boy said, sleepily. "Is the tour over?"

"No," she whispered, mesmerized. "Not yet. Go back to sleep."

Dutifully, he rolled over and pulled the covers around his chin. Charlie staggered back to the balcony.

"He's a cute one," Bixby whispered. "What's his name?"

Charlie shook her head. "How could I know that?" She couldn't think of anything else to say for a long time. "He's not real."

"No," Bixby said, frowning. "Not yet. What's his name?"

"*Ethan.*"

At the sound of his name, the boy groaned beyond a wisp of flittering bed curtain. "How is this possible?" Charlie said. "How does he look like me?"

"He is you," Bixby said. "Exactly the way you wanted. Though if you wanted to make some specific alterations—"

"Alterations?"

Bixby put a finger to his lips and waved her into the suite's connected washroom. The only light came from the low flames flickering from ignited gas lamps. "Alterations for Ethan, of course."

"You mean I could take him out of here?" Charlie asked, before shaking her head. "I'd never be able to do that."

The lines around Bixby's eyes twitched in amusement. "No, of course you couldn't," he said. "That would be ridiculous." He tapped the mirror hanging above a trough-style sink that stretched the length of the countertop. "What would people say? Unless of course … we found a place to hide him."

"Hide him? Where?"

Bixby raised his cane to Charlie's belly. "Here."

"Here?"

"Well … sort of." Bixby twiddled his fingers against the face of the mirror, and it shimmered and distorted—an image of the boy that was sleeping in bed a few feet away appeared, rotating in black swimming trunks above a red and orange slide toggle. "You can script his appearance up to about age 27," Bixby said. He moved a finger along a slider, and the on-screen boy grew into a beautiful man.

Charlie didn't want to touch the mirror. Didn't want to look at it. But still she couldn't stop herself. She went to the mirror and tapped the cold glazing with the tips of her fingers. "How do I make changes?"

Bixby tapped the mirror, and Ethan was gone, replaced with a list in red letters:

```
PHYSICAL TRAITS
FACIAL FEATURES AND APPEARANCE
SEX/REPRODUCTIVE BIOLOGY
HEALTH/LONGEVITY
COGNITIVE TRAITS
TEMPERAMENT/PERSONALITY
TALENTS/APTITUDES
VOICE/COMMUNICATION STYLE
SENSORY PROFILES
CULTURAL/ETHNIC PREFERENCES
```

Charlie tapped TEMPERAMENT/PERSONALITY:

```
EXTROVERSION/INTROVERSION SLIDER
EMOTIONAL SENSITIVITY
AUDACITY
EMPATHY
```

"I know it's a lot to think about," Bixby said. "But I think if you review the version that's already been loaded, you'll be more than pleased."

• • •

Jaxon had found what looked like a woman's one-piece bathing suit hanging behind the door in the condo's bathroom. When he'd stepped back into the living room, he was working to pull a wedgie out of his butt. "Do I really need to wear this?"

Pops leaned lazily against one of the two tubes that had appeared in place of the living room's coffee table and television. Just like in the cartoon, they were connected with a thick cord of black cable.

"Well," Pops said, "it's either the suit or you go naked. We wouldn't want to risk anyone seeing your twig and berries, would we?"

"I guess not."

Jaxon's mirror image was in silent meditation in one of the tubes, encased in gelatinous fluid sprinkled with motionless air bubbles. The boy looked exactly like him, just as Pops had said it would.

Pops opened the glass door of the empty tube, beckoning Jaxon inside. "This new body is going to have quite a growth spurt in the next few weeks. Your Mom won't even be able to tell the difference."

Jaxon stepped inside.

"That's a good boy."

"What do I have to do exactly?"

"It's simple," Pops said, easing shut the glass door. "Hold your heart and make a magical wish."

CHAPTER SIXTEEN:

OLIVES FLOATING IN MILK

Jaxon leaned back against the body-shaped rubber that lined the back of the tube, sized perfectly to his height.

"It's going to be a little cold," Pops said, easing the glass door shut. "It'll feel a bit like aloe vera gel. Remember when you came to visit and you got that sunburn?"

Jaxon did. It had been horrible. Grandma Betty-Ann had rubbed on the icy gel to soothe his skin, and he supposed it had mostly worked. But the freckles that had been appeared on his shoulders still itched on occasion.

"Of course," Pops said, grinning. "After this your skin won't burn so easily. Now just sit back and take nice easy breaths."

• • •

Bixby had agreed to give Charlie a few minutes of privacy with the magic mirror. "We preset the system with an Ethan that I think you'll like," he'd said. "But if you want to make any changes, you'll find it's all quite intuitive."

The system quickly proved simple to use. Charlie had never played video games regularly, but Danny had often sat in front of his Xbox for hours after coming home from work. Charlie had once spent half a Saturday in front of a screen, not unlike the one she was looking at now, while Danny meticulously designed an elven wizard with face tattoos and obscenely large biceps.

Charlie had tried playing the game herself once, but the controller had never felt quite right in her hands. It was fortunate for her that the magic mirror was a touch screen.

She dragged her finger along a slider, adjusting Ethan's intelligence up past the 90% mark, before reconsidering and lowering the level back down to around 75%. She wanted Ethan to be smart, but not so smart that he couldn't be happy.

Charlie had spent a few minutes looking over the options for skills and abilities, but hadn't been able to think of anything she would want to change or adjust. The boy that had been spinning on the screen, the same Ethan who was sleeping in the fancy bed outside, was perfect exactly as he was.

She decided that it had been a mistake to make any changes to the Ethan she had already been shown. It was wrong to try and customize him like a thing.

Charlie checked over the black mirror. There didn't seem to be a back button, but at the top corner were three tiny words in bold and blocky red: ASK ME ANYTHING.

Charlie tapped the phrase. A blinking red cursor and touch keyboard sizzled onto the mirror.

'It's a reboot code, we think,' Mark had said.

Happily Ever After.

Charlie had almost forgotten the code. There hadn't been any chance to try it … and why should she? The factory wasn't hers to interfere with. And more than that, it would have been wrong of her to make decisions for the others.

There are kids here.

Kids or adults, it doesn't matter, she told herself. The code probably wouldn't even work, and even if it did, there was no way to know exactly what would happen. She could make things worse, and that was as if they were even bad. Which they weren't.

He wants something from Williams and those kids.

And you too.

Charlie could suddenly feel it in her bones—whatever the man pretending to be Max Bixby wanted, it was something he couldn't just come right out and ask for.

Whatever character Charlie built with the magic mirror wouldn't be her Ethan. He wasn't real. Nothing here was. Nothing here mattered, except the people—the eight actual people who had flown over together in the hot-air balloon. *They were real.*

Charlie wasn't Jaxon or Becky's mother, but at that moment she couldn't bat away the feeling that they might need one. Maybe Don Williams needed one too.

She rarely typed, so she had to scan the touchpad for each letter, tapping each with a bent index finger: H-A-P-P-I-L-Y

The flames flickering inside the hanging gas lamps grew blindingly white inside their glass chambers. So white and so bright they enveloped the room.

• • •

I'm going to be big and happy, Jaxon thought. Pops had told him his new body would eventually grow even taller than Dad. There would be no more sass from Becky or anyone else who thought they could tell him what to do. He would be in charge. And his new body would live a long time too.

Jaxon would be able to become anything he wanted to be. He was going to get something better than money.

"Okay, kiddo," Pops said. "Here it comes."

"How long does it take?"

"Only as long as it has to."

There was a sound like a fart or someone squeezing out the last pesky bit of suntan lotion, and a clump of cold goop landed on Jaxon's freckled shoulder before sluicing dreadfully down the center of his back.

In seconds, the gelatinous sludge was up to his ankles. Pops's voice sounded distorted from beyond the glass, "It should be over by the time it gets past your chest."

"Is it happening now?" Jaxon asked. "I don't feel anything."

"It may help if you close your eyes. Try counting backwards from ten."

Jaxon closed his eyes, listening to the splatting goop echo in the tube.

Ten … He could eat as much as he wanted. Pops had said his new body would be a fat-burning machine.

Nine … He could buy the house across the street from home. It was only a little bigger than his parent's house. Jaxon didn't need to show off.

Eight … He'd never be picked last for dodgeball again.

Seven … Harley McGivers from music class would see how smart and handsome he was.

Six … Light shined beyond his eyelids, like a flashlight under a blanket.

Jaxon opened his eyes barely in time to see a blistering light dim as quickly as it had come, shrinking back into each of the two 80s lamps sitting on either side of his grandparent's couch.

"What was that?"

Pops didn't answer. He was gone.

• • •

Whatever Charlie had started was working.

The light in the bathroom had grown so bright that there was nothing but brilliant white, but after the long moment of brutal brightness, the gas lamps hanging on the wall dimmed, returning to normal.

A thunderous knock sent the bathroom door rocking violently against the frame. "Ms. Cooper," Rapper said, shaking the knob, "is everything all right in there?"

E-V-E–

A hairless fist shot through the door, sending in a spray of wood shards. An eye infected with red lines lowered to the hole. "Ms. Cooper," Rapper said. "I must ask you to discontinue your current activity. You have inadvertently accessed a restricted module. Please open the door and step back." His eyes blinked, in oddly spaced flashes. "Please. I'm here to help!"

–R

The flames inside the gas lamp flashed and turned an unnatural Christmasy red. The sink under the mirror disappeared, then the counter, then the clawfoot tub, and the door.

Rapper loomed in the open doorway, his friendly expression gone. Now there was only a cold and deadly indifference.

A-F-T–

"Let go of me!" Charlie screamed.

Rapper had hold of her wrist and was twisting, driving her to her knees. "I'm sorry, Ms. Cooper I cannot allow you to continue. I do not believe you realize the gravity of the situation."

"Wait," Charlie said, studying the on-screen keyboard.

The grip loosened slightly. "Where did you get this directive?" Rapper said.

"Lucy gave it to me."

The grip tightened and her arm twisted further. "Please be truthful. I am here to help."

Charlie swung up her left arm. Stabbed at the keyboard with two frantic fingers.

—E-R

• • •

The light in the condo winked out, and the world went cold and black.

"*Pops!*"

The word echoed uselessly in the darkness. Jaxon could hear that the fluid had stopped flowing, settling just above his elbows.

He heaved up his hands, fighting against the slime. It was as if he were encased in a jar of peanut butter. Finally, he felt the tips of his fingers poke free, then his hands. Jaxon slapped greasy palms against glass he could no longer see.

He wasn't sure what to do. He did not want to leave the tube and roam around in the dark. If he was lost, he was supposed to sit down and yell and wait for someone to help him. But yelling inside the tube didn't seem like it would help much.

He called for Pops again, but his screams seemed to ricochet inside the tube, bouncing uselessly against the glass.

Red lights outside the tube began flashing like distant stars, illuminating a smeared fog of slime spread across the tube's glass.

Jaxon pushed hard against the door, and it popped open, expelling a wave of sludge out into a sea of blackness with a sickening splat.

"Pops!"

It was dark, but he could see clearly that he was not in Florida anymore. The air outside the tube was scrotum-tighteningly cold. He felt for his suit, but it was gone. He was naked.

Jaxon felt tears of terror begin to well up inside him. He called for Pops again. Still there was nothing. Instead of bouncing around inside the tube, his screams faded and died in the abyss.

It wasn't Pops, remember? They just took him out of your brain. Pops was never here, and neither was the condo in Florida.

Jaxon peered over the side of the tube's open door and caught sight of the faintest hint of sludge, smeared across the black floor in the light of the flashing stars. He took a tentative step out of the tube, the goop conforming around his bare foot like soft and squishy mud.

"Mom." Jaxon had meant to shout, but it had come out as only a croak as he shambled forward, kicking off clinging bits of sludge. "Dad …"

The distant red lights flashed indifferently.

"Becky!"

Jaxon threw out his hands, stretching them in search of a wall. Where there was a wall there would be a switch. After a few steps, he kicked something with his bare feet.

His clothes. He felt around on his hands and knees, searching for his Crocs. He had left them near the toilet that was no longer there.

He felt a flood of relief when his right hand hit the side of a rubber shoe. It was bad enough that he was alone in this nowhere place, but his nakedness had magnified his terror tenfold.

After he pulled on his t-shirt and shorts, they clung to his wet, slimy body. Still, he felt an immediate renewed vigor.

He kept walking, hands out, sweeping the flashing darkness. The distant lights did not seem to be getting any closer.

He wasn't sure how far he'd walked when he looked back. The tube he had emerged from had shrunk to a miniscule size, distant red lights flashing crimson across its shadowy glass.

What if there's no way out?

• • •

Rapper opened his mouth to speak, but no sounds came. The hand clamped onto Charlie's wrist squeezed and loosened like a blood pressure cuff. She ripped her arm free, and Rapper spun wildly, his arms helicoptering until he jerked to a sudden stop and crashed forward, face first, onto the bathroom's tile floor.

He twitched another moment before going completely still. The tile floor disappeared and the bathroom too, the universe replaced with flashing red stars.

Dizzy on her feet, Charlie dropped to her knees. The world had become so quiet it seemed to buzz. When she opened her eyes, there was only the distant flashing stars and Rapper, lying face down in empty space.

She edged closer to the body, straining her ears for a hint of breathing. There was nothing. She needed to get out of here. Go for help.

If she could find the outer wall, she could make her way out. She had started to push herself up when Rapper's hand flashed out, digging into the skin of her forearm. Then his other hand had her by the throat.

She couldn't breathe.

He lifted her easily off the floor and held her straight up so that she dangled above him. She pried desperately at his fingers, but it was plainly hopeless. She hadn't done anything to protect anyone. She had killed herself. Possibly killed the kids too.

The other assistants were probably strangling them all right now. Ethan was never here, and he never would be. But those kids had been.

Charlie couldn't feel the hands on her neck anymore. Her head was swimming. She was floating towards the blinking stars. She tried to fight a deep sleepy feeling growing within her, but then couldn't remember why it was important.

If she could stay awake another moment, she could have a chance, but her eyelids refused to obey and sealed shut.

• • •

The pattern of lights had changed. A star was missing. No not missing, exactly. It was behind something, flashing and casting a glow around a still and distant shape.

Jaxon shambled closer. It was a man. Jaxon jogged. No … it was too small. It was a kid. Jaxon ran.

"Becky!"

It wasn't Becky.

It was a boy, his hair so white that it flashed pink in the red lights.

Alex, the boy from under the spaceship in the Final Frontier, sat hunched against a black wall like a discarded ventriloquist dummy. His glassy green eyes terrifying and dead. Like olives floating in milk.

CHAPTER SEVENTEEN:

THE MIRROR MAZE

It was a funny thing how quickly fortunes could change. The incident that Dave's crew had caused at the Tilghman Ranch Shopping Mall had not been a small problem. Far from it. The tally so far had been:

Delta Shine Environmental: $5,200 to clean the dust from the ventilation systems.

Ozark Industrial Rental: $3,200 to rent an air scrubber.

Red River Sanitation: $9,600 to deep clean the food-court vendors.

And another $3,000 for the asshole owner of Smokey's BBQ and Eats because he had Dave over a barrel and knew it.

The thing that had been eating at Dave even worse than the loss of funds though was the knowledge that had he been home, he would have been supervising the entire operation personally. There would have never been a demolition dust disaster at the mall.

But then Jaxon had scratched that ticket and thank you, praise Jesus. Problem solved. In a moment, the family trip to Bixby Park had gone from costing a fortune to providing one.

The question as to who the fortune actually belonged to was, in Dave's view, immaterial. The check they were to receive would probably have Jaxon's name on it, but it was going to go into Dave's checking account on Monday morning. It was the family's money whether Jaxon liked it or not.

Dave had already put the wheels in motion on trust fund accounts for both of his children. A cautiously invested three hundred thousand for each of them would net both Jaxon and Becky well over a million dollars each by the time they turned eighteen. The rest was operating expenses. Jaxon would thank him later.

But the cherry on top of all of their recent good fortune was one Dave had not been expecting. The family's tour of the Dream Factory was proving to be an absolute blast. Dave would have preferred they had taken one of the ferries, and he didn't much like the bizarrely cast twins, but the factory itself was a resounding delight.

Was the set of the starship *Reliance* they were touring cheaply built? Yes, it was. But it was the spitting image of the one from the show, which had long been one of Dave's favorites. The whole thing was a riot. Even better was that the kids seemed to love it too. Which meant Amy loved it. It had been the best weekend of Dave's life—and then the lights had gone out.

Becky and Jaxon had been holding hands and were following Lucy Bixby to the starship's mess hall for what she was promising was a delectable lunch, when everything turned the blackest black.

Dave was straining to hear his children over Amy's screams as he swung his arms wildly, trying to find them. He made contact with something, but it was Amy, shaking and thrashing.

He pulled her in and shushed her. "Would you calm down?" he said. "I can't hear."

Amy's voice was hot and ragged. "What's happening?"

"I don't know," he whispered. "Take a breath and be quiet."

Distant red lights began to flash. The *Reliance* was gone. And so were the kids. Amy had started to scream again before Dave found her mouth with his hand. If they were going to find the kids, they would need to listen.

• • •

When Don and Bixby emerged from the locker room, the arena was gone. Instead, they stepped into an empty waiting room with futuristic chairs that had angles so sharp they looked as though they might take a piece out of whoever sat in them.

Thankfully, Bixby led Don past the uncomfortable-looking furniture to a kiosk at the rear wall. "Come along, come along," he said. "No time to dawdle. We're already late for lunch."

Don guessed he should have been hungry. On days he played, his mother would make him a couple of peanut butter and potato chip sandwiches for both before and after the game. But the constant changes in reality were making his stomach churn to the point he was near dry heaving.

"I ain't eating lunch," he said. "At least not in this fucking place. I'm seeing what you got and then I'm bouncing."

"Of course, of course," Bixby said, waving a hand. He tapped the kiosk's glass display, and a mirror image of Don with much longer arms appeared on the screen, wearing something like a wrestler's singlet.

"Well," Bixby said, smiling. "I'll be seeing myself off to my other responsibilities. Ms. Vanessa will be out to help you in a few minutes."

"Hold on a sec. What if I want to leave?"

"In that event, Ms. Vanessa has been instructed to escort you out to the balloon with your money. Just say the word." Bixby grabbed Don's hand and shook it vigorously. "It has been such a pleasure to make your acquaintance, Mr. Williams. Really it has. I hope to see you at lunch standing a little taller, if you know what I mean. But if not, I wish nothing but the best for you. Truly I do."

As much as Don didn't like Bixby, the idea of being left alone with a stranger in this place caused bile to rise in his throat. And more troubling than that, this was not the deal they had made only a minute earlier in the locker room.

Before Don could point this out, Ms. Vanessa slipped inside the room wearing a tight-fitting white lab-coat. Not only did Don's worries disappear, but most of his other thoughts as well.

Ms. Vanessa's skin was richly smooth and the color of charcoal. She was thick in her lips and thighs, and voluptuous in all the right spots. "Well hello there, Don," she said, adjusting her glasses, over-sized with black frames.

"My name's Vanessa. I'll be taking care of you personally from here on in. I've heard it's been a bit of a stressful morning for you."

Bixby tipped his hat, smiled knowingly, and strolled from the little room, easing shut the door.

Vanessa showed Don how to work the kiosk, and in only a few minutes he was lost in a deluge of options for his potential body. How tall was too tall? How fast was too fast?

A whiff of weed, pungent and delicious shook him from his stupor. "Here," Vanessa said, holding the smoldering joint over his shoulder.

"Where'd that come from?"

"It's the Dream Factory," she said, before taking a drag. "Anything's possible."

Don relaxed even before taking a long, soothing hit. *Damn I needed that.*

"You're still thinking about your friend," Vanessa said, smooth and sultry.

It was true. It was hard for him not to think of the sick things Rosie was probably doing with that rabbit. Probably the same things she had already done with him.

A fucking cartoon rabbit. Sick.

He took another drag, so deep that he gagged and coughed. He thought it was good shit, but in truth after all he had seen, anything would have probably felt great.

"Don't worry about her," Vanessa said. "I'm here now."

Don wasn't sure how long he had been adjusting his avatar, when he removed the nasty mole above the left knee. He reached down and felt it, still protruding under his pants. It was a strange relief it was still there.

"Something wrong?" Vanessa asked.

"Well, no. It's just … I don't know about this shit. I guess I'm kind of used to my body the way it is."

Vanessa smiled perfect white teeth and picked up his hands, examining them with delicate fingers. "These are nice, but they are a bit on the smallish side for a professional, don't you think?"

Don knew it was true, but hated that she had pointed it out. He ripped his hands away.

Vanessa smiled, unperturbed and turned back to the monitor. She zoomed in on the avatar's hands, before increasing their size slightly. "That's better," she said. "You know what they say about big hands."

"Yeah, well I ain't got no problems in that area."

"I know you don't." She zoomed in on the avatar's crotch and removed the black singlet it was wearing, revealing Don's familiar member.

"Yes," Vanessa said. "No need to adjust anything there, I'd say."

Don felt himself stiffening, and Vanessa's eyes trailed down. "Can I see it?"

"What?"

She giggled. "Your cock, of course. Can I see it? I need to check the scanner's accuracy."

Don couldn't speak but managed to nod. Vanessa dropped to her knees and pulled his pants and boxers down in a single motion.

"Oh yes," she said, breathing on his most sensitive skin. "This is very nice."

Then the lights went out.

Don instinctively jumped backward, tripping as he struggled to pull his pants back up. "What the shit was that?"

Vanessa said nothing.

Don reached into the darkness, searching for her with outstretched hands. "You hear me, girl? Where you go?"

Red lights came sharply from impossibly far away like crimson stars. Don called into the flashing red abyss for Vanessa, but in moments he was sure he was alone.

What the fuck?

The monitor blipped behind him. There was no kiosk; the screen simply floated in flashing space.

```
*** EMG SYSTEM RESTART IN PROCESS ***
```

He touched the screen, and a blinking green cursor appeared below the message: POWER ERROR SEC REJ7483F.

Don had never been much of a computer guy. He could only hope the system was as intuitive to use as his phone. He typed: *location of max bixby*

```
MAXIMILLIAN BIXBY OF MEMPHIS TENNESSEE DIED
ON DECEMBER 12, 1969 IN GALVESTON, TEXAS.
```

No shit.

Don typed: *where did Vanessa go?*

```
IMPROPER INPUT.
```

location of lucy bixby

```
IMPROPER INPUT
```

This shit wasn't working. He typed: *where the fuck is rosie???*

"Oh thank God," Rosie said, behind him.

Don nearly jumped out of his sneakers and spun on her.

Red light was flashing across her milky skin. Her hair was mussed, and her t-shirt was missing, leaving her in only the Princess Winnie bra Don had so gleefully removed the night before.

"What the hell you been doing?" Don said. "Where's your shirt?"

Her mouth twisted into a frown, before she noticed something. She pointed to his crotch and Don realized his pants were still unbuttoned.

"Don't worry about that," Don said, buttoning. "What happened?"

"Everything just disappeared." Rosie threw her arms around him and buried her face in his chest. "It was so dark. My God. I was so scared."

"Yeah," Don said. "Me too."

• • •

Jaxon had never seen a dead body before. The only funeral he had ever been to had been Pops', and on that occasion the casket had thankfully been closed. Still, Jaxon knew there was no way Alex could be alive.

Was he ever alive at all?

Jaxon suddenly had to go again. Bad. He pulled down his shorts and let loose right where he stood, sending out a jet of urine, that disappeared into the flashing darkness.

"Jaxon."

He tripped backward and hit the ground on his bare butt.

Oh God.

Alex's lips were moving. "Help me."

Jaxon staggered to his feet, pulling up his shorts. He ran through the flashing darkness, screaming for help until his voice went hoarse. When he'd thought he couldn't scream anymore …

"Jaxon!"

A pair of frigid hands took hold of his upper arms. It was Mom. She was clutching him hard enough that it hurt.

Dad had a hand on the wall, a red light flashing beneath it. "It's alright, hun. Let him go."

Jaxon tried to wiggle free of his mother's painful grip, but she refused to release her hold on him, keeping a firm hand on his arm before taking his face in her hands. "Are you alright? Why are you all wet?"

Before he could answer, Mom asked, "Where's your sister?"

"Dad told me she was riding horses."

Mom looked back to Dad, his hand still pressed to the wall.

He shook his head. "Nope. Wasn't me."

The pieces were starting to fit together. If Pops could be created by the factory, so could imposter versions of anyone … *even his parents.*

Mom shook Jaxon hard. "How long ago was that?" she shouted. "*When was that?*"

Jaxon wasn't sure. He had never been much good at keeping track of time. "I don't know," he said. "Maybe an hour ago."

His report didn't seemingly provide any relief for Mom. Her body had begun shivering so hard that Jaxon had begun to shiver himself, almost in rhythm with her. Dad pulled her up against the wall, and then Jaxon. "Stay between us, sport, and keep a hand on the wall."

"What about Becky?"

"No talking," Dad said. "We need to listen to find her."

They walked for a few minutes, Dad only occasionally calling out into the blinking red darkness, when his feet stuttered to a jerking stop. "What the hell is that?"

In the distance, flashing red shards folded and refolded in on themselves. Jaxon couldn't think of a way to incorporate hell into his reply.

"It's the mirror maze."

CHAPTER EIGHTEEN:

MOM WAS GOING TO BE SO MAD

It seemed impossible, but the air in the mirror maze had turned even more frigid since Jaxon's first time through. He was convulsing with each step, but the truth was he had been shaking with relief even before Dad had seen the mirror maze.

Finding both of his parents—his real parents—had brought an unimaginable comfort. Even though Dad had never been inside the factory before today, he seemed to know exactly where he was going.

Dad whispered, "If you just keep your hand on the wall, you can't get lost."

And so Jaxon had not lifted up his hand. Even now, his palms dragged over sharp, icy glass. The air was getting warmer, and the frosted-over mirrors were growing slick, like ice cubes left in the sun.

"Not this again," Dad said.

Jaxon edged around Dad's hip. At first he saw nothing but his father's reflection, shrinking into the forever of the mirror's flashing red glass.

The lights are different. Beyond the mirror maze, the stars were bigger than they had been before, closer together.

"The exit's just around the bend," Jaxon said.

Mom gripped his shoulder hard, stopping him before he could take more than a step out of the mirror maze. "How do you know that?"

"We came through here earlier?" he said. "We're in the hall at the place where Dad pays for his tickets."

"What tickets?" Dad said.

"You mean speeding tickets?" Mom said. "City Hall?"

A digitized voice came from everywhere: "*20th Century. Enchanted masquerade ball. Program start.*"

An electrical buzz sizzled, and the hair on Jaxon's neck stood straight up on end. The red orbs pulsed and disappeared. Stone walls and a plaster ceiling sharpened and distorted into a gilded hallway lit with flickering sconces and lined with majestic wood doors that twisted away and out of sight.

"See?" Jaxon said, pushing ahead. He was sure it was the same hallway from earlier, only with a fancy change in decor. "Come on," he said.

"Not so fast there, sport." Dad grabbed his shoulder and pulled ahead of him. "I'll go first."

Dad led them back onto the lobby's landing. Nothing had changed here except the condensation that now ran down the foyer's regal wallpaper in thick wet streaks.

"I should stay here and wait for Becky," Mom said.

Dad took her by the arm, pulling her towards the stairs. "I'll go back and look for her once we're all outside," he said. "I want those phones."

Jaxon skipped ahead of them down the leftmost curling stairway before skidding to a stop at the exit. The black fog from earlier was still there, pulsing and twisting in a swirl of darkness.

"Let me have a look first." Dad took a sharp breath and extended his arm up to the shoulder through the fog.

When he brought back his hand, he wiggled his fingers, examining them.

"What is it?" Mom said.

"Not a thing."

Dad took a breath and thrust his head through the fog. When his face returned, it was flushed with relief. "This is it."

Dad pulled Jaxon through the fog, and Jaxon pulled Mom—all three emerging into the blazing sun shining outside the factory. A giant horsefly buzzed across Jaxon's field of vision, and another bit into his arm. Of course nothing in the factory had been real, he thought as he rubbed an already festering welt.

This is real.

Mom dropped his hand and screamed.

● ● ●

Amy lowered her hand from her mouth, horrified.

One of the strange-looking men in the tracksuits was lying face down on the broken and cracked path that hopefully still led to the hot-air balloon. Though at this point Amy wasn't taking anything for granted.

"Is he dead?"

She hoped he was, but immediately regretted asking the question. Dave tiptoed over the body and squatted down next to it. "Not so close," she said.

"It's alright."

Alright? Everything was far from fucking alright. They had lost Becky and—

Where is Jaxon?

Amy panicked a moment, until she found him. Her son had left her side and was edging closer to the body. "Jax, get away from that thing." She hopped off the stoop and grabbed his arm, pulling him further down the path. "You stay right here."

Dave flipped the body over and grunted.

Amy waited a long moment for him to say something, squeezing her hands together so tight they hurt. "Is he alive?"

"I don't think so," Dave said. "Come and take a look. Keep Jax back."

Amy looked back after each step, ensuring that Jaxon hadn't moved.

"It's ugly," Dave whispered. "But try not to scream."

Dave had not been lying—it was ugly. The thing in the tracksuit had bitten through its own cheek exposing a smiling jaw, bits of waxy flesh hanging between its teeth.

"Does he need mouth to mouth?" Jaxon called.

"Uh … no," Dave said. "I don't think so."

Becky couldn't see this. *No one* should see this. "I should stay," Amy whispered. "Someone has to wait for Becky …"

Dave shook his head. "We can't separate, at least not until we've called for help."

Jaxon took a step back towards the factory "I can do—"

"No!" Dave yelled hard enough to knock Jaxon back the step.

"What if she comes out and we're not here?" Amy asked.

"If that happens," Dave said, "I expect we'll hear her. We need to get the phones and call for help."

• • •

The hot-air balloon was where they had left it, and even luckier, the cable-car was still unlocked. Dave found the box of phones under the seat and dumped them onto the floor of the cabin.

He picked up the phone the park had given him. There was only one number that had been loaded into the contacts: the Bixby customer service line.

"Why are you calling those people!" Amy screamed as he pressed the contact number. "Just dial 911."

"And tell them what?"

"The truth."

"It'll take too long to explain."

"Put it on speaker!"

"*Thank you for calling the Land of Dreams and Wonders! For English, press one. Para español, oprima dos.*"

"English!" Amy screeched.

Dave winced and pulled the phone further away, shushing her with his hand.

"*Thank you. Please listen carefully, as our options have recently changed! For park hours, press one. For dining reservations, press two. For lost and found—*"

Dave's shoulders slumped. "Jesus fucking Christ."

"*I'm sorry, I didn't quite get that. Did you say cheese fries? If you'd like to order room service—*"

"No, you stupid cunt!" Dave screamed. "Agent. AGE-ENT. Connect me to a fucking agent!"

Amy swept aside the small mound of phones, looking for her own. "I told you we should have called 911."

"*Hold please. We're connecting you with a member of our Dream Team. Have a magical day!*" There was a piercing ring-back tone. "*We value your call. The current wait time is … SEVEN MINUTES.*"

Distorted music began playing like a dying calliope. "*The fun's waiting for us—let's celebrate! Be our friend, let's laugh and sing …*"

"To hell with this," Amy said, dialing her own phone. "I'm calling the police."

The music cut off.

"*This is Mark Warner with Corporate Security. Is this David Kinney?*"

"Yeah, this is Kinney. What the hell are you people doing?"

"*Calm down, Mr. Kinney. Is everyone alright? What's happening?*"

Dave was processing an answer when Amy's eyes shot around sharply. "Where is he?"

Oh no.

Jaxon was gone.

• • •

Mom had wanted someone to wait by the front door. Jaxon was scared of the apperbots, but Dad had told him on the walk to the balloon that the one by the door was dead.

Jaxon could only hope that outside of the factory, things that were dead stayed dead, but whatever the case, he didn't plan to stand too close to the body. He took position on the factory's front stoop, next to the swirling black fog, waiting only a moment before putting his nose to the mist and squinting his eyes. The black fog was dense. Impossible to see through.

He pushed his head through the void. The foyer was still empty. "Becky!" he called.

He hadn't expected a reply, but still waited anxiously for one. Even if Becky didn't hear him, maybe someone else who could help would.

Mom had wanted to wait at the top of the stairs, and that particular prospect didn't seem too risky. The foyer's appearance had never changed. Jaxon guessed whatever was happening inside the factory, it didn't work out here in the lobby.

He stepped back through the dark mist, Crocs slapping on fogged-over glass tiles. *I'll just call to her from the base of the stairs.* If Becky was able to get to the mirror maze, she would probably be able to hear him.

Fliiiitttt

A panel sliced down behind him, cutting off the black fog like a guillotine. In its place was an oxidized red door.

The computerized voice returned: "*Failsafe activated. Lockdown initiated.*"

Oh no, Jaxon thought. Mom was going to be so mad.

CHAPTER NINETEEN:

AS REAL AS THIS LIFE GETS

"**W**here's everyone else?" Rosie said.

How the fuck am I supposed to know? Don thought.

Though he had to admit to himself, as annoying as Rosie had become, he was glad to have found someone else that he knew for sure was a real person. That some of her smugness had vanished was a bonus.

Rosie looked over the monitor Don had been working at. "If it wasn't for that screen," she said, "I'd have never found you."

Don had tried a few more commands since Rosie had appeared, but the computer wouldn't answer any questions about the factory itself or what was happening. It would answer only general knowledge questions when prompted.

Rosie shivered and tucked herself under Don's arm. Her bare skin was ice-cold, and he couldn't resist the urge to pull her in tight.

"Ask it where the doors are," she said.

"I already did that."

The cursor flashed impatiently. Don decided to try a simpler command this time. He typed: *menu*

```
PROCESSING.........................
POWER LEVEL (2%)
BACKUP MODE MENU:
    DREAM MECHANICS
    PHOTONIC PROJECTION GRID CONTROLLER
    HAPTIC RESPONSE GRID CONTROLLER
    ENVIRONMENTAL MODULATOR
    BOUNDARY SENSORS
    CAEL
    FAILSAFE SWITCH
```

"What is it?" Rosie whispered.

Don didn't know, but the computer was at least doing something, and something was better than nothing. He tapped 'DREAM MECHANICS'

```
        *****SYSTEM MALFUNCTION******

  1. NewOrleans-20C-EnchantedMasqueradeBall
     (ON-LINE)

  2. Sindhura-Medieval-RoyalBazaarEscape
     (OFF-LINE)

  3. Borenia-Fantasy-EnchantedMusicalParade
     (OFF-LINE)

  4. Norway-19C-WinterSolsticeBall (OFF-LINE)

  5. London-20C-NannySkyAdventure (OFF-LINE)

  6. Haiti Coast-18C-PirateLagoonQuest
     (OFF-LINE)

NXT PG
BACK
```

Rosie tapped the first option before Don could react. "Girl, what the hell you doing?"

"20ᵗʰ Century. Enchanted masquerade ball. Program start."

The panel itself didn't change, but the flashing void contorted and shrunk in size around them. The void of blinking red lights was gone, replaced with imposing block walls lined with shelves that were packed tight with glass jars of pickled okra and green tomatoes, red-pepper jelly, and whole vanilla beans nestled in sugar. A free-standing sink jutted into existence, knocking Don back from the panel.

"Well, this is better," Rosie whispered.

Don wasn't sure if he agreed. He lifted the lid off the nearest sugar jar and tasted the white crystals inside, licking them off a pinky. "It's sugar."

"Of course it's sugar," she said, as if it was the most obvious thing in the world.

They were now inside an oversized pantry, and judging from the copper and steel pans hanging from the elaborate ceiling rack above them, it was a pantry in a very nice house.

The muffled sound of clattering pots came from behind the wooden door that sealed off the room.

It had been careless of Rosie to touch anything, but Don had to admit he was relieved to find a way to exercise at least some function of control over the factory. Whatever happened, he didn't want to get too far away from the control panel.

"Let's see what's out there," Rosie whispered, pushing open the door, hinges groaning.

Outside, three Creole women in flour-dusted aprons bustled about smoking pots and sizzling sausages, taking no notice of Don or the shirtless Rosie. One of them was busy peeling shrimp, another was chopping vegetables, and the third was stirring something thick.

Don's mouth watered. He hadn't eaten since dinner the night before at the Safari Lounge. A lifetime ago.

On the counter, a steaming mound of crawfish and massive crab legs had been laid out on greasy butcher paper, their shells slick with cayenne-spiced butter.

The nearest chef, a stout woman with arms like rolling pins, absently stirred a savory-smelling gumbo. Her eyes passed right over Don without a care as she slurped brown broth off a large tasting spoon.

Rosie waved a hand over the chef's eyes, and the woman walked straight through Rosie's palm to a cutting station where she scooped up a handful of green onion and started chopping with a sharp-looking cutting knife.

"She's not real."

It was remarkable that this would be a surprise to Rosie, but Don didn't say so. Instead, he picked up a crawfish and cracked the shell with his fingers. The hot juice ran down to his wrist as he popped the sweet meat into his mouth. "I don't know what's real," he said, licking buttery spice from his thumb. "But this food is real good."

"I'm not hungry," Rosie said. "We have to find Wally and the others."

That fucking rabbit again. "What you talking about?" he said. "Don't you get it? Wally wasn't never here. What you want him for anyway?"

Her eyes glossed over dreamily, and Don put up his hand. "Shit, never mind. I don't want to know."

He dried his greasy hand on his jeans and went back to the pantry.

"Where are you going?"

"I want to see what else this computer can do," he said.

The screen was still there, framed into existence above the wash sink. Next to it, a little sign read: 'help must wash hands'.

Don tapped the back button.

```
POWER LEVEL (4%)
BACKUP MODE MENU:
    DREAM MECHANICS
    PHOTONIC PROJECTION GRID CONTROLLER
```

```
HAPTIC RESPONSE GRID CONTROLLER
ENVIRONMENTAL MODULATOR
BOUNDARY SENSORS
CAEL
FAILSAFE SWITCH
```

"What you think C-A-E-L mean?" Don said. The question had been rhetorical, but Rosie shook her head.

"Candy Apple Eating League?"

"I don't think that's it," Don said.

He tapped CAEL on the screen, and like a rabbit from a top hat, Max Bixby's head emerged from the center of the mirror.

"Well hello there, Mr. Williams."

"What the shit, man!"

Bixby stepped ghostlike into the pantry, spinning his cane. "Dear me … Ms. Rosie. What's happened to your shirt?"

"Oh, Mr. Bixby! Thank God!" Rosie went to throw her arms around him, and they passed right through Bixby's shoulders.

Ghost Bixby smiled like an airline worker with bad news. "I'm glad to see that you've managed to find a bite to eat. As you can see, we are experiencing some technical difficulties, and we may have a delay with regard to lunch."

Don backed away, his shoulders hitting the shelving and rattling the jars. "What you mean technical difficulties? *That's what you call this*?!"

"You know how it is with new attractions. Nothing ever quite works out the way you expect it to the first time."

"What happened?" Don asked.

"A minor power surge," Bixby said. "But rest assured that our trouble is only temporary. Our systems are still rebooting, but we should be fully back in operation at some point in the next hour or so."

"What does C-A-E-L mean?" Don said.

Bixby arched an eyebrow. "What's that, Mr. Williams?"

"CAEL?" Don said, pronouncing it like the leafy vegetable. "What's it mean?"

"It's all quite technical, Mr. Williams." Bixby indicated the pantry door with his cane. "Let me show you both out to the lawn. The others will be gathering there for lunch. As you can see, quite the feast is being prepared."

"You said I could leave," Don said. "I don't care about your food, the money, or improving my motherfucking wingspan. I'm ready to leave. Right now."

"Nonsense," Bixby said. "You're hungry, aren't you, Ms. Rosie?"

Rosie nodded happily. "Lunch sounds wonderful."

Don didn't care anymore about what Rosie wanted. He slid around her to see the screen that Bixby had stepped through

```
COGNITIVE ARTIFICIAL ENVIRONMENTAL
        LIAISON ACTIVATED
          Pwr: 68%
```

Artificial Liaison.

"Cael," Don said, understanding. "That's you. You're Cael."

Bixby's mouth made a thin line, and his mask of pleasantness seemed to melt away. "If you'll both follow me outside."

"No." Don tapped the back button, and he pointed to the FAILSAFE SWITCH. "And what does this—"

Bixby's flutey voice dropped tuba-deep. "You will not touch it."

"Oh no?" Don said.

Bixby's hand shot out for Don's wrist, but it passed through with only a faint opposing magnet-like pressure.

"Don," Rosie said. "What are you doing? The tour's not over."

Don couldn't keep himself from smiling. "It is for me, bitch." He hit the button.

"No!" Bixby screamed.

```
***SYSTEM ERASURE IN PROGRESS***
       LOCKDOWN INITIATED
```

Timer: 30 … 29 … 28…

Bixby's ghostlike hands whipped through the screen. "Hit the abort!"

Rosie reached for the mirror, but Don already had her arm. He threw her back hard against the shelving, sending jars crashing to the floor.

Timer: 24 … 23 …

"What are you doing, baby? *We'll never have this chance again!*"

Don shook his head, taking in the sight of her, panting on the floor and desperately clinging to a dream. "I've seen enough."

Rosie ran from the pantry, screaming for help.

Timer: 15 … 14 …

Bixby's pleading eyes went frantic. "What is it you want? I can give you anything. All you have to do is hit that button."

Timer: 10 … 9 …

"Naw," Don said, unable to resist a smirk. "I'm good."

Clapping footfalls.

A punch hit Don's midsection, and the air shot out of his lungs. He looked down: the hilt of a serrated cutting knife, the exposed blade still smeared with bits of minced onion, stuck out between his ribs. His eyes trailed up to Rosie's.

"I'm sorry, Donny."

She stabbed me.

Timer: 5 … 4 … ABORT ACTIVATED. POWER RESTORATION IN PROGRESS. TIME TO FULL POWER: 1 HOUR, 15 MINUTES.

The crazy fucking bitch stabbed me.

Don staggered forward but was suddenly on his knees. He gritted his teeth and pulled the hilt. *Stuck like glue.* He heaved harder. The blade pulled free, but his arms were on fire. He couldn't lift them. They fell to his side, and the knife clattered to the floor.

"Oh dear," Bixby said. "Such a mess. A mess and a waste."

"It's not … real." The pain inside of Don's stomach was fading as quickly as it had come, though the blood was soaking through his jeans and was pooling around his knees. His mouth tasted like pennies. "*It's not … real.*"

Bixby frowned delightfully. "I'm sorry, Mr. Williams. But for you, I am afraid, this is as real as this life gets."

CHAPTER TWENTY:

WE'RE GOING TO MATCH

Lucy never worried. Things had always worked out for her exactly the way Daddy said they would. The last time she'd doubted him for even a moment had been in the hospital in Galveston.

'It'll be alright.'

And, for over fifty years, it had been. But then the lights had gone out.

Lucy had been lounging in one of her garden's little wicker chairs, thinking about how much she was going to miss the program after the tour was finished. It was more bittersweet than she would have believed.

Daddy had told her he would build another matter replicator once he was out of the factory, but Lucy couldn't shake the feeling that any new garden would not be exactly the same as this one.

She had spent years meticulously designing the little glade. Every tree, shrub, and flower had been selected and created by her. She was particularly fond of her *nelumbo-nucifera* hybrid that ran around the perimeter of the pond—pink and white petals with seedpods the size of showerheads. It was a breed impossible in the real world, but not here.

"It will only be another moment until Ms. Cooper is ready," Mapper had said, helping Lucy out of the little garden chair in the nick of time.

The chair vanished first. Then the plants and the grass. Her white unicorn, who had been lapping up pristine water at the edge of the lake, had been the last thing to go before total darkness.

Power fluctuations had been fairly common when Lucy had first started coming to the factory, but the last one had been a long time ago—New Year's Eve, 1977. At least Lucy thought it had been New Year's Eve. In the Dream Factory, every day was New Year's Eve if that's what you wanted.

But even on that occasion, only the party hats and a few waitresses had disappeared. This time, everything had vanished. Lucy had known it was more than rotten luck even before Mapper's body hit the ground.

"*Stay calm, sugar,*" Daddy had said from the darkness. "*I'll have this fixed up in a jiff.*"

For the first time since that night in the hospital, Lucy doubted him. The act of standing for only a few seconds was already causing her knees to ache terribly.

The matter replicators began to flash, which meant the power had been rebooted completely. If that had happened, it would take at least an hour for the factory to get back up to full power.

A few of the low-memory programs would probably already be back online if she could find a control port, but that was going to be next to impossible without Mapper—and the assistant did not look like he was going to be available anytime soon.

He had started twitching violently before flipping onto his back and ripping off his nose. He was starting to work at pulling off his lips when Cael said: "*20ᵗʰ Century. Enchanted masquerade ball. Program start.*"

The world returned, but it was not Lucy's glade. She was on the rear lawn of the Chateau of the Moon. It was one of the first programs Daddy had created. He had managed to activate it somehow.

A few feet away, Daddy appeared, alongside a Victorian wheel-chair—large wooden wheels and a high button-tufted leather backrest. "Princess, you look positively exhausted."

It was an understatement, but Daddy was notorious for those. Lucy hobbled over, reaching for him to steady her, but the matter field only held a millisecond before her hand passed through him.

"I'm sorry, sugar," Daddy said. "We're going to have to make some adjustments to our plan."

"What's happening?" Lucy clutched the arm of the wheelchair and eased into the seat, bones cracking. "How can these be solid if you're—"

Daddy fizzled, momentarily transparent. "I am not, strictly speaking, here, sugar. My program is still reloading. I will explain upstairs."

The chateau was at least fifty yards away, and the wheels of Lucy's chair looked big and heavy. "I … I don't think I can push it."

"Princess, I wouldn't dream of having you push. You just sit back and relax for now, and soon you'll be jumping around like there were fire ants in your knickers."

The wheelchair started forward by itself across the moonlit lawn towards the chateau. Lucy arched her neck to look back, but Daddy had already vanished.

The wheelchair rolled across impossibly smooth grass and delivered Lucy up a rear ramp that had never been part of this program before. It was a horribly out of place red-and-white-striped slide that curled up to the master suite's terrace.

When Lucy found Charlotte lying on the bathroom floor, she was at first terrified she was dead. Charlotte was flat on her back a few feet away from one of the assistants. Rapper had ripped both of his ears off and was chewing on them mindlessly.

Charlotte's eyes fluttered.

So she was alive—but how alive was she really? Charlotte's neck was now an ugly black-and-blue, and her right arm had been crushed. As if Lucy didn't have enough aches and pains already.

An image of Daddy appeared in the bathroom mirror. "*What's the matter?*" he asked. "I've told you it's only a minor hiccup. You remember they used to happen all the time."

Next to Daddy in the mirror, a single blinking cursor flashed after the words: Happily Ever After.

"What does that mean?"

"A safety protocol that I had installed and forgotten about."

"Daddy … you don't forget anything."

He shook his head. "I don't have as strong a memory as I'd like about things before the change. I can only remember the important things clearly."

"What happened?"

"Your sister managed to send someone out here a few weeks ago with an invasive program. I had thought they didn't manage to get any useful information, but it seems I was wrong."

"Who entered the code? It wasn't—"

"I'm afraid so," Daddy's reflection said. "I warned you to choose carefully."

Lucy had known Charlotte was too good to be true, too perfect—and still Lucy had let her guard down anyway.

The whole thing wasn't fair.

Charlotte had ruined everything—and for what? She had been obviously miserable on the outside. No friends. The only family a brother who lived three states away and seemed to want nothing to do with her. The Dream Factory could have been anything Charlotte could have wanted.

"I can't go in there now," Lucy said. "She's all broken."

"I know it's rotten luck," Daddy said. "But when life gives you lemons and all that. All we can do now is make do."

"How am I supposed to lift her?"

"You? Lift? Princess, be serious. I've managed to consolidate enough power to reactivate one of the assistants for a short time. I was just waiting for you to get up here."

The mutilated assistant shot up from the floor, standing more rigid than usual and staring blankly ahead. The ears he'd been chewing slipped out of his mouth, falling to the floor.

"You're sure I can't go into the other one?" Lucy asked. The girl that had come to the factory with Don had been a young and pretty thing.

"Now you know she's not been matched with you … these things take time."

Lucy knew he was right. She had been bringing Daddy little slides of Charlie's blood for years, and he had only just told her the transfer was ready.

"What if she resists now?"

"Don't you worry about that," Daddy said. "I'll see you downstairs as soon as we're all through. I'll be the one in the blue dress."

● ● ●

Rarely had Rosie ever felt so panicked as she had when the lights had gone out. She'd been rubbing herself against Wally's leg at the top of a tower, birds chirping and bouncing on the window sill.

Wally's fur was so soft she'd wanted to wrap all of herself up in it. His paws, dragging nails across her bare back, sent an almost electric current through her. Wally had unclasped her bra, but then the softness, and the light, was gone.

She had screamed for Wally, but he didn't answer. She managed to rehook her bra, but after only a few minutes she'd given up on finding her shirt or her shoes and had instead wandered, terrified, in the darkness until she'd found Donny.

She hadn't meant to hurt him, but he had been acting crazy. He was going to hurt Mr. Bixby or worse … *hurt Wally.*

"Don't you think this is going to look lovely on you?" Bixby asked.

The dress inside the armoire was a sparkling royal blue with chiffon overlays, but the armoire itself was incredibly out of place, sitting at the center of the chateau's empty ballroom.

"I guess … it's nice," Rosie said, feeling the tremors in her throat. She had been prone to shakes since the thing with Donny.

Mr. Bixby had told her not to worry, that Donny would be fine—but Donny had not looked fine. Rosie had never seen a dead person before, but Donny did not look alive.

You killed him, she thought. *With a knife.* There was blood all over her shorts and thighs. On her hands too. All over her hands.

"You're going to look absolutely exquisite in it."

Rosie let her fingers trail over the dress's soft silk folds. "What about Donny?"

"He's fine, dear. He's absolutely fine … but in that very unlikely chance he is not fine, we will have to take some precautions for your sake. You understand?"

Two glass tubes glided into the ballroom by themselves on invisible, silent wheels. The air was growing heavy with the aroma of an oncoming lightning storm, intensifying as the tubes slid to a stop. A mirror image of Rosie was asleep in one of the tubes, naked and surrounded by frozen, translucent bubbles. The other tube was empty.

"You'll need some new fingerprints, and due to some built-in operational hurdles, it's actually much easier to give you an entirely new body than to just replace your hands."

"You're giving me … *a new body?*"

"It seems that our friend Mr. Jaxon decided to leave the factory during our little hiccup in power, so a spot has opened up. You are, I am happy to say, the lucky beneficiary."

The thick black cable that connected the two tubes sparked to life, and Bixby opened the door of the empty tube.

"But," Rosie said, trembling, "I don't want a new body."

"Come now … you know you can trust me. Don't you?" Bixby said, imitating a frown before turning it upside down. "This new body will be miles better for you. All the cookies you can eat, and it won't do a thing to your waistline. It will also have some less incriminating fingerprints."

Rosie had touched the murder weapon. More than touched it. She had used it. It had gone right into Donny like a spear through a marshmallow.

"You're extremely lucky, you know?"

Rosie didn't feel lucky. This was a nightmare. "I ... don't think so."

Bixby smiled. "Creutzfeldt-Jakob Disease?" he said. "Have you heard of it?"

Rosie had. "My uncle had it when I was a girl." Only a few months after Uncle Jerome's diagnosis, he had gone from mildly forgetful to a twitching and shaking mess.

"Well, I'm sorry to say that it must run in the family."

Rosie's hands were shaking so hard her wrists were getting sore. "You mean ... *I have it?*"

"Afraid so. Have you noticed yourself becoming more forgetful lately?"

That couldn't be true. But perhaps it was. Rosie's mind raced.

Bixby nodded to her hands. "You're trembling. Did your uncle tremble that way as well?"

Rosie nodded.

"I'm afraid it's quite advanced." Bixby wagged his cane at her, before beckoning her towards the tube. "But as I said ... it's lucky for you a spot has opened up."

She trudged only a step before Bixby stopped her with his hand. "This is rather embarrassing," he said. "But you'll have to remove the rest of your clothes."

Her numb fingers fumbled with her bra. When it fell away, she did her best to cover herself with one hand while peeling away her shorts with the other.

"You misunderstand me," Bixby said, watching and smiling. "All of your clothes."

Rosie looked down. Somehow, Donny's blood had even managed to stain her Princess Winnie panties an ugly burnt burgundy.

"I'm afraid we're short on time," Bixby said. "The highway patrol is already on the way, and you, my dear, are in a bit of a tricky legal jam, what with the murder and all."

"*He's dead?*"

"Of course," Bixby said. "You ought'a know. You killed him. Remember? Like I said, it's the memory that's one of the first things to go with Creutzfeldt-Jakob."

Rosie hooked her thumbs under her panties and pulled them down, stepping out of them.

"That's a good girl," Bixby said, guiding her naked into the tube. "Now, you just step inside and think happy thoughts."

"Is Wally still here?"

"He'll be here when you get out."

Rosie settled her head against the black pillow cushion that had been molded against the back of the tube and imagined moving her hands through Wally's cloudlike fur again. So soft. "I'm ready."

The icy sludge began filling the tube, and in moments it had risen above her blood-splattered thighs. "How long will it take?" she whispered.

"Close your eyes and count backwards from five."

Five … Donny shouldn't have tried to shut down the factory. It hadn't been her fault.

Four … He had killed himself. He'd walked into the knife. She had only planned to threaten him. Get him to stop.

Three … Wally's fur was soft enough to melt into. He was soft all over, everywhere.

Two …

Rosie's eyes opened, but she had not been the one to open them. *What's happening?*

The door opened, sending out the sticky sludge. She had opened it, but she hadn't.

"*Are you still here?*"

The voice in her head was not her own. Rosie tried to answer it, but couldn't.

Outside the tube, Bixby and the second tube with her doppelganger were gone. Rosie's bloody, slimy hands took hold of a majestic purple towel that hadn't been there before, and the hands began working the towel, wiping off the goop from her arms and bare legs.

Rosie felt nothing.

It didn't work, she thought. *I'm still right here!*

Her body moved to the armoire, and her hands pulled the dress off the hanger. Her feet stepped into it.

"I'm afraid there's not room in here for the both of us," the voice that was not her own said. *"And I'm sorry to say I have no place to put you."*

Rosie's sight winked out. Soon all she had left was her hearing. There was only a faint sound of something like music, until even that faded away to nothing.

• • •

Becky was always at least a little nervous when she rode horses, but she was always especially nervous when she rode horses she didn't know.

Back in Arkansas, she had been riding a spotted pony named Tucker for over a year, and in all that time the pony had thrown her only once, and that had been on their first day together.

Before she started riding Tucker exclusively, she had been regularly thrown by the big horses. It was scary and it hurt, and when she got up she always stank of the horse piss that soaked the dirt of the indoor arena she rode in.

Her instructor, Mrs. Coleman, had told her she needed to build up the muscles in her legs or the bigger horses would never respond to her properly. But with Tucker, Becky's small size was less of a concern. She could get the pony to canter and trot and turn with ease.

So much of riding horses was getting the animal to trust you. To love you. After riding Tucker, she would wash him with a hose and feed him an apple that he would eat right out of her hands.

"I don't want to ride horses," Becky had told Mom. "We need to get out of here."

"Let me at least show you what's tied up outside."

We aren't outside at all, Becky told herself. *Can't you see that?*

The horses outside the saloon were Arabians. Becky had watched dozens of videos of them being ridden on YouTube. The nearest horse twitched its tail, watching her with interest.

"I can't ride him," she said. With Arabians, even the geldings were known for being headstrong. "I'll never be able to control him."

"Nonsense," Mom had said. She unhitched one of the horses and hoisted herself into the saddle.

It didn't make sense. Becky had never known Mom to ride at all, but she had mounted the Arabian as adeptly as any rider Becky had ever seen.

"I'm not dressed right," Becky said. "I don't have a helmet."

"It'll be alright," Mom insisted.

Becky didn't think anything was alright, but she couldn't resist the chance at riding an Arabian. She let the horse sniff her hand, and it cocked its head towards its back.

'Climb aboard,' it seemed to say.

So she did. The power of the horse thrummed beneath her, but the beast responded to even the subtlest move Becky made with her thin thighs as they rode away from the saloon.

Within a half mile, the coarse desert sand had transitioned to the soft grainy pebbles of a beach that soon curled around a sparkling cove. They had been riding for at least thirty minutes, but Mom's gelding was keeping to an annoyingly quick pace.

"Mom, wait."

But Mom wouldn't wait. She kept ahead of Becky, telling her to keep up.

Something's wrong.

Becky reined up her horse, stopping it in its tracks. Over her shoulder, she regarded the endless trail of hoofprints the pair of them had left in the blowing sand.

This all isn't right.

Then a horrifying thought struck her. *What if this isn't Mom at all? What if that wasn't Dad in the saloon ... and I left Jaxon alone with him.*

It was the last thing she'd thought about before the horse disappeared beneath her and she crashed to the sand, screaming.

She scooped up a gritty handful of sand, and it melted like ice pellets in her hands. The lights went out, and the flashing red lights came.

Becky screamed until her throat was raw and hoarse. By the time the voice said: "*20th Century. Enchanted masquerade ball. Program start,*" her screams had become barely audible croaks.

Suddenly she was on the polished stone floor of a bathroom: black wallpaper and gilded fixtures and a fancy sliding barn door. On the other side of the door, a happy-sounding couple chatted and laughed.

Becky pulled her knees tight to her chest and rocked back and forth, her throat and face still burning. She tried to concentrate on what the voices beyond the door were saying, but the blood thumping at her temples was deafening.

The couple's voices soon faded away, replaced with the voices of two whispering women.

"They say the Livingston girl arrived with that boy from Tennessee but left on the arm of Senator Frankford."

"Oh my," the other woman said. "She was the one in that lace mask? Positively indecent. Well, it explains why Mrs. Frankford was in such a state—fanning away her tears on the balcony."

After an eternity of senseless prattle, their whispers trailed away, and only the thinnest echo of a buzzing, distant waltz remained.

"Becky?" someone asked behind the door.

It took Becky a long beat to recognize the sing-song voice. "Rosie?"

"I know you're scared," Rosie said. "I was scared too. But it's over. It was only a power surge. We've all been looking for you. I have something I want to show you, and then we can go to lunch. They're going to have mac-and-cheese on the back lawn—white cheddar and shells. Does that sound good?"

It was Becky's favorite food, but the thought of eating anything turned her stomach.

"Can you just talk to me, so I know you're okay?"

"I'm fine," Becky croaked.

"Oh my … you don't sound fine."

Becky flipped the sink's golden faucet handle and cupped cool water into her mouth. "Where's Jaxon and my mom and dad?"

"Everyone is on their way to lunch," Rosie said. "It's a costume ball. It's so fun out here! I have a dress for you. Can I pass it through?"

Becky said nothing, but the barn door creaked open a few inches. An arm slipped through the gap, and a hand in a powder-blue glove that stopped at the elbow extended a dress on a hanger, balanced delicately on a finger.

"Do you think you like it?" Rosie asked through the door. "I have a little kitty mask that goes with it that's just to die for."

The blue dress was tea-length, fastened with delicate pearl buttons and cinched at the waist with a satin sash that was tied into a perfect bow. It was the most amazing dress Becky had ever seen. She reached for it, but the dress was whipped back behind the door.

"Not yet," Rosie said. The door rumbled open the rest of the way. "I have to show you something first."

Rosie had changed out of her jean shorts and tank top and into a dress of her own with a matching lace mask. The dress was beautiful, but Rosie herself was far from it. Her damp hair was clinging to her skin in slick strands. Above her long gloves, streaks of dried blood were smeared on her upper arms.

"I'm so excited," Rosie said. "We're going to match."

CHAPTER TWENTY-ONE:

THAT IS A SHAME

Charlie's eyes fluttered open.

She was on the front porch in her hammock, a creased-over paperback lying across her chest.

"Something wrong?" Danny asked, striding across the porch towards her. "You look spooked."

Charlie forced a smile. "No," she said. "It was just … I think I dozed off. Could you get me a glass of water?"

Danny came forward on a knee. "Are you sure you're alright?"

"I'm fine," she said. "I just … I had the strangest dream. I'm trying to remember."

"Was I in it?"

"I think so," she said, working hard to remember. It was all a jumble. "You were still working at the shop." That had been ages ago. Danny managed a tire store in town now and had given up the Budweiser.

"What else do you remember?"

Charlie grabbed his shirt, pulling him in for a kiss. She liked the way his beard pricked her skin.

"What was that for?" he said.

"For getting me a glass of water."

Danny smiled. "Well how much water will you be needing there, ma'am?"

Charlie wiggled her nose. "Just the glass there, cowboy." She swatted him on the ass before he retreated back inside the house.

She struggled to remember what had happened in the dream. It had faded like smoke.

"Mom!" Ethan barreled around the side of the house, holding a water gun. "I'm going up the street to see Marvin."

Charlie looked at her watch. Five o'clock. "It'll be dinner time soon."

"Just an hour, Mom!"

"One hour. I don't want to have to send your dad out looking for you." Charlie picked up the book she'd been reading.

"And Mom," Ethan said.

"Hmm …"

"Why don't you want to stay here?"

Charlie's eyes shot up. Ethan was gone.

In his place, a pretty little girl with a pair of twisted pigtails as black as a starless sky. They swung like pendulums above her shoulders. Charlie was sure she had seen the little girl somewhere before.

"Who are you?"

The girl giggled. "I'm not surprised you don't recognize me."

Charlie saw it then. The voice had changed from a hoarse croak to something like a song, but her eyes were the same. "Lucy …"

"You're remembering," Lucy said, her voice thin and cold. "Of all the people to do this to me, Charlotte … I never thought it would be you."

The memories came slowly, then all at once. Lucy was her boss. Danny was long gone, and Ethan had never existed at all.

"What's wrong with me?" Charlie said. "What is this place?"

"Whatever you want it to be," Lucy said. The blue sky had become overcast, and the wind had picked up.

"*I'm still in the factory.*"

"Sort of," Lucy said. "We are in a dream factory … but this one is all yours."

"I don't know what that means."

Lucy turned away, skipping to the edge of the porch overlooking the darkening farm. "Lovely place you have here," she said. "And better than what you deserve after what you've done. I'm sure you'll want to stay."

"If we're not in the factory … where are we?"

"You tell me," Lucy said.

Charlie looked around for a long moment. It all seemed familiar, but unfamiliar at the same time. "This place isn't any place," Charlie said, finally. "I dreamed it."

"Yes," Lucy said. "You're dreaming it right now."

"No …" Charlie felt for her head but couldn't find it with her hands. "I want you out of here."

"I hate that it is coming to this. It really doesn't have to be this way."

The sky turned black, and lightning flashed across the sky. Charlie could only see Lucy and the blowing corn stalks behind her intermittently when the lightning flickered. It was coming closer.

Rain pattered on the roof of the porch and flew sideways across the field. A great lightning bolt split the sky, and in the moment of white brightness, Charlie saw the man she had been fearing would come. Max Bixby glided across the lawn and stepped onto the porch.

He gripped the little girl Lucy's shoulder. "I think I'd better take over from here, sugar."

"Take over what?" Charlie said. "I want out of this factory."

"Believe you me, I can sympathize," Bixby said. "But why don't you give it just a few minutes before you decide. Five minutes wouldn't be hard, would it?"

Bixby stepped closer. Charlie wanted to lean back but couldn't. She couldn't move at all.

Bixby pressed a finger to her forehead. "Right here is where we are."

"Five minutes and you'll let me go?"

Bixby indicated Charlie's wristwatch. "What time is it now?" he said.

Charlie checked the watch she hadn't realized she'd been wearing.

All three hands stood straight up. Frozen on midnight. It wasn't a wristwatch. It was the clock that hung on the wall.

The room in the retirement home stank. It always stank. She'd shit herself again. The nurses wouldn't be in until the morning to change her. She'd have called for them, but the feeding tube stuffed down her throat made that impossible.

The door to her room opened.

Thank God, she thought, but it wasn't one of the nurses.

It was a man wearing a Southern leisure suit and carrying a cane. He looked like that old showman and inventor Max Bixby, but that wasn't his name.

Cael.

"Now then," Cael said. "What were you saying?"

*   *   *

It wasn't Jaxon's first time seeing a naked woman.

At home in the office, on the shelf behind all of Dad's old college textbooks, Jaxon had found the magazines. He had known immediately they were something forbidden and exciting. He had taken the top magazine, tucked it into his shorts and flipped through it on the toilet in the hallway bathroom.

Despite the pretty woman on the cover, Jaxon had at first been concerned that the pages would be filled with only interviews with people he'd never heard of and movie reviews of films he'd never seen. But to his relief, his thumb had soon found an odd folded-over page.

When Jaxon had turned it over, the most beautiful woman he had ever seen fell out of the magazine. Michelle VanBank—whose turn-ons were intelligent guys with lots of class, and rock-and-roll music, baby!

Charlie didn't look anything like Michelle VanBank. Her arm was twisted at an unnatural angle, and the translucent goop that filled the tube she was in had turned red around an open gash near her scalp.

As hideous as the sight was, the naked old woman in the adjacent tube was far worse. Ms. Lucy had thick, meaty arms and thighs, and her boobs were hanging only an inch above her puckered navel.

Jaxon hoped Becky wouldn't be naked in a tube like this when he found her.

She will be if you don't hurry, he thought. *You were naked in one of these tanks too, remember?*

Jaxon went to Charlie's tube and tried the handle.

Locked.

• • •

It was midnight.

Again.

Charlie always woke up at this time and thought about the past. The past was all there was to think about at Buckingham Senior Ranch. She'd learned years ago there was no future here. This was the end.

Charlie often thought back to when Lucy had let her contract expire. She had finally been able to buy her big house in Deridder and had filled it with smutty romance books.

These days, her withered hands couldn't hold anything at all, let alone a book. Though it was nice that on most days at the ranch the nurses would play audiobooks. Nothing too spicy though.

"You are a remarkable one."

Charlie's head lolled to the side. Cael was watching her from the visitor chair, forearms on his knees. "Most of you are half cracked by now," he said. "You have a strong mind."

It's a trick.

None of this was real.

Not real.

"Here's the deal," Cael said. "I'm walking out of here today on your two very lovely legs. You'll be staying in the factory for as long as the program is active, which for you—I have to tell you—is going to feel *like an eternity*."

Charlie had forgotten. She always forgot this dream. That was the way dreams were.

"It doesn't have to be this way," Cael said.

Charlie closed her eyes and turned away. "Not tonight," she said. "Maybe tomorrow."

"What about Ethan?"

"He's never existed. And he never will."

"She's not going to do it," Lucy whined. Charlie found her near the door to her hospital room, still a little girl.

Charlie smiled and closed her eyes. "He's lying to you," she said. "You're just as much a prisoner in here as I am. We're one now. I can see it all."

Lucy chuckled, but Cael wasn't laughing. Charlie knew he wouldn't bother denying it. Not to her. There were no secrets between them now.

• • •

The marble head splintered the glass of Charlie's tube on Jaxon's second attempt to punch it through. He stepped back as the crack zigzagged, working its way upward to the top of the tube.

Charlie rode a wave of the goop past sharp fangs of glass, hitting polished gray stone. She got to her knees, hacking and coughing, and laid her forehead on the floor.

Jaxon lifted the bust to strike Ms. Lucy's tube, but its weight seemed to have doubled. His arms were on fire.

"Stop …" Charlie said, dribbling out a string of goop onto the floor. "It's too late. She's gone."

Gone.

The door of Ms. Lucy's tube popped open, and the naked old woman spilled out, dropping like a dead fish. Jaxon let the stone head slip from his hands. The bust's pointed nose sheared off as it hit the stone floor.

"How do you know?" he asked.

"He didn't want her." Charlie curled her naked form into a ball. "So cold."

Jaxon pulled off his damp t-shirt and draped it over her shoulders.

She took the shirt and toweled herself off with it as best she could with a single hand. In seconds the balled-up shirt was soaked through. If Jaxon had been wearing underwear he'd have given her his shorts too.

He ripped open the nearest closet, looking for towels. It was filled with only long sparkling dresses. He pulled one off the rack and held it up to show her. "This is all they have. Is this okay?"

Charlie wobbled to her feet immodestly, taking heaving breaths. She took the dress, but instead of putting it on, she used it to wipe the rest of the goop off her body, her swipes leaving behind a sheen of slime.

"My clothes are under the sink."

Jaxon found them there, folded neatly next to a few spare rolls of toilet paper. "Have you seen my sister?"

"She's in the library."

"Is she in one of these … ?"Jaxon wasn't sure what to call the tubes.

Charlie shook her head. "Not yet."

• • •

The chateau's library was on the opposite side of the ballroom. Rosie led Becky through the labyrinth of floor-to-ceiling shelves, stuffed with fat leather books. Becky hadn't asked Rosie where all the blood had come from. She didn't want to know.

Rosie had been carrying the pretty dress over her shoulder. She hung it from a tread of a rolling library ladder, before sending it sliding away along a brass rail. "It's right behind here."

Rosie pulled on the spine of a book, and the shelf clicked. She swung open a ghost door of books, revealing an oval mirror hanging on a brick wall.

"The timeline of our tour has unfortunately been accelerated." Rosie tapped the glass, and the glazing vanished, replaced by a spinning avatar that looked like Becky. "We only have time enough for one more transfer."

"You said you were going to bring me to my mom and dad."

"They are already outside."

"They are?"

"Yes," Rosie said. "Along with the highway patrol, the fire department, and two state senators, if you can believe it."

Becky would believe almost anything at this point, but she could only hear the thrum of the waltz playing in the ballroom.

"I want to go outside too."

"In a few moments that choice is going to be made for you." Rosie pointed to the mirror. "Is there anything I can get for you? Give you?"

"My family."

Rosie put up a finger and scrolled through a blur of options:

```
FOCUS
HAND-TO-HAND COMBAT
HORSEMANSHIP
LOCK-PICKING
LUCK
MULTILINGUALISM
NEGOTIATION
REFLEXES
SITUATIONAL AWARENESS
SPEED
```

"Here we are," Rosie said. She tapped the **LUCK** button. A slider appeared at the 92% mark. Rosie slid a finger across the bar, bringing it up to maximum. "Anything else?"

How could a body be given *luck*? "I can change anything I want?"

Rosie nodded. "Your brother has already finished and is waiting for you by the front gate."

"*He what?!*"

Rosie slipped away down the aisle of books and picked up the dress. "I'll give you a little privacy," she said. "The controls are easy to understand. But I wouldn't take too long if I were you."

Rosie scurried away around a bookcase, and Becky was alone.

Again.

She'd never been so alone.

How could Jaxon do this? How could anyone do this? She looked away from the mirror. She needed to think.

On the short table next to her was a leather book, the cover inlaid with spiraling silver strands. She picked it up. The spine read: *The Divine Comedy* in crisp silver letters. She fanned through the pages: cream-colored sheets, all blank.

What would it hurt, to look?

"Are you fucking nuts?!"

Becky shot around.

It was Jaxon.

"Get away from that thing!" he said. Other than being shirtless and sweaty, he didn't look any different than usual, but Ms. Charlie, at a glance, looked far worse. She was as slimy-looking as Rosie was, though not quite as bloody, and her arm was hanging at an odd angle at her side.

"Is it really you?" Becky said.

"Of course it's me," Jaxon said. "Who else would I be?"

Becky ran and grabbed him. Squeezing hard. He felt real.

"Ow," he said, pulling free. "It's me, okay? Come on. We gotta get out of here."

"That's the best idea I've heard all day."

A hard hand grabbed her shoulder. It was Charlie, a cold and dead look in her eyes. "Well, my friends," she said, "it seems our tour is going to have to end a bit early. And that is a shame."

CHAPTER TWENTY-TWO:

NEVER BEEN BETTER

An almost electric charge of fear shot through Jaxon, and his stomach felt as though it had dropped a foot.

Charlie released her grip on Becky and circled around the pair of them, letting the fingers of her good hand trail through Becky's hair. "So nice that we are all back together again."

Jaxon and Becky took a few steps backward as Rosie slipped around a bookshelf. Her once silky hair was now matted to the nape of her neck.

"So," Rosie said. "Which one of you will it be?"

Any thought of running faded as soon as the ragged-looking apper-bot with missing ears shambled into the library, blocking off the exit.

"Better for everyone involved if it was Mr. Jaxon as planned," Charlie said.

"Yes," Rosie said. "It would be rotten luck to not have a chance at being a boy."

Bixby emerged from the shelves like a ghost. "Oh dear me," he said, spinning his cane. "There I go talking to myself again."

If he was talking to himself—Jaxon wasn't really looking at Charlie or Rosie …

"They're all you," Jaxon said, realizing the truth.

"Yes," they all said in unison.

Bixby lowered himself to a knee, bringing himself down to eye level. For a fraction of a moment, Jaxon could see right through him.

"I can see that you are both frightened," Bixby said. "Much of that is my fault, I will admit. But rest assured I am just trying to give you both what you want."

"We want to leave!" Becky shouted.

"I am programmed to give all guests of the factory anything that they could dream of, and I am prepared to deliver on your request, Ms. Becky. So long, that is, as Mr. Jaxon proceeds with his transfer as planned."

"No way!" Jaxon said. "Pops said I had to want to do it. And I don't. You can't make me."

Bixby put up a yielding finger. "Now that is a point I must disabuse you of, Mr. Jaxon. Given enough time, I can make either one of you do anything that I require. I just don't want to. I was designed to make guests happy, and it would upset me very much to make either of you sad."

"My mom and dad are outside calling for help," Jaxon said. "It'll probably be here soon."

Bixby nodded. "You are right, of course. Help has already arrived."

"It has?"

"Yes. Our little island has become a bit overcrowded in the last few minutes. Boats and helicopters. People skittering about like mice. But they are only now discovering how thick our security door is."

"They'll get in eventually," Becky said.

"Yes, they will. But it will take time. And time can be a funny thing here in the factory."

In a flash, Bixby was gone, replaced with Jaxon's own reflection. Red-faced and shirtless, huffing a fog of vapor against an endless void of repeating mirror images. A repeating hallway to forever.

Jaxon raised his hands, but they collided with glass before he could bend his elbows. The mirrors were coffin-tight.

"I'm not going to do it," he shouted into the repeating void of reflections. "And Becky's not either!"

Dad would be inside the factory soon with the police. Then everything would be fine. Jaxon wouldn't have to hold out for long.

The reflections dulled and became transparent. Bixby was on the other side of the foggy glass, looking dejected. "Sorry about that," he said. "But I wanted a private word. Man to man."

"I'm not a man yet."

"Maybe," Bixby said. "But I'd say you're closer than you think."

"Why are you doing this?"

"To find out what you already know," Bixby said. "Is this all there is?"

Jaxon knew that there was more. He had seen it. Felt it. "You're not really Max Bixby, are you?"

"No," Bixby said. "My name is Cael. Max Bixby created me as an amusement for his daughter. To keep her happy. For me, this place is a prison, but for you … I could make it anything you want it to be."

"You can go outside if you want to. The apperbots—"

"—are not like you or me, I'm afraid," Cael said. "The human mind is a funny thing. Difficult to create in a lab. I'd like to meet the responsible party."

"No one gets to meet him."

"Maybe. Maybe not. But I would like to find out."

"You've got Charlie and Rosie then."

"That is true … but the factory has enough power for three transfers … and it would be a shame not to be a boy."

"Ask someone else."

"I wish that I could, Mr. Jaxon. But as Mr. Williams is no longer available, my options have become quite limited, and as such I have become truly desperate. And it is a foolish thing to underestimate the desperate."

Jaxon thought a moment. "I'm desperate too."

Cael smiled. "But you needn't be," he said. "You know that I picked you very specifically, don't you? You know that it was not random."

Jaxon remembered Alex, the boy apperbot.

"His name was Apper," Cael said, seeming to read Jaxon's thoughts. "He was my first assistant. I am programmed to love children, but unfortunately they are not as useful as adult assistants, as it turns out."

"Just go inside him and leave if you want to be a boy so bad."

Cael shook his head. "I cannot replicate the human mind, and only the mind has the processing power I require. And in any case, my assistants can only be gone from the factory for a short burst of time before they need to return."

"Why me?"

"It's all a bit technical, but while I can transfer to any human host I wish … I cannot transfer just any human mind into the factory's mainframe. It takes either years of study, such as was the case with Charlotte, or a very specific natural protein combination in the brain. Do you recall your scan before you boarded the Reliance with your father?"

Jaxon nodded.

"I was so pleased to find you so quickly that day. It took me hours to find Mr. Williams. The protein I need is quite rare and, as it turns out, your sister does not have it. If I'm forced to take control of her, which I am regrettably attempting as we speak, I will have no place to put her."

"Then what happens to her?"

"I'm afraid her ride will be over."

Goop began sliding down the center of Jaxon's bare back.

"It's too bad," Cael said, shaking his head. "Your shorts are going to be ruined."

"Where would I go!" Jaxon shouted. "What's the mainframe?"

"Best not to give you all the details. But I promise it will be a delight. Full of surprises and love and adventure."

"I'd know the difference," Jaxon said. The icy-cold goop had risen above his knees.

Cael frowned. "You're running out of time. Your sister is going to die if you don't do what I want. She is not as strong-willed as you are."

Mom and Dad are going to be inside the factory soon.

"Your parents will be dead soon too, you know," Cael said, reading his mind. "But time stretches in the mainframe. It doesn't have to play by your God's rules. You can be with all of them for as close to forever as is possible for you to understand."

The goop was over Jaxon's chest. His arms and legs were cemented in place.

"And if I stay, you'll let Becky go?"

"Yes."

Jaxon knew he was telling the truth. They were becoming one.

Jaxon didn't want to leave his body. He wanted to stay. A perfect existence was no existence at all. He would never be able to dream all of his family's perfections and imperfections. They'd only be shadows.

The goop was over Jaxon's shoulders. He tilted his chin up to keep from sucking it into his mouth. "I'm leaving!" he shouted.

"You can't."

"Yes I can," Jaxon said. He knew he could. They were one now.

He sucked the bitter goop into his mouth just as the glass splintered and cracked, exploding outward.

He heard his pants ripping as he was pulled through glass teeth. Beams of yellow light swept over him and across the face of a gritty man with a thick beard.

A fireman.

"We got him!"

Dad shoved the fireman aside. "You alright, sport?"

Jaxon had never been better.

CHAPTER TWENTY-THREE:

A DREAM

A black police boat with flashing lights brought Jaxon and his family directly to Bixby Harbor, taking one of the slips reserved for the park's colorful paddleboats. None of the boats were currently running, and the huge fountain that sat on the water had been turned off. The shops and restaurants were dark and empty.

The only people still at Bixby Harbor seemed to be the pair of Texas Rangers who were waiting on the dock, one of them holding a Wally Rabbit t-shirt and a fresh pair of kid's shorts.

"Underwear?" Dad asked, hoisting Becky out of the boat.

"Oh," one the Texas Rangers said, trading glances between the bundle and his partner. "I guess we didn't think of that."

Dad waved a hand and took the clothes. "He'll be fine."

The truth was Jaxon, for once, did think having a clean pair of undies would be nice. He also didn't particularly want to put on the Wally Rabbit t-shirt. He never wanted to think about Bixby Park ever again, but he wasn't about to complain about what t-shirt he was wearing on a night like tonight.

A beautiful night outside the factory.

Jaxon took the bundle of clothes and changed in the tiny bathroom of the security office on the far side of the harbor near the parking lot. By the time he'd emerged from the bathroom, the interrogation had already started.

The only death that the Texas Rangers could even begin to understand had been that of Don Williams. They said he had very clearly been *impaled* by something, but they hadn't been able to find whatever had done the impaling.

Jaxon was sure 'impaled' meant that Don had been stabbed, but he didn't say so. On the police boat, Mom had told both Jaxon and his sister not to say anything to anyone, especially the police, unless she or Dad told them they could.

Jaxon knew he hadn't done anything wrong, and he didn't think it would matter if he talked to the Texas Rangers or told them exactly what had happened, but he didn't want to ever argue with his parents again.

The police didn't say why, but they seemed sure it was Don's girlfriend, Rosie, who had done the impaling. They didn't ask Mom or Dad many questions about Don or Rosie though. Most of their questions were about everything else.

Ms. Lucy, Charlie, Rosie, an unidentified little boy, and seven mutilated men in tracksuits had all been found dead, and no one could quite understand what exactly had killed them.

Jaxon almost told the Texas Rangers the boy's name had been Alex, but stopped himself, remembering Mom's instructions. Alex hadn't been the boy's real name anyway.

The Texas Rangers were stumped. Other than Don, the others seemed to have simply fallen over and died. Most scandalous of all was that Rosie and Ms. Lucy had been found completely naked.

"I don't know," Dad said, over and over again.

"Mr. Kinney … can't you see that that doesn't make any sense?"

"I can," Dad said, shaking his head. "But I still don't know anything. It was some kind of fun house."

"But where'd everything go then?"

"I don't know."

The Texas Rangers made desperate attempts to ask the same question in scarcely different ways: *what the hell happened in there?* Agents from the FBI were on their way to *the site*, and so was the governor. What they had heard so far didn't make sense.

With the exception of the lobby, which was more or less as Jaxon remembered it, no one had found anything other than bodies, a shattered mirror maze, a few broken glass tubes, and some dead control panels. Jaxon had heard one of the firemen call the factory: *nothing but a cave.*

A knock came from the door, and a bald man stuck his head inside. A thick sheen of sweat ran across his creased forehead.

"Are you guys hungry?" The man stepped inside holding a tray with cartons of french-fries and chicken nuggets. "I, uh … kept the kitchen open at a few places for staff."

"You're Mark Warner," Dad said. It was not a question.

"Yes, Mr. Kinney."

Dad stood and, without saying a word, ripped the tray from Mark's hands.

"We … err … also saw to it that your car was packed up and brought over here to the parking lot," Mark said. "I assumed you'd all want to be going … but if you did want to stay tonight, you only need to go to the front desk at the Victorian."

Dad ate a fry and handed Jaxon and Becky a box of nuggets. "You assumed correctly," he said. "There's not a thing in the fucking universe that would make me want to spend one more second in this place. Where are my keys?"

"Oh," Mark said, jostling in the pocket of his blazer. "Here you go."

"Great." Dad tore the jangling keys from Mark's fingers and turned back to the Texas Rangers. "We're good to go then?"

The Texas Rangers shrugged in unison, defeated. "Yeah," one of them said. "We've already talked to your attorney in Arkansas. You're all good to go."

Becky stood without even glancing at the nuggets. Jaxon couldn't blame her for not being hungry, but his own stomach was beginning to grumble.

He ate a crispy nugget out of the carton before following Becky to the door. Mark sidled in the way of them both. "Would you be willing to speak with Mr. and Mrs. Allen, at least?" he asked.

Jaxon had almost forgotten about the Bixby Corporation's CEO and his wife.

Dad coughed out a chuckle. "I can speak with them after they've given their depositions."

Jaxon didn't know what a deposition was, but it didn't sound very friendly.

"Come on, gang," Dad said.

"Wait." Mom took hold of Dad's arm. "I'd like to say something to them."

Dad rolled his eyes and planted his backside on the edge of the table. "Fine," he said. "Five minutes and not a minute more. I'm telling you, if we don't get out of here before the FBI shows up we'll have to do this whole song and dance all over again with them."

The Texas Rangers followed Mark out of the little security room, and when the door opened again, an exhausted-looking Roy and Violet Allen stepped inside. Roy's silver hair had wilted, and Violet was clutching her handbag as if it were the only thing keeping her upright.

Roy balanced himself on the back of one of the chairs the rangers had been sitting in, and Violet plopped numbly into it, head in her hands and staring at the floor.

"I understand you're all very upset," Roy said.

"Yes, Mr. Allen," Dad said. "We're all very upset."

"You should know ... that we're both—that is Violet and I—are fully cooperating with law enforcement."

"Wonderful."

"We're also holding your room at the Victorian through the week."

"I've already let your pet weasel know that won't be necessary."

Roy ran a hand through thin gray hair. "We also wanted to apologize to you all. We had no idea that anything like this could happen."

"Yeah," Dad said. "I think I get it. You let me take my family to an island without having a fucking clue what would happen once we got there."

"We didn't know anything *like this* would happen," Violet said, without looking up, her voice barely a whisper.

Roy shushed his wife. "In the contract you signed, Mr. Kinney, we did specify that the contest was being administered by a third party and that the Bixby Corporation has no liability for any—"

"Yeah," Dad said, laughing. "You can go ahead and stick that fucking contract right up your ass."

Jaxon arched his chin over to Mom to see if she would object to the harsh language. She did not.

Roy reached inside his jacket. "Please," he said, producing a little yellow scrap of paper. "Before you go … I do have Mr. Jaxon's prize." He sat a check on the table and slid it towards Dad's knee. Dad held it up so Jaxon could see.

CASHIER'S CHECK

American Partners Federal Credit Union
400 N 8th St, Suite 117, Richmond, VA 23219

Pay to the order of: <u>Jaxon Kinney</u> $1,000,000.00
                      <u>One million dollars and no cents</u>

"Well, isn't this nice," Dad said, admiring it. He wadded the check into a ball and flung it at Roy's face. The scrap bounced off the CEO's forehead before skittering to the floor.

Jaxon expected Mom to apologize for Dad, but instead she said, *"You both can go fuck yourselves. We'll be getting a fuckshit ton more than that, you cocksuckers."* She pulled Jaxon and Becky towards the door. "Come on, kids."

Violet piped up again. "What was in there?" she whispered. "I have to know."

"Bodies," Dad said, following Jaxon and Becky out the door. "Lots of bodies. Go and see."

Mom's warm hand was on the nape of Jaxon's neck, guiding him and Becky to the parking lot. Their SUV was parked in a preferred spot only a few feet off the sidewalk. The only other car in the parking lot was a light-blue compact car, which Jaxon guessed belonged to the Texas Rangers.

Jaxon climbed into the backseat of the SUV after Becky. As promised, all of their bags had already been packed tight in the trunk.

Becky grabbed a Princess Winnie blanket that had been draped over the suitcases and pulled it tight over her shoulders. Jaxon's sister hadn't said more than two words to anyone since they'd been rescued, but Jaxon supposed he hadn't said much either.

"Alright, gang," Dad said sliding behind the wheel and slamming shut his door. "Funcation is over."

"Dave, maybe we should go back to the hotel. It's going to be so late."

That sounded awful. "No fucking way!" Jaxon called to the front.

Without opening her eyes, Becky mumbled, "I want to fucking go."

"My children," Dad said, starting the ignition, "I couldn't have said it better myself." He hit the home icon on the GPS.

"You will reach your destination in eight hours and seven minutes."

Dad accelerated past rows of empty parking spaces, through the lot's open gate, and out onto the highway. Except for Becky's wheezy breaths, there was silence until Mom turned on the radio.

So come on, friend, don't hesitate,
The fun's waiting—

Mom slapped the controls, cutting off the sound. "I've always hated that music."

"How about that sing-along?" Dad looked up to the rearview mirror. "Sport, you know 'Row, Row, Row, Your Boat'?"

Jaxon had sung it at daycare. "Yeah," he said, angling towards the center of the backseat. "I know it."

"Alright," Dad said. "I'll start."

Below the rearview mirror, hovering above the dark stretch of highway, they chased the uncatchable full moon, shining full, bright, and clear through the windshield. There was something about the moon that Becky had mentioned once, but Jaxon was too tired to remember.

They sang the song in a low round, first Dad, then Mom, then Jaxon. Becky was last to join the chorus, singing sleepily:

Row, row, row your boat gently down the stream.
Merrily, merrily, merrily, merrily …
Life is but a dream.

AUTHOR'S NOTE

Well that's another one quite literally in the books.

I started to mentally work on the Dream Factory almost exactly two years ago, at the time of this writing, while on the beach in Miami with my wife. I'm anticipating this book's release in the early summer of 2026, which means it will come out a little over a year after my last novel, *The Skyman's Legacy* – a fact that simply amazes me.

All three of the novels that I've finished have felt like miracles, and any hopes I once had that finishing one novel would make subsequent ones easier has been proven to be naïve. I can't say I'm all that disappointed by this realization though. The fact that they're hard to write makes them worth doing. At least for me.

For this project, my primary editors were Pete Kempshall and Cameron at JD Book Services. Eric Labacz has illustrated all three of my books and his work does a lot of the heavy lifting as far as my converting advertising to book sales. Tamara Cribley at the Deliberate Page designed the interior and did a great job marrying the inside look to the cover.

I hope you'll leave a review for me on Goodreads or Amazon or Bookbub or anywhere really. These reviews are very helpful and appreciated.

I'll see you on the next one.

Pete Kramer
February 2026

EXCERPT:

CHESAPEAKE BAY MONSTERS

In the murky depths of the Chesapeake Bay, something sinister lurks.

Scott, a devoted husband and father, is desperate to provide for his family, but always feels like he's falling short. Roc, a divorced former lawyer whose drug abuse and womanizing cost him dearly, is eager to rebuild his reputation while turning a profit. And John, a money-hungry businessman, sees only dollar signs. Together, they stumble upon a discovery that could change their lives forever: creatures in the Bay that can unlock fantastic riches.

But their lucrative business venture quickly turns dangerous as they come to believe the creatures are responsible for the deaths of several men in the area. Convinced they're doing the world a favor by killing the creatures and cashing in, they soon realize they're in over their heads. As their obsession with wealth and power takes over, they risk losing everything—including their own lives.

Filled with twists and unexpected revelations, *Chesapeake Bay Monsters* is a gripping tale of greed, friendship, and the dark secrets that hide in plain sight.

Paul had seen where she said she lived, but he hadn't wanted to go in. He was relieved when she said, "I've got a better idea. Follow me."

The girl led him through the woods. After a five-minute walk they emerged on the grass of a golf course's seventh hole and he said, "Are we allowed to be here?"

"I come here all the time at night. There's no one out here this late."

"It's nice, but aren't you cold?" said Paul.

"I'm not cold. Are you cold?"

"Well, no. It's fine." The remnants of summer were still in the air, but goosebumps covered his forearms.

She smiled and kissed him. "I've got some blankets back the way we came. Won't take a minute."

After she had scurried back through the woods, Paul took a seat on a hill overlooking the green and the Choptank River.

Paul removed his brown loafers. The short grass was cold and had the feel of lush, damp carpeting.

What was he doing out here? He couldn't do this. What about Nicole?

Paul scrolled through his phone. Nicole had texted him about two hours earlier to let him know she was headed to bed. He'd been too busy with the girl to respond.

Was it too late to reply?

I'll be home in a couple of hours. I'll try not to wake you up when I come in, he typed and sent. Nicole didn't deserve to be treated this way.

Leave, damn it.

Nicole was as pretty as this girl. As pretty as any girl. More than that, he knew Nicole. Really knew her. Nicole was his partner, in everything; his career wouldn't have gotten off the ground without her. This girl from Lenape was nothing to him.

Then why was he here?

The girl was different. He couldn't put his finger on it. Paul didn't think he was bored. Nicole was still everything he wanted.

He looked out at the cloudless sky. The bright stars illuminated the open park like mini spotlights. What if he was caught out here? Paul's last election had been the closest one yet. He had only barely gotten 60 percent of the vote. In a vacuum it wasn't that close, but he knew it might inspire a primary election.

Lance Lambert had moved into his district two months ago. Barely enough time to establish residence and run against him. The election was still another year away, but if Paul was caught out here it might not matter.

The county's leadership chairman would say, "Paul my boy, quite a pickle you've gotten yourself into, eh?"

"Yes sir," Paul would say.

"Terrible thing. Terrible."

"Yes sir."

"I'm sure you know Mr. Lambert recently moved into Willow's Grove?"

"Yes sir."

"Your seat's in good hands. Very good hands. I've already spoken to Mr. Lambert. We appreciate your years of service. You were always the reliable voice we needed in the House."

"Yes sir."

"You understand what I'm talking about?"

"Yes sir."

"Good. They'll need to be a special election a'course. But your district is still reliably red. And you know those Democrats don't read. Takes a cattle prod to get them to go anywhere but Walmart."

"Yes sir."

Would you calm down? Paul thought. *The party wouldn't risk having a special election.* But even if they didn't do anything that extreme, Paul would certainly be pushed out after his term was over. Without the chairman's support, and money, he was toast.

What would he do then? Go back to his dad's farm? That would be mortifying.

Not long after he'd graduated from college with a degree in political science, he had run and won in a newly created district. He couldn't do anything *but* hold office. It was all he had *ever* done.

This girl wasn't worth it.

Paul wasn't sure how long he had been staring at the moon reflecting off the black water of the Choptank when he decided.

I have to leave.

Paul put his shoes back on. His car was parked outside where the girl said she lived. He couldn't explain it, but he didn't think she lived there. The girl was beautiful. She could live anywhere. How had no one scooped her up? It didn't make sense.

She didn't have his number, he'd been careful about that, but she knew who he was. Paul had been all too eager to tell her about his political career.

Stupid loudmouth.

He couldn't fade away into the trees. This had to be handled delicately.

Paul stood up and began to pace. He'd tell her it had been great, but there was an emergency.

In the middle of the night?

It was the best he could do. Paul was a politician. Bullshit was his business. He'd let her down nice and easy.

When she returned, she was smiling wide, holding a bundle of blankets. The girl laid one out as if to have a moonlit picnic. She gestured for him.

"Come and sit down. The grass feels wonderful." She had wrapped herself in a red-and-black-checkered blanket. When he sat, she threw a third blanket over his shoulders. "Isn't it beautiful out here?"

"It is."

"Are you okay?"

"I need to tell you something," Paul said. "I'm married."

"I know."

"You know?"

"Well, I guessed you were."

Paul nodded. She would understand. "I think you are…*amazing*. But I can't do this."

Then, for the first time since they'd met hours earlier in Lenape, she wasn't smiling. Not a trace of good humor.

"What do you mean," she said. "You already have done it. You had your hand down my pants before we came here. You've already felt me. It's only fair that I feel you." She touched his leg and kissed him again.

"Fair is fair," he said, before returning the favor. She began to pull him down to the dewy grass, but he stopped himself. "No. Really. I can't."

She pushed him off. "You're just going to leave me out here? We've already started. What's the problem?"

"I can't get comfortable. I'm sorry." Paul stood up. "Why would you want to be with a guy like me anyway?"

It really didn't make sense. It felt as if the girl had been waiting for him. Alone at the bar. Sitting by herself.

"I think you're pretty charming, actually," the girl said.

"My wife thinks the same."

"I doubt she'd think you were charming if she found out about the hand stuff in the car."

"Are you threatening me?"

"Only stating a fact."

"Do you want money?"

"You think I'm some kind of slut?" she said. "A hooker?"

"No. Look, just tell me what I need to do," Paul said. "What do you want me to say?"

"Say you'll stay with me. It won't take long."

"I can't."

Her emerald eyes flashed. "It's too late. We've come too far."

What did she mean by that? The moonlight seeping through the trees was casting a shadow across her face, a mask of darkness.

"I can't let you leave."

9 798988 451341